★ THAT ★
BOTTOM STEP

EVERETT DURHAM

AUTHOR'S NOTE

CHAPTER 1

A FUNERAL AND A MEMORY

Everyone sat encompassed by the tragedy of this day's funeral. It was the sad and unpredicted end to a story that was almost two and a half decades in the making. Sitting there on the flimsy-bottomed black plastic chairs were some of her closest friends. Marsha sat directly beside her, and on the other side were Mama and Da. Also, there were a number of Gus 3's friends, his cadet family, and many others, both old and young. The commandant of West Point was there. His eyes were sad, but his tall body stood erect, and his face offered little emotion. He was joined by General Hrabal. The general was older and was in fact a retiree, but was also a tall and emotionless figure. He had done this before. There were many there whom she did not know. She reckoned it was a group of those close, those he had accumulated during the short twenty-two years of his life. Each person there had played a part that blended into this end. This small-town cemetery offered a solemn and eerie canvas upon which to paint this event.

The service was almost over. It had not been a military funeral like Gus's but still had many of the same participants, plus many formal contributions provided by West Point. There was a color guard with the U.S. flag and the West Point flag as well. It was very formal, and even the cadet who had spoken at the church portion of the funeral was precise and militarily correct. It was all about to end. The funeral director carried a flag, folded just as the one she had received when Gus died. He knelt before her and began. "A grateful nation…" As those words dissolved into the sound of taps, she could think only that she had heard them before. Her mind wandered back to a place where she would be totally engulfed in a memory. It was a place that she must peer back upon alone.

It was in the fall of 1970. The many trees on the courthouse square in Cowan, North Carolina, had already begun to turn into the fall's red-and-yellow backdrop. Aggie was the picture of a cheerleader. She was just a little taller than the other girls and wore her auburn hair pulled into a ponytail. It was the last period at Cowan High School on that Friday. The students and teachers joined in the gym to be a part of a great and exciting event. These gatherings were much welcomed by the students because they got them out of class. Cheers led by an elite group of uniformed ladies, a few words from the coach, and a silent group of young men sitting on the front row of the student-lined bleachers wearing their football jerseys all made this pep rally perfect. They were ready to play ball. The players and the cheerleaders would ride the athletic bus to that night's game. It was just less than one hour's drive in a car, but the old bus stretched it into almost two. They were sent on that trip in grand style. Pom-poms, short white dresses with red sweaters, and red bullhorns identified the cheerleaders. All were vivacious, all were excited, and all were chanting and cheering as they left the gym. Aggie was one of those cheerleaders and fit perfectly into the part she played. The ball players were much more composed. All had serious faces. All seemed to follow the coaches' every instruction as they lined up and entered the bus. This was a serious undertaking, and it was all about winning tonight's game.

A little shy of two hours later, they arrived at the ball field where they were to play. The players, coaches, and managers all exited the bus and went into the locker room. The cheerleaders stayed in their seats as the bus drove on to a nearby drive-in so they could grab a burger. The players had all had a special lunch earlier. As always before a game, they ate their fill of roast beef with potatoes and a salad. Apple pie was always the dessert of choice. It had been served just before the pep rally in the school cafeteria. All of that had taken place, and the game was just minutes away. A crowd gathered on the sidelines as each of the two teams prepared for the kickoff. It was time now.

The cheerleaders jumped, yelled, and waved their pom-poms as those sitting on the sideline bleachers joined the yelling and stood to watch the kickoff. A short time later, it was halftime. Then just as quickly, the game was over. The team had not won, but the coach used this time to begin preparation for next week.

The coach's efforts were to motivate his players in an attempt to create a different outcome. "You are measured by how you played the game and how you learn from that," the coach stated. On the opposite side of the field, the opposition's coach told his players that their win was a great feat. How no one could take away that feeling. Both coaches were doing their job as best they could.

On the way back, the bus was very quiet and dark. Some of the players found their way to a seat beside one of the cheerleaders. Kissing, wandering hands, and promises made with the slightest of whisper were the conversation of those so lucky to have such a seat. Those who had secured no such place could only wish that they had done so and look forward to a time when they might. One young man took a chance. He got up, walked the several rows ahead, and asked Aggie if he might sit with her. He was in his last year of high school and was one of the most popular young men in his class. His six-foot-two-inch frame was hard and muscled from football practice. His face was a little of a baby face, but his dark eyes and equally dark black hair gave him the look of a college student. He was, in those cheerleaders' terms, a "good-looking hunk." She, just like he, was a senior. He was very popular, an only child, and he had his own car. She was much the same, but had no car. She agreed and asked her friend to move to another seat so she and Gus could share that spot. Aggie and Gus had known each other since the first grade. The two of them together could not have been a better matchup for an "all-around American couple." One of her friends looked back at the two of them and said to a group at the front of the bus as she pointed to them, "That is the start of something."

This was their first real conversation, and it seemed that the talk came easily. Both enjoyed the ride home. Nothing but conversation, and so quickly they were back at their school. As they exited the bus, Gus asked Aggie to let him take her home. She told one of the other cheerleaders, a close friend whom she was to ride home with, that she would instead ride with Gus. She did not think her mom and dad would mind, and besides, it was almost an hour before she had to be home.

Gus was waiting as she finished talking with her friend. Aggie's friend smiled at her, giving her a sneaky little grin as if to say, "Be careful, but have fun."

Gus had waited by his passenger door and opened it for her. That caught the eyes of some of the other guys standing around. "Wow," one of them said in a sarcastic way, "she must have really rung his bell." He walked around to the other side and endured the shouts and looks from those others as he entered the driver's side. He tried to ignore them.

In a couple of minutes, they were on their way. The conversation picked up and continued just as easily as it had developed on the bus. After riding around a bit, it was time for her to go home. They pulled up in front of her house. He got out of the car, walked to her side, opened the door, and extended his hand to help her from the car. He held tight to her hand as they walked the short distance to her house. Her dad peered out of the front window. When he saw this, he turned to her mom and said, "I have not seen Gus with her before, but I think I like him; he opened her door and helped her out of the car."

Gus walked her to the porch and stopped just shy of the front steps. He felt a little more comfortable saying good night just out of the bright lights on the porch. Just beside the bottom step where she stood, he took her hand and looked square into her eyes. His hands were warm and gentle and much larger than hers. She looked up into his eyes as he peered into her very soul. She had never been looked at like that before. His eyes seemed to examine every aspect of her. She felt as if she may be melting and began to realize in that minute that this could be a turning point in her life. He now held both hands and said, "Aggie, I do not know why I have never asked you out before, but this night is one of the best I have ever had. I would like very much to see you again and hope you will let me give you a call." Aggie could barely speak. Her heart pounded in a way it had never pounded before. There had been no awkward kissing or any gestures or attempts made other than those of sharing. It had been a night she would never forget. A night wedged into perfection by those moments that required nothing but having been a part.

As she turned and went into the house, suddenly she realized she may not have answered his question. Neither was he sure if she had answered, but based on Aggie's smile, he assumed she wouldn't mind if he called. He walked back to his car and pulled away. Life had never seemed better.

She entered the house to the usual questions about who won the game, did you have fun, and was that Gus Johnson who brought you home. Before she had time to think, she turned and looked directly at her mom. She was a woman who had enjoyed the years of her life. She had never had to work outside the home except during the war when almost everyone was working. Aggie's mom was exactly the way Aggie wanted her to be. It was as if her father wasn't even in the room. She said to her mom firmly and with total conviction, "I think that is the man I am going to marry."

Her dad began to laugh and said, "Tonight, young lady, it is time for bed. You and Mama can discuss getting married tomorrow."

All day she stayed inside the house. She helped her mom with the usual chores but failed to go out on afternoon trips as she usually would have. She did not say it—in fact, she may not have even realized it herself—but she was waiting on a phone call. A little after five, the phone finally rang. It was Gus. He indicated he had been working with his dad at the drugstore all day. He had no plans for this night, and wondered if he could come over and just visit for a while. Aggie replied, "Just so happens that I do not have any plans either. Come on over, and we'll hang out." And hang out they did. They were very seldom apart from that time through the end of school.

THIS MAN'S NAVY

After school everyone was making plans to go off to college or to start new jobs. Gus wasn't sure exactly what he wanted to do, but he was sure that it included Aggie. Aggie was just as sure that she wanted to be included in his plans.

The war in Vietnam was raging, and a number of his friends were there. The draft was in high gear, and young men he knew were being called every day. He knew he could take his chances on the draft or that he could join and have some say in which service he was going to enter. His father had been in the Navy, and he was pretty sure that was what he wanted as well.

He joined and was to be shipped off in two weeks. For those two weeks, he and Aggie were together almost every minute. They were very much in love but had never been intimate. They had some pretty steamy moments when alone, but had never gone beyond that. He would be leaving on Monday and knew only that he should be able to come home at the end of the two months of basic training. Sunday would be spent with the both of them being surrounded by family and friends. It was Saturday night, and this would begin the longest time they had been apart since that Friday night football game.

They went to a favorite and secluded spot. It was on a piece of land his father owned about twelve miles from home. It was July and still pretty warm. The lane into the property had a locked gate about twenty or so yards from the main road. He left his car sitting at the gate, and they walked hand in hand down the lane, which ended at a favorite swimming hole. It was in a creek that bordered the back side of that property. Aggie had been swimming there several times, but this was her first time at night. The cooler evening air allowed them to enjoy that walk and their conversation. They had carried a blanket to sit on and did so when they came to an opening alongside the swimming area. There were a million stars that lit the otherwise dark night. Again, he took both of her hands into his. It was much like the first time they were together, only this time a promise was whispered. "You are the best thing to ever happen to me. I cannot even imagine what it would be like not to have you in my life. No matter where I am or what I am doing, you will exist within my every heartbeat. I want you to wait for me so that we can be together forever."

Almost as a confirmation of what she had known since that first Friday night, her answer was a very simple, "You know I will."

With that, he took her into his arms and held her in a way he had never held her before. His lips brushed lightly over hers as she slightly gasped. Pushing her back, he again looked into her eyes. Neither said a word, but both surrendered to that time and place. This would be the night that they bonded in a way that only the purest of love can bring. They would share each other as if they were one. It was as if each knew exactly what the other's slightest of moves would be. There was nothing left when that night ended. Every single pleasure that a man and woman can imagine within the bounds of love, they had shared. This union was the welding of a true and lasting love that would never be broken.

The night ended as sweetly as it had begun. A perfect blend of all that is right with the world. He would be away for a while, but she would hold him in her heart no less tightly than she had held him this night. This night they had allowed themselves to be consumed by their never-ending love.

YOU GOT A CALL, JOHNSON

There were only a few days left in Gus's basic training. One night, just after chow, another sailor from the end of the barracks called out, "Johnson, you got a call."

Gus thought that it must be Aggie. He went to the phone. He could tell she was upset. He had never heard that break in her voice before. He knew by instinct that it wasn't a happy call. She began, "I have something to tell you. I know that we did not plan this and that you have to complete your Navy training. But I—we—are going to have a baby. I just found out for sure this afternoon. I just wanted you to know." He did not allow her to say another word.

Without any hesitation, he told her in no uncertain terms that he would be home the following week. That she should go ahead and make whatever plans were necessary for them to get married as soon as he arrived. He was going to be home for two weeks, and that would give them the opportunity to make plans about how they would live. He assured her he was not unhappy and was glad she was to be the mom of his baby.

FURLOUGH

The two weeks following were like a whirlwind. A short marriage service was held in the church where she and her family attended. It was both of their families joining with a few friends. The service was as pure and sweet as had been their entire relationship. A honeymoon followed but was somewhat shortened as it must exist within the confines of a navy salary. He—they—would not allow either of their parents to foot any of the bill. This was their life and their start. It was during that last week of the two-week furlough that they told their parents about the baby. Her family first, then his. Aggie and Gus both took part in those conversations and sat side by side as they informed their families.

At Aggie's house, they were very surprised when her parents did not seem to react as she told them about the baby. Aggie's mom was the first to speak. "I have known this for a while. I told your father so he has also known. Do not ask me how, but I could tell by looking at you. We may have wished things to be different, but we are not mad at you or Gus." She then addressed Gus, "There is just one thing, though, that we would like to insist upon. We want Aggie to continue to live here with us until she is able to join with you. She needs to be in a safe and familiar place. Here is where she belongs." All four agreed.

They left her parents' house and went straight to his home to have the same conversation. His parents were older. They asked both of his parents to join them in the living room. Again, they sat side by side as they began the conversation. As Gus spoke, he looked directly at them both, but his eyes seemed to focus on his dad. They had been so close through the years that it seemed as if each knew what the other was thinking. This was no exception. Neither of his parents seemed shocked.

The first words were, and they came from his dad, "You know you may stay here with us, Aggie. You are our daughter now, and this home is yours." She explained how her folks had offered the same opportunity and that she would stay with them. She went on to say how much she appreciated that gesture and she surely considered herself lucky to be a part of Gus's family.

With this behind them, they had but to enjoy each other and family for the following week. He was to head to Fort Sam Houston, Texas, to be trained as a Navy corpsman. His experience working with his dad at the drugstore seemed to make that a perfect fit. The training was to be nineteen weeks, but he would be able to come home during Christmas, and that was only a couple of months away.

AGGIE, THE BABY, AND CHRISTMAS

Aggie missed Gus so very much. They wrote to each other every day. She wrote about how she could feel that there was a new life inside her and was starting to get a pretty big belly. He told her about his training and how he could easily see himself in a career that would involve medicine. He also indicated that there may be some issues involving his being able to be home during Christmas. He, just as he knew she would be, was heartbroken about that. He could not give her the details. He could tell her only that he had been selected as a member of an important new unit that was preparing for deployment and that she did not need to worry about him, because, and this was the only thing he could tell her, he would not be put in harm's way.

About a week later, he confirmed to her that he would not be home for the holidays. He would probably be gone when the new baby arrived. He told her that he had received a promotion, that his address was also new, and that letters should be addressed to HM3 Gus Johnson, The USS *Sanctuary*, U.S. Naval Command, Norfolk,

Virginia. A letter went to him every day. Her tears were often and her heart ached, as she hoped she would see him soon.

His ship steamed from the San Diego Naval Yard on December 21, 1971. The last five weeks of his training would be aboard ship as they sailed to their destination. Onboard training was a must for their mission. He was on his way, but still could not provide more information. He could not tell anyone, but his ship was to sail to Southeast Asia. There it would slowly travel in a never-ending maneuver in the waters just off the coast of Vietnam. The movement would provide safety from shelling or attack as the location would continually vary. U.S. Army helicopters would transport wounded soldiers to their ship directly from the battle zones where those injuries took place. The ship had seventeen doctors along with 120 corpsmen to treat those injured. Treatment would be fast, professional, and safe. Hospital Corpsman Third Class Gus Johnson was part of an exciting new program that was designed to save lives. Even Aggie did not know his exact whereabouts or the job he was doing. Letters to her were upbeat and frequent, but shrouded in secrecy.

Gus was engulfed by his work. He loved it. Not the work so much as the good he felt he was doing. It came natural to him, and he was promoted to Petty Officer Gus Johnson very soon after their arrival in that war zone. He was now a "team leader" and would command a group as they secured the injured from the arriving medical evacuation choppers. "Medevac" was the official way to identify those choppers over the radio. Gus would direct the wounded soldiers to the appropriate location aboard ship for their treatment. There was a constant flow of choppers, and with them, every injury imaginable was received aboard.

He began to recognize and know some of those chopper pilots and their crews as they continued to bring in the injured. That was true of the chopper coming in for a landing on his early morning shift.

It was a little after daybreak. His headset allowed him to monitor the information from the chopper as it made its way to the landing on the ship's deck. He knew there would be two injured on the incoming flight. The "Huey" had taken small arms fire as it made the rescue, but was intact and performing as needed. He and his crew were waiting as the chopper touched down on the deck. Quickly, the two injured soldiers were taken from the open interior of the craft. They were transferred onto waiting gurneys. Those injured were whisked away to a waiting doctor for treatment. As soon as one stretcher was removed, a new one was put on the chopper in its place. The drill was precise and left little room for error. The chopper could then quickly depart back into battle to pick up more damaged young Americans.

Just as Gus helped insert the second stretcher into the flat, open service area of the medevac chopper, he noticed the young army medic aboard groan in pain and bend over. From the blood, he quickly saw that the medic had been shot in his leg. The medic had not mentioned his injury as his duty was to the two injured soldiers under his care. They were his priority.

Gus helped the medic from the chopper, got him onto a gurney, and was directing that he be sent to one of the ship's gunshot trauma specialists. As all that was happening, Gus heard a call on the radio of the chopper. "Medevac, medevac, this is control. We have an urgent evacuation need about six clicks south and west of Nha Trang. Repeat, immediate medical evac six clicks south and west of Nha Trang."

CHAPTER 2

ENJOY THE FLIGHT

The deck officer of the *Sanctuary* had come to Gus's station on the ship. He was concerned as to why the chopper was taking so long to off-load. As soon as he saw the army medic on the gurney, he knew. He also heard the radio request. The pilot, in a very distressed tone responded, "This is ME 207. We have lost our onboard doc. We have had no ability to respond."

The radio voice responded, "Roger, no doc available. We have no other unit available for that evac. We need a responding unit." The message went out over the airways as the operator emphasized, "Anyone, we need a responder. We have multiple civilian casualties, including small children."

Gus's mind could think only of his small child waiting to be born back home. He yelled to Warrant Officer Jordan, the pilot, "I will go!"

"Not without ranking permission, you will not," was the pilot's reply. Gus turned to the deck officer as if the question had already been asked.

Gus simply spread his arms and uttered, "Sir?"

The deck officer reluctantly replied, "Go ahead, Corpsman, but when the captain finds out about this, he will have both our asses." Gus's quick response was, "He'll never know. We will be back in less than thirty minutes."

Gus jumped aboard as the chopper lifted from the deck of the ship. He hooked the seatbelt and put on the aviation helmet the army medic had been wearing. First, he heard his pilot telling the evacuation control operator that they were on their way with a nine-minute touch. In a lighthearted tone, he then addressed Gus, "Welcome aboard, swab. First time in a chopper?"

Gus responded that it was, and the pilot made another lighthearted statement as he said, "We are less than six minutes out. Enjoy the flight."

Gus did. It was a calm morning with unlimited visibility. He could see the white sand beaches and the palm trees that nearly touched the water's edge. The lush jungle behind was green as far as he could see. He wondered how a place so beautiful could be so full of death.

In a very few minutes he heard the pilot as he responded back to the medevac controller. "We are less than a minute out. Please notify ground force that we are friendly and that we need smoke near the best location for touch." In a few seconds, they were on the ground. Villagers began to bring civilian women and children to the chopper. Gus began to administer whatever aid he could to them. They were burned and dazed from a planted bomb. The bomb had hurt no Americans but instead just those Vietnamese who were there, at their homes. By default, they had been made part of this war and now had become its casualties.

The chopper was revving to lift the injured group from the floor of the jungle when Gus saw a young girl running toward the chopper. "Wait, wait," Gus spoke into his helmet radio, "there is one more." The pilot hesitated. Gus looked directly into her young eyes as she ran toward the chopper. She could not have been more than twelve or thirteen years old. Gus reached to take her hand into his so he could pull her aboard the chopper. He was looking directly at her when she lobbed a blue-colored grenade from her hand into the chopper. Before anyone had time to react, the chopper exploded. Gus felt a burning force jam him against the wall of the craft. His only thought was of the face of that young girl. It was his last thought.

Back aboard ship, no one knew what had happened. All that seemed to matter was that Petty Officer Johnson was missing. This was a very important happening on a naval ship. The first thought was that he had fallen overboard. The captain who was in the bridge was notified immediately. He called for the on-duty staff during the time that Johnson had his last duty and also called for anyone who might have information regarding Petty Officer Johnson. Ensign Palmer had information. It was he who had been on duty as deck officer. It was he who had given Petty Officer Johnson permission to board the medevac unit. He told the growingly irate captain the details about how Petty Officer Johnson boarded the medevac. He explained about how the normal medic for that flight had been shot and how the call had come in from medevac control. He explained to the captain how that specific chopper was the only one available for that mission. Without Johnson being allowed to board and take part in the mission, it would not have taken place.

"Sir," he said, almost as a plea, "there were wounded children. I gave permission to Petty Officer Johnson to make that flight. I take full responsibility for that choice, and there is none other than me to blame."

PROTOCOL

The captain went ballistic. He cussed as he told his radioman to contact medevac control and ask if there had been any problems connected to that flight. When the radioman finished that transmission with the word "over," there was no response. Silence filled the room with an eerie and stagnant stall. The captain told the operator to ask again.

This time a response came back, "Stand by." In just a moment, another voice filled the airway.

"Captain, this is Major Seawell of the 305th medevac unit. Sir, I regret to inform you that chopper exploded while lifting off from a mission earlier this morning. There were the remains of a number of civilians who were onboard, the onboard doc, and the chopper pilot. We are attempting to locate the dog tags at this time and will notify you as soon as we have more information. All aboard that flight were killed."

The captain then took the radio mic and responded that the normal medic for that flight was onboard his ship being treated for gunshot trauma. "I repeat, your medic was not one of those killed. One of the souls onboard was Petty Officer Johnson, a sailor based on the USS *Sanctuary*." After that, silence again filled the bridge area. Formal military inquiries would be what remained of this incident.

The fact that a naval corpsman was on an army chopper presented some real issues. It was a highly unusual fit. In fact, no one remembered an incident like this happening before. Later that day, the captain called the young ensign into his sea cabin. His face held a scowl, and his glasses were low on his nose as he was peering downward at a typed page. No one could question his authority.

"Sit, Ensign." He finished a document he was reading and signed it. He looked up at the ensign, laid his glasses on his desk, then began, "What you did this morning was way beyond your authority. Only the ship's captain can authorize the departure of any personnel from a U.S. Navy ship. If pursued, your career will end in a very negative way. Because Johnson should have known that, his career will be just as tarnished. The naval hearing will conclude that because of you and Johnson, a petty officer, an army warrant officer, and a number of Vietnamese civilians are now dead. A much-needed and expensive piece of military equipment has been destroyed. Had the chopper sat on deck, this would not have taken place. I have researched all my options in an attempt to try and clean this thing up. You have created a situation that gives me no choice but to now put my ass on the line alongside you and Johnson. Understand clearly what I am about to say. I have given my staff orders to create a written order, dated and timed prior to the flight of that chopper from this deck. It will be signed by me. Never, and I mean never, take this kind of initiative again. Dismissed." The young ensign was exactly what you may think Tom Sawyer would have looked like, the difference being that instead of wearing cutoff jeans, he was a polished and perfectly dressed U.S. Naval officer.

Palmer stood, saluted, and with a clear and firm voice, responded, "Yes, sir." He turned to leave the cabin. Without looking up from his desk, the captain said in a loud voice, "Palmer, you did what I would have done."

CHAPTER 3

HEARTBREAK DELIVERED

Less than thirty-six hours later, in fact, about 6:00 the next evening, there was a knock at the front door of Aggie's parents' home. Her mother answered the door. As she walked to the door, she noticed a grey sedan sitting in the drive. It was not until she answered the door that she connected that car to what would become this day's horror. Two young navy officers were standing at her front door. Both wore perfectly prepared full-dress uniforms. They asked if she was Mrs. Gus Johnson. She could hardly reply.

"No. Honey," she hollered, "find Aggie and bring her here quick!" She asked the two to enter the front door.

In a moment, Aggie and her dad entered the room. Her father knew immediately what this was about. Aggie did not. She walked up to the young men, extended her hand, and spoke, almost gleefully, "I am Aggie Johnson."

With a somber but official voice he stated, "Mrs. Johnson, the Secretary of the Navy has asked us to deliver this letter and to inform you that your husband, Petty Officer Johnson, has died in action in Southeast Asia. He was killed early yesterday. It happened while he was on a heroic and compassionate mission. That is all the information we have at this moment but more will be following. You will be notified as it is available. A military chaplain will be put at your disposal to help you through this time. Is there anything we can do for you?"

Aggie could offer no answer. She could not even think much less respond. She was nothing but a shell of a woman standing helplessly abandoned as she stared at the two sailors. She felt unable to function in any way. Her only reaction was that she pressed both hands and held them against her slightly larger stomach.

Her mother put her arms around Aggie, and the first words from her mouth were, "We must tell Gus's parents immediately."

Aggie's dad said to the two sailors, "If you will accompany me to Gus's home, we will notify his parents." They agreed even though it was not part of their official duty.

The grey car pulled into the drive while Mr. and Mrs. Johnson were sitting on the porch. When they looked and saw the two sailors and Aggie's dad exit the grey car, they both froze. The three walked up and onto the porch. Aggie's dad looked directly at the two parents who remained seated and said, "These gentlemen bring unbearable news. We have lost Gus."

Trying to relieve some of the pressure from Aggie's dad, the older of the two officers followed, "As we informed his wife, Corpsman Johnson died a heroic death while trying to save others. He has made the ultimate sacrifice for his country, and this country is forever grateful. We have no further information available at this time. As it becomes available, it will follow."

Mr. Johnson rose and walked directly to where the three were standing. He looked at Aggie's dad and said to him, "You need to go and be with Aggie." He then turned to the two sailors, extended his hand to them, and without any break in his voice told them that he knew they had performed a task today that no man should ever have to undertake. He told them that he appreciated their being there but he and Mrs. Johnson would prefer to be left alone now. With that the two sailors returned Aggie's father to his home.

The two officers departed to go to their next location to deliver a similar message to another young wife. It never got easier, no matter how many times they did it. The training they undertook required that they never exhibit emotion, that they never make any physical contact, and that they maintain absolute military professionalism during a notification. They had done this one by the book.

Mr. and Mrs. Johnson continued to sit on the porch. Neither said a word. She was crying. While neither spoke, thoughts were running through her head at lightning speed. She was wishing that he would begin crying. She knew that he would hold this pain in his heart as he always did. She also knew that nothing in the life of her husband could provide more of that pain than the news he was just given. His son was his life, his best friend, was all that he had ever hoped a son could be, and most importantly, it was Gus who would carry his name forward. She knew that the grief he would bear would tear him apart. Gus would be irreplaceable. "Please, Lord, let him release his pain, so as to relieve it." That was her prayer, and she said it aloud. That day, her prayer was not answered.

A few blocks away, Aggie's dad entered the house to an eerie silence. He walked to Aggie's room and saw her lying there with her mom. He knew she was in good hands. He went back into the living room where he sat, wide awake, for the remainder of that night.

WE WILL LEARN TOGETHER

The next day, soon after lunch, another grey car pulled into the drive of Aggie's home. That time, her dad saw it first and made his way to the front porch. Again, a tall young naval officer exited the car and started to the steps. He looked as if he could have come directly off a recruiting poster. He was erect, perfectly polished, and every item of his uniform was exactly where and how it should be. He had on his cap, but took it off as he approached the porch.

"Are you Mr. Johnson?" he asked.

"No, I am Harvel Croom. My daughter was married to Petty Officer Johnson."

"Sir," he began, "I have been sent by the U.S. Navy to offer assistance to Mrs. Johnson and other family as they may require."

"Son, I do not know of anything you can do, but come in and make yourself at home. I will go and see if Aggie," he corrected himself, "Mrs. Johnson will see you. Have a seat here in the living room and I will be back in a moment." Aggie was not ready to see anyone, but did suggest to her dad that he ask the chaplain to go and speak to the Johnsons.

Her father did so and the lieutenant agreed that would be a good start. It was the lieutenant's first time at this chore. He would learn as he proceeded.

The short drive took less than a few minutes. Again, he exited the sedan, adjusted his uniform, and walked to the front door of the Johnson home. He knocked and within a couple of moments, a tall and obviously sad man made his way to the front door. Each step he took seemed pained. His shoulders drooped, and his head tilted downward. When he got to the door, he expressed no emotion. Without the officer having to say a word, Mr. Johnson opened the screen door and said, "Come in. Please have a seat and tell me if you have any more details about how our son died." He did have additional details and was about to begin them when Mr. Johnson said, "Wait, let me get my wife."

She joined them after he called her. Lieutenant Morgan began again, "According to the information available at this time, it would appear that your son was given permission to board a U.S. Army helicopter to assist in a rescue mission in Vietnam. He was serving on a rescue ship operating in that area. The normal medic for that flight had been wounded. A mission was called for, and since there was no normal medic, he was allowed, at his request, to join that rescue.

"Everything appeared to be normal until the flight exploded as it was about to begin to lift off with evacuees onboard. All on the flight lost their lives. That is all of the information that is available. There is no question, Mr. and Mrs. Johnson, your son is truly a hero. He gave his life in an attempt to save others. He went far beyond what his normal duties required. He will be receiving a Silver Star from the U.S. Navy, a U.S. Army Commendation Medal, and will be issued a Silver Star by the South Vietnamese government. I know that none of this can replace your son. I hope it will give you ease in the future to understand that your son did in fact make the ultimate sacrifice for his country. No greater honor can be achieved."

All of this information was later shared with Aggie and her family. It is information like this that one day may help someone cope with the loss of a loved one. It had no value that day.

The time surrounding Gus's death and burial was much like a fog for Aggie. She remembered it, but it was as if it were happening to someone else. The dull and constant pain quite literally caused her heart to ache. When her pain would reach a point that she could no longer bear it, she would think of the baby inside her. It was a sign that she must continue. The most important obligation of her life was about to begin, and she must persevere. Gus would have had it no other way.

Her parents, even though they shared the horrible reality of that time, held strong for her benefit. Gus's parents also offered her much support. Everyone agreed that the baby was the most important task at hand.

Many friends in the small town surrounded her with whatever they could offer. She was never alone for any moment other than those she chose.

Lieutenant Morgan did everything for her that he possibly could. He helped her through a lot of the business details, which involved insurance, naval assistance, and other issues as they related to the fact that she was now a U.S. Navy widow. He helped her plan the funeral.

A GRATEFUL NATION

The day of the funeral, Mr. and Mrs. Johnson came to Aggie's house. Gus's dad seemed much older. He had not eaten since he had heard the news about his son. His horror of this time was held within, and those who knew him could see it. Gus's mom brought food as she knew a crowd would stop by after the funeral to pay their respects. It was always her intent to do more than her part. A long black Cadillac pulled into the driveway, and Mr. Rimons, who was the local funeral director, came onto the front porch where the family was all gathered. Lt. Morgan was there too.

The director said in a voice just loud enough for everyone to hear, "Folks, it is time for the service. We need to go."

All stood except Mr. Johnson. He looked at everyone, and for the first time that they could hear, he spoke, "This is the hardest thing I have ever done. Standing now and getting into that car will be confirmation that this not a dream; it is real." He sat for a moment before rising from the rocker.

The brick church was only a few blocks away. It was a Presbyterian church and had been kept perfectly through the years. The grounds, the building, and even the bell tower looked just as they had since it was built during the early 1900s. As soon as they arrived, they entered the double doors into the sanctuary. The U.S. flag covered the grey coffin at the front. It was closed. The family was the last to enter, and a couple of pews at the front were marked off with small red, white, and blue bows. Music played softly on the organ. When they entered the door, everyone else stood. As the family sat, so did the congregation. That prompted the music to end. The preacher, who knew them all very well, stood and began with a prayer. He prayed the family would find peace during this time. So far, Aggie had not. Somewhere between a fallen hero and the miracle of the baby within her was a conflict as she tried to find peace with this horror. Today was about the loss.

After talking about all the wonderful things Gus had done, he asked if there was anyone who would like to have a word. A young soldier in his dress uniform, sitting near the back, rose and said, "Yes, sir, I would."

The soldier moved toward the front of the church. He walked with a walking stick and limped. He went to the front but did not go into the pulpit. He turned and spoke. No one knew who this young man was. His words were loud and clear. "I am Specialist Bert White. I am the soldier who was the medic assigned to the helicopter that crashed, the one Petty Officer Johnson was on. I knew him from the frequent times we worked together on his ship. He would often be the leader of the team that took casualties from our Huey when we landed on the USS *Sanctuary*. He was kind while being professional. He was friendly while being absolute about his drill. He was the one who discovered I had been shot. He was the one who forced me onto a gurney and into appropriate care. He was the one," he hesitated as emotion took over but then continued in a broken voice, "who took my place on that flight. He did so because a call had come in for evac needed for a group of civilians, mostly women and children. Had he not insisted on getting on that chopper in my place, those folks would have had no chance for help. In trying to save the lives of people he did not know, Petty Officer Johnson gave his life. Thank you for listening to what I have said."

With that, he turned, came to attention, and saluted the flag-draped coffin. He then gently placed his hand on the casket. He turned and walked back to his seat. He was a big man, and big tears flowed from his eyes.

A sailor Aggie did not know sang "God Bless America." It was the song she had suggested to Lt. Morgan because she knew that Gus loved it so much. After another prayer, they were instructed that the service would conclude at the grave site. A group of Gus's friends from high school came to the front of the church and took his coffin to the waiting hearse. When they got to the cemetery, that same group took the coffin from the hearse and then to the grave. It was then that the military took over. Lt. Morgan stood at full attention at the end of the row of seats where Aggie sat.

A color guard, which would have normally been four soldiers, was now five. The flag of the United States of America and a naval flag would normally be the only two, but this time a U.S. Army flag was also carried. A sailor with a shouldered firearm stood on each side of those three flags. There was a firing party of seven sailors who would fire the twenty-one-gun salute. Each of them would fire three volleys. At the command of "ready," they would raise their weapons to firing position. "Aim" would be the second command and would be followed by "fire." Each time the weapons would fire, those in attendance would flinch as the report would confirm the realization of their friend or family member's lost life.

A separate detail then took the flag from the casket and folded it into a triangular shape. The commander of the detail handed three of the empty shell casings to one of the sailors who had folded the flag. That sailor inserted them into the triangular fold. He then handed the folded flag to Lt. Morgan, who inspected it to ensure it was folded perfectly. He then walked with stiff precision to just in front of where Aggie sat. Her family sat on one side while Gus's family sat on the other. He knelt in front of her, handed her the flag, and as he placed it in her hands, he began to speak: "On behalf of the president of the United States, the United States Navy, the United States Army, and a grateful nation, please accept this flag as a symbol of our appreciation for your loved one's honorable and faithful service."

He stood and saluted her as "Taps" played in the distance. The color guard lowered the U.S. Navy and the U.S. Army flags to full retreat while the U.S. flag was lowered to half retreat. It was horrible but beautiful. It was torment but offered relief. The fog of sadness began to lift, but with that came the realization of a grief that would persist for many years. Now Aggie must see her way forward. She knew she had no choice but to make it through this. The life inside her, that life that she and Gus had made, demanded nothing less.

LIFE BEGINS AT THIS END

For the next few months of her pregnancy, Aggie tried as hard as she could to move on with her life. It seemed that she could never really separate herself from her memories of Gus. She relived every moment of their brief life together. She would see him at a store or in a car only to understand in a flash that it was not really him. All of these things were normal, and she very openly discussed them with her mom. Those discussions were probably her best healing tool.

Gus Sr., however, was not faring as well. His failure to discuss the loss of his son was allowing that trauma to eat away at his very being. His wife and others who were close to him would talk about the upcoming birth and about how the new child would be a replacement for Gus. Gus would want his father to be as much of a dad to this new baby as he was to him. He heard those words and agreed with them as they were spoken. But as quickly as reality resurfaced, they would wash from his mind and he would shrink back into the darkness of his son's death. His grief was taking a toll on his physical well-being. All of a sudden, Gus Blake Johnson Sr. was becoming an old man.

"Mr. Johnson, Andy is waiting to see you. I know he is a good friend of yours so I let him sit in your office and wait." Those were the words he heard as he walked into his drugstore this morning.

He made his way to his office with a freshly poured cup of coffee in his hand. His first words, even prior to saying hello, were, "Will you have a cup?" After a nod of his guest's head, "G," as he was known to his workers, turned and asked the lady who had told him about his visitor if she would get Andy a cup of coffee.

Soon both were sitting across the desk from each other. He and Anderson (Andy) Powell had known each other for years. Andy called on Johnson Drug Company as a salesman for many years. As such, he watched as Gus grew up, knew G's wife well, and was to all of them a good friend.

After a discussion about Gus's death and about how moving on was so tough for all concerned, Andy came to a quick point, "G, your heart is not in this business anymore. You are older now, and besides, you will soon have a new baby in your life. You should devote time to the new grandchild. That will help you as you struggle with your loss.

"As you probably remember, one of my best friends founded the Medical Center Pharmacy chain some years ago. He asked that I speak to you. He knows that you and I are close friends. They now have forty-nine stores and would like for your store to become the fiftieth. They are well aware that your store is very profitable and as such is quite valuable. They feel it would be a perfect fit for their chain. Only the name will change. They will keep the same employees, rent your building from you, and most importantly of all, will pay you very well for that purchase."

Gus Sr. heard and understood every word that had been said. He sat for a minute with no response. He then looked directly at Andy and replied, "Andy, I will need to talk with my wife about this, and I would also like to talk with my attorney before I respond."

Andy assured him that was by far the best way to proceed from this initial conversation. G replied, "I will call you soon with an answer either way."

He stood as if to say *we are done now.* They exchanged good-byes, and Andy left the office. G could hear Andy on his way out speaking to all the employees whom he had known for the many years he had called on them at Johnson Drug.

That evening, G and Mrs. Johnson spoke about the visit from Andy. He told her what Andy had proposed. Her response to him was just as it had always been in those kind of matters: an almost flippant, "That's up to you." He called and set an appointment for the following day with his attorney.

G arrived at Robert Neece's office a few minutes early. He noticed that the usual receptionist did not greet him in the waiting room. He also noticed that Robert's office door was open. From his desk, Robert could see G waiting and waved him in.

"Where is Rebecca?" G asked.

"She retired and moved to Green Forrest to be with her oldest daughter. She wants to be with her grandkids," responded Robert. They talked for a minute, and then G went into the conversation about the sale of the drugstore. He also indicated that he had wanted to stop by for some time. He wanted to be sure that the new grandchild would be the benefactor of his and his wife's estate. Robert seemed to weigh those words very seriously. "You are making good decisions, G, and this is all very important. But it must be done right. Here is the way I would like to proceed. Bring Aggie by with you and your wife next week. We will all sit down and talk about how best to make this work. It is important to bring Aggie into this as she will be responsible to administer any estate left to her child. It must be done in a way that serves to benefit the needs of that child and her ability to provide for it."

They agreed and the appointment was set. If Aggie agreed, the meeting would be the following Thursday.

Robert Neece had been Gus Johnson's attorney for many years. He was also his tax accountant and had been a part of almost every decision G had made over the last thirty-plus years. He could well remember when G came to him and wanted to open his pharmacy. G had been working as the pharmacist at the only drugstore in town. He wanted to open a new and more modern store, and the owners of the older drugstore did not mind. They were ready to retire and move on. They did, he did, and all had worked out for the very best with the new store.

His new store had done very well. He had invested well and bought property, including a farm nearby that he rented out. The farm also served as a retreat for him as one of his greatest pleasures was hunting. Especially when Gus had gotten old enough to join him on those adventures. There they could bird hunt with their Pointer, "Toy." He was a great dog, and the hours he and Gus spent with that dog were among the best of his life. Their dog could also track a deer. Toy was the best of companions as the three of them enjoyed the life and balance of nature. There were ducks on the five-acre pond, and fishing there could always produce a good string of bream, just the right size for a frying pan. Being less than fifteen miles from town gave them very easy access. It was their small piece of heaven on earth. He and Gus knew—and had enjoyed—every nook and cranny!

GET A JOB

Aggie arrived at Attorney Neece's office a few minutes before G and Mrs. Johnson. She walked into the empty waiting room just as G had done the week before. Mr. Neece noticed her enter and motioned her into his office. "I am really glad you are here early," he said. "I have an issue I would like to discuss with you." He nodded toward her bump. "You are very soon to be a mom. I know that you have your folks to help with the baby and I also know that you do not need to start work for a couple of months after having your baby. With all of that, I am going to need a new receptionist. I can do well without one for a couple of months but do need to go ahead and look for someone to fill that spot. If you will agree that you may like to give it a try, I would like for you to have that job. You can type, can't you?"

She smiled and then responded to his question with a yes.

"I am not as busy as I used to be. If you have to miss a day or two for some reason with your new baby, that will be okay. I just need someone I can trust and who knows most of the folks around here. You, young lady, are that person."

His question was the first thing that had happened since she found out that Gus had been killed that made her feel as if she mattered. This would be a perfect situation for her. Her quick reply was, "Yes, I look forward to that opportunity." They were both pleased with the potential of this relationship.

Mrs. Johnson and G soon arrived and entered directly into Robert's office, where they joined Aggie. Aggie stood, and both Mrs. Johnson and G hugged her tightly. They had become very fond of each other. After a short conversation, all agreed to the basic issues involving the documents Robert was to draw up. Aggie said very little.

She had not expected anything to this degree. A little information was discussed about the size of the Johnsons' estate. She knew they were well off, but had no idea as to the amount of wealth they had created. It was more than she could have dreamed.

"I promise that our baby will be well taken care of," she assured everyone. And that was just what the Johnsons wanted to hear. She felt she owed them at least some explanation of what her financial status was so she offered some details. She did not get deeply into her parents' finances as they were pretty obvious. Her dad was a retired lineman who had done a good job with managing his income so that neither he nor his wife would ever be a burden on Aggie. Their wealth was nothing like that of the Johnsons, but they were assured her family was very secure.

She spoke quickly of that part and then went into a discussion about what the Navy had provided. She had navigated these issues with the aid of Lieutenant Morgan.

All remembered who he was. He was a great guy and a great help to that end. She remembered him well as she was his first assignment, and he wanted everything to be perfect. Also, his kindness during this time was a blessing to her. Aggie received a fairly large cash benefit. It had all been put into the bank and into an investment fund. That fund would be used to educate the new baby. In addition, she did not incur any debt related to Gus's burial. She would also receive full medical payment for her care and the baby's during the birth. There would also be a benefit from Social Security until the baby reached the age of eighteen. With a job, she could raise her child very comfortably. With what the Johnsons were offering, she and her new baby would be more than comfortable. "None of this will replace Gus," she went on, "but it will remind us daily that he is still very much a part of our lives."

CHAPTER 4

BABY IS HERE

On March 12, Aggie awoke to a wet bed. She was beginning to have pains and knew immediately what was about to take place. Her parents got her to the hospital. That trip had been rehearsed several times. Also, her dad remembered the drill, having made that same trip eighteen years ago. Mr. and Mrs. Johnson were notified and soon arrived in the waiting room. The four of them sat for what seemed to be hours. A couple of Aggie's friends showed up, and everyone awaited the magic moment. Only Aggie's mom was allowed in the birthing center. When she came out all smiles, everyone knew.

She announced that they would get to see the new "son" in a few minutes. He was being cleaned and readied for his grand introduction into his new life. At that moment, there was no emotion in the room other than joy. In a few minutes, a nurse came through the double doors and told them that two of them at a time could come in and see the baby.

First, though, Aggie would like for Mr. Johnson to come in alone. With a wondering face, he entered. He did so very shyly as he was not accustomed to entering a place where so much was going on and with babies being born. He felt that was a place where men just did not belong. At least that was the way it was when he came along.

As he entered the room, Aggie was sitting on the bed with the back inclined. In her arms, tightly wrapped, was the new baby. She smiled at him and said, "This is your new grandson. I know how very close you and Gus were. I ask this favor, and if you say no, I will understand. I would like to give our new son your and Gus's name. I know you gave your name to Gus, and I feel he would want it to be his son's name as well." G could not speak; he just looked at her and nodded yes. He turned and left the room without saying a word. Just as he was about to close the door behind him, she spoke to him again, "I think we'll just call him 'Gus 3.'"

When he reentered the waiting room, all looked at him as if to ask what that was all about. He simply smiled and said, "Gus the third, no, 'Gus 3' is waiting to meet you all." With that, he sat on one of the pale green plastic couches, put his face into his hands, and sobbed like a baby.

The next two months were filled with washing diapers, making formula, answering the call of a crying baby during the night, and changing diapers almost constantly. Aggie never asked her mom or anyone else to do any of those duties. She did them and also helped her mom around the house. She did not want to be a burden. The Johnsons came over every day. The one thing that required little to none of her time was rocking the baby. That was a grandparent joy. It was only late at night after she had fed Gus 3 that she was able to hold him and rock. The bond that formed between them was equal to the one she had shared with Gus. It was forever.

Two months went by quickly, and Aggie went to visit with Attorney Neece. She asked if his offer was still open. "Of course it is. When will you be ready to start?" he replied. She answered, "In a week, on Monday, June first."

Aggie's mom had insisted that she did not want Gus 3 at a nursery. She was very capable of taking care of him and she would have plenty of help. All four grandparents were excited about the task. "It certainly will not be the first diaper any of us have ever changed," she said.

BEGINNING AGAIN

On June 1, Aggie left home about 8:30 a.m. The office would open at 9:00, and she wanted to be there to do that. When she left her home, she felt a number of emotions, but was excited to get back into the world and start this new era of her life. But being apart from Gus 3 for the first time was distressing. Even knowing that everything could not be better positioned, she still felt an ache in her heart as she walked to the porch. When she stepped down from the bottom step, she suddenly relived that moment when Gus had first looked into her eyes and held her hands. It was almost as if he stood there now. He would be saying to her that she must move on and embrace every opportunity that awaited her and his namesake. She felt he would have wanted her to be that same Aggie he had fallen for. The one he had gotten up enough nerve to ask to sit beside that Friday night, just a few months over a year ago.

Aggie's new job was perfect for her. Mr. Neece was very impressed with her and the way she handled the clients who came into the office. Her secretarial duties were all done to perfection, and her work ethic was one of the best he had ever seen. She was a perfect fit for his practice—his new right hand.

Aggie began to think the world of Mr. Neece. She had never known a nicer man. He seemed to understand her better than anyone. He went out of his way to ensure that she never became involved with anyone who may be less than a perfect client. His practice had few to no criminal clients, and most of his work was either civil or with the tax accounting needs of those clients. Soon, she was able to understand and do much of the busy work required with preparing tax returns. She loved to do that and did it well.

Gus 3 was also doing well. He was beginning to stand and was very close to taking a first step. That would be bittersweet. As soon as he started walking, he would begin exploring his new world. Time would accelerate, and soon he would no longer be "mom's baby." One evening she got home at the usual time of about 5:30. Gus 3 and her mom were sitting on the bottom step of the front porch.

She got out of her car and started up the walk. After she took just a couple of steps, Gus 3 stood up and began to walk toward her. He stumbled several times and fell, but each time he would get up and try again. He had taken his first steps! She could not have been prouder. That spot created a special memory again. Her son's first step was taken by that same step where she and Gus had stood. She could feel Gus there again this time, smiling and as proud as she was.

Aggie and Gus 3 would take a walk almost every night after dinner. Mom and toddler moved at a toddler's pace. Her folks still ate dinner between 5:30 and 6:00 so there was plenty of time for them to share. He would hold her hand when they walked. Then more and more often, he started to pull away. It would be to look at a flower or pick up a rock. He began to notice a world around him that offered endless magic.

His first words all related to family. He called Aggie "Mom," her mother was "Mama," and her father was "Da." He was very close to both of them. If you were to paint a picture of the perfect grandparents, Aggie's folks would look and act the part. Both with knowing and experienced depths of wisdom in their kind eyes. The look of a warm home and loving family would be the best way to describe them. The Johnsons were "Memaw" and "G." It was as if he knew the exact role each played in his young life. He could say all of their names well. After all, Gus 3 had given them those names. On one evening as he and his mom were walking, he looked through a fence at some boys playing basketball. He turned to Aggie as if he was telling her something she did not know. He simply pointed and said "ball." It wasn't long before he was speaking short sentences. Those short sentences created a new level of the closeness of their bond. They were becoming friends as well.

He was close to and loved all his family. The bond that was building between Aggie and Gus 3 was hard to explain. It was as if he was giving her all of the love he would have normally shared with both his mom and his dad. He had no dad, so all of that went to her. He had never known a dad. That issue created no particular sorrow for him. He could sense that there was a hole left empty by the one they all called Gus. It was not until later that he understood just what that hole had held. For now, his mom filled every empty spot within him that required love with no bounds.

Gus 3 grew like a weed. He had become aware of things like Christmas and Santa. He looked forward to the Easter Bunny. One of his favorite things was watching cartoons. He loved watching one particular show over and over on the TV: *Batman with Robin, the Boy Wonder.* Memaw made him a black cape just like the one Batman wore. She even cut out the shape of a bat and sewed it on his cape for him. It had a button in front, and he could wear it all day. His backyard was "Gottum." That was as close as he could come to saying Gotham City. He righted many wrongs and saved many a damsel. Later, he would have a newfound friend and Memaw would fashion her a Robin cape. Together they controlled crime in the neighborhood. He had toy cars and trucks. He also had begun to develop a group of other friends. There were several boys and girls in his neighborhood about his same age.

He had met "Robin" while walking one day with his mom. They had walked two doors down from their house. Another mom was standing next to a young girl who was playing. She had toy cars and trucks and was rolling them on the ground. Gus 3's mom and the other mom spoke as they knew each other. They had both had their children on almost the same day. The little girl got up and walked to just in front of Gus 3. Aggie spoke up and said, "Gus 3, this is Marsha. She is your same age." He looked at her with eager eyes. In a way that cannot be explained to adults, he knew she would provide a wonderful comrade with whom to share his youth. With that introduction, Marsha looked curiously at this young stranger. He was a person just the right size for her.

She said, "Will you be my friend?" He was excited, and a lifelong relationship was born then and there. She never called him Gus 3, though. She named him simply G3. It was easier for her to say. That name stuck with all but Gus 3's mom. From that day forward, G3 and Marsha were never less than best friends.

They played together and enjoyed a life free of any obligation except that of just living. All of this would soon change. School was to begin in a few weeks. One day Mama was sitting on the porch while Marsha and G3 played in the front yard. They had been joined by two other boys who also lived in the neighborhood.

All four of them were sitting on the ground. They had created roads and a town using the small cars and trucks that were their toys. They talked about what they wanted to be when they grew up.

"A fireman," shouted the first young boy.

"I want to drive a bulldozer," followed the second.

Marsha (the only girl in the group) was next and she thought a minute. "I want to be a doctor at the hospital," was her reply.

It was G3's time to respond. "I want to be a hero," he said. They all looked at him and none of them had any idea what that meant.

Marsha asked, "What do you mean, G3?"

"Well, Mom and Mama and Da and even Memaw and G all say my dad was a hero. He was riding in a helicopter when he left to go to heaven. They said God needed him worse than we did so He took him up there. Since I would love to ride in a helicopter, and the preacher says every Sunday that we should all try to go to heaven,

I guess being a hero is the best way to do both of those. So, yeah, I want to be a hero." All seemed to understand, including Mama sitting on the bottom step of the porch a few feet away.

SCHOOL

Gus 3 had his sixth birthday on March 12. Then it had been a wonderful summer. It was almost fall, and he and Marsha were looking forward to starting school at Cowan Elementary. It was the same school that Gus 3's mom and dad had both attended. School was to begin the next day. Aggie had taken the morning off to go with him on that first day. It was the first grade and it was at the same school where she had gone her first day. In fact, it was the same room. When she stepped inside, she recognized the smell and the view from the windows. They were much the same. Different furniture and chalkboards but still the same room. G3 saw Marsha and her mom a few feet away. Pulling on his mom's hand, he led her to that place. He and Marsha were best friends. They were both excited to be in the same room. Soon the teacher began to welcome everyone. She said that the first order would be to get the students into their seats.

The teacher began, "I am Mrs. McCullen. As I call your name, please take a seat at the desk I am standing by. Remember that this will be your seat every day." All of the students nodded that they understood and would remember. Their teacher knew better. When she got about halfway through the second row, she read from the roll, "Gus Johnson." Gus 3 did not move. His mom tugged his arm, but still he did not move. Again, she said, "Gus Johnson." He didn't even flinch.

Knowing full well who he was, Mrs. McCullen walked over to him and said, "Gus, will you come with me to your seat?"

With his big eyes and already handsome face, he looked directly at her and said, "I am not Gus Johnson. I am G3." Some of the other moms grinned, and Aggie wasn't sure whether to grin or cry.

The teacher, knowing his situation very well, simply looked down and said, "Well then, G3, will you go to your seat with me?"

"Yes, Mrs. McCullen," he said and walked to it without her. The roll call continued, and soon they were all seated.

The next order of business was to talk about lunch and snacks and the rules for parents. The students were to be picked up each day at 2:00, and only a person who had been pre-approved would be allowed to pick up a child. Aggie made sure that she and the four grandparents were all on the list. She and Marsha's mom agreed that the two of them should each be on the other's list. That would make the pickup much easier as they could swap pickup days. Marsha's mom even asked that G3's grandparents be put on Marsha's list as well. She trusted them without condition. The first grade was a little different from when she attended years ago. Anyway, it seemed like a great first morning, and Aggie was soon off to the law offices of attorney Robert Neece.

When she got to the office, Robert was very inquisitive about the morning's activities. He and his wife, Marylin, never had a child. He was not familiar with the issues involving children. G3 would be the closest thing he could have that he and Marylin could enjoy in that way. Aggie told him about the Gus Johnson/G3 issue, and he laughed. "Good for him. A man has to learn to stand up for himself," he said. She made a funny face when he said that.

"It's not time to start using the 'man' word," she responded. "He is only six."

Robert looked back at her and said, "Yeah, six going on twenty-six." She wasn't sure she liked the way that sounded either, but said nothing. She, much to her regret, knew exactly what he meant. The remainder of her day was full. She sat in with her boss and several of his clients as they went over various issues. She had learned shorthand in high school, and it helped a great deal in client meetings.

CHAPTER 5

A GOOD PLACE TO WORK

Robert Neece and Aggie were developing a special relationship. They had become very close friends. They shared details about their lives. A familiarity was forming that would become the cornerstone of a long-lasting relationship. He was very knowledgeable about her family history, and she knew about his. His wife was very active with social activities, and was involved with many charities and clubs. While they were very happy together, they did not spend a great deal of time together and had few of the same interests. He liked to read and take walks. She liked to be entertained and take trips. Aggie shared more of the same interests as he did. All that worked well into building a special friendship but neither allowed it to interfere in any way with their professional relationship. Robert and Aggie were as close as any two could be without ever crossing that thin line between friendship and courtship. That line stayed in place the entirety of their time together.

The summer after first grade, Gus 3 decided he wanted to play t-ball. Marsha and some of his other friends were all going to play, and he wanted to do so as well. G took G3 to his first practice. The coach was one of the best. He had been coaching for several years. He made a great effort in teaching the fundamentals of the game. G3 caught on quickly and was one of the early stars of the league. He could hit, catch a ball, and he understood the reason for the game. He wanted to win.

The late afternoons of summer were filled with ball games. G3's mom, his four grandparents, and now Mr. Neece and Mrs. Marylin would all be in attendance. Marsha's mom would be there, but not her dad. All wondered why. It was fun for the adults to watch, fun for the kids to play, but most of all, it was the best of times for those players when they got refreshments after each game. During that summer and the next one, t-ball filled most of the late afternoons.

G3 had begun to fish some with G. They were getting to be good buddies. G did not seem to mind when G3 would ask if Marsha could come along. After all, she was his very best friend and she loved to fish and go to the farm with them. Her mom certainly did not mind as she knew the Johnsons very well. Her dad never seemed to be around or spend any time with her. Marsha never talked about him, and the only time G3 had ever seen him was when he was asleep in the chair in front of the TV. He later learned that Marsha's dad had three basic parts to his life: his job at the town garage, going to the bar on the way home, and then drinking beer as he watched TV. He did not seem to be much of a dad. But then, how could G3 know what a dad should be?

Marsha went with them to the farm often, but not all of the time. It seemed that when it was just G3 and his granddaddy, they enjoyed a special time. G would talk to him as if he were a grown man. They talked about baseball, about cowboys, but most important of all, they talked about Gus. G told stories about how Gus could hunt so well. That he could shoot down a quail as it rose in front of their pointer's stand. How Toy would find the bird, take it in his mouth, and bring it back to Gus and drop it at his feet. He showed G3 where Gus had killed his first deer. It was a "forked horn." He laughed as he told G3 how he had marked Gus's face with blood from that first kill. He explained, "You do that to honor the life of the deer. We will do that when you kill your first one." G3 gobbled up every detail of those stories. This place was G and G3's little piece of heaven on earth.

He looked up at his granddad and said in a tone of total sincerity, "I would like to go hunting with you just like my dad did."

G said, "Son, I was a much younger man then. I cannot walk like I could then. We no longer have a dog to hunt with. I am pretty much relegated to playing golf with my older friends. With golf we can ride on a cart and go as slow as we like."

With all of the excitement a new adventure can offer, G3 said, "Well then, I would like to ride on a cart, G. I can go slow. I want to learn how to play golf with you."

STAY ON THE PATH

The next Saturday, G picked up G3 at his house before he even had a chance to eat breakfast. G assured everyone not to worry about that; he had it covered. They walked into Nick's Diner a few minutes later. A group of three men were sitting at the table near the back. They waved to G and G3 and motioned for them to come on back. It was the group they were going to play golf with. G had told them about G3's statement, and they all agreed that he should bring him on this Saturday.

Pancakes and sausage soon sat in front of G3. The men all had coffee. The waitress put orange juice in front of G3. He told his granddad that he wanted to have coffee just like the rest of them. G ordered it. G poured in as much cream as the cup would hold. He then started pouring sugar. G3 noticed that it was not from a dish like the one they had at home. It was a jar that had a top on it with a hole in it. The sugar just ran out as you turned it on its end. G put a lot of sugar in it for him. It was good, and he drank it all. It made him feel like he was "one of the guys."

G remembered that was the same way Gus had liked his coffee when he was a boy about that same age. Two of the other three men talked about how they had played golf with their sons. One who they all called Joanus must not have had a son. The other two men's sons were now grown, and they seldom even saw them, much less played golf. They talked on about how they missed those days.

Back in the car, Gus 3 began to ask a question. "G, do you wish you were playing golf with my dad? I bet you would rather be playing golf with him than me."

G waited a minute before he answered. "That is a tough question, and it is an important question. Listen to what I am going to say. It is important for you to know, and I want you to remember what I am about to tell you. Yes, I would love for Gus to be here. He and I never played golf together. There is nothing I, or he, would love more than for him to be here with you and me today. That cannot happen. It is just you and me. I promise that being here with you is the very best thing that I could be doing. I miss Gus with all my heart. God sent you to take his place. Instead of taking his place, you have created a new place. Now, I have you both. Nothing in this life is more important than our time together. Our golf game today is much more than just a game. This day will become a memory that you and I will share."

Cowan Golf and Country Club was less than a mile away. They pulled into the parking lot, walked over and got a cart, and put G's clubs on the back. They joined the other three and rode away. All of them were about the same age as G. Just regular guys out for a Saturday morning golf game, dressed in khakis and a golf shirt. As soon as they were out of sight of the clubhouse, G let G3 drive the cart. G operated the pedals, and G3 steered. Their cart was all over the place at first. After a couple of holes, G3 could follow the cart path as well as any man there. After the first nine, G let his grandson operate the pedals too. Life was surely good for them both.

They started playing golf often. G3 was learning to hit the ball pretty well, and even had his own set of golf clubs. For them, those golf games became another small piece of heaven on earth.

ON MY HONOR

Near the end of summer that year, a man came to see Aggie. Gus 3 could hear them talking from his room. He was asking her if she would be willing to become involved with the Cub Scout troop. It would be the one that her son could join that year. She could hardly say no. Besides, that would give them a great deal of time together. She agreed, and in a few days, she and Gus 3 were sitting in a room full of young boys all dressed in blue uniforms.

He did not have one yet, but he would by the next week. Mama would see to that. She would take him to the department store where they sold them and get him one that fit just right. She would then sew all of the numbers and badges they brought home on that first night onto the uniform.

This would all be done before next week's meeting. He would be one of the Cub pack. He quickly learned the handshake, the salute, and the Scout Oath. He learned to say the Pledge of Allegiance while standing and saluting the flag. They made things from popsicle sticks and did other crafts too. Just like t-ball, the refreshments at the end were the highlight of the pack meetings.

Tonight's meeting was a special night. Each Cub would receive his pinewood derby kit. From that, each would form a car that would then be raced on a special track. This was one of the year's biggest events for the Cubs.

Da would help Gus 3 with his car. He had a shop behind his house, and he worked on things all the time. In fact, a special time for them both was when they had such a project. Often Marsha would join them on those projects. She seemed to love all the same things he did. Nothing could be more pleasing to Da than to help his grandson on this project. The same night that Gus 3 had picked up his car kit, a mom from one of the other packs came to his house.

The lady had known Aggie for a long time. She also had a son in the Cub Scouts. That was not why she was there. One of the young men in her Cub pack had recently lost his dad.

Or at least sort of lost him. His father had to go to prison for two years. He had been caught for drunk driving. The problem was that it was not his first time. The boy, along with three other kids, had to be without a dad for those two years. Since his grandparents were gone, he had no one to help with his derby car. Word had gotten around that Da was really great with kids that age, and since Da was going to be helping his own grandson with a pinewood derby car, she hoped he would not mind helping that young man too. Aggie was sure he would not mind, but indicated that they should ask him.

They walked to the shop in back and spoke with Da about that request. He could hardly say no, but wanted to include G3 in the decision. All agreed to move forward with that plan and so they did. Da did have one request. He would like to have one more of those derby kits. Da helped G3 and the young Cub, whose name was Addison, with their cars. Addison was about the same height as G3, but looked thinner. He was a nice young man, but it was obvious that he was carrying a little bit of his dad's situation around with him. His feelings were somewhere between shame and sadness. The young man was bearing a heavier burden than he should. G3 and Marsha both sensed that and tried to cheer him up. Marsha came over almost every afternoon while they worked. She wished she could be a Cub Scout instead of in the Brownies so she could race a car too. Even though she could not be in the race, Da helped her make a car too. That was the reason for the third kit. Just like the boys. Soon they finished, and all three cars looked great. It was about time for the big race.

Moms and Cubs gathered as the race was about to begin on the long-sloped track. It was the same track they had used for years. It was thirty-five feet long and made of wood. The races were run quickly. Cars were placed at the top. When a bar was raised, both cars would leave the starting position at the same time. The first car to reach the bottom was the winner. Winners raced again. The losers got to race again as well—to be disqualified, a car had to lose at least two times. All the races were done. Each of the four dens had held its own races, and the winners of those races would now race for the championship.

Dads, the ones who had done the work on those cars, were right in the middle. In fact, most of the young Cubs had not even worked on their car. That was not true of the cars that G3 and Addison raced that night. Da had ensured each one of them had done most of the work. He had a couple of secrets, though, that he shared with them to use on their cars. One was to drill holes in the wood and insert an exact amount of weight so the car would be as heavy as allowed. The extra weight was to pull it down the hill. The other was to polish the axels the plastic wheels turned on. Candle wax was then followed by a coat of three-in-one oil on those wheels. Each of the cars had been enhanced by a "secret trick." In the end, four young Cubs stood proudly holding their prized cars in hand. One from each Cub pack.

The names were read. Cub Randall, Cub Addison, Cub Michael, and Cub G3. Of all the things that could happen, the two cars that Da had helped build were both in the race. The race-off was about to begin, and tensions were high. Families cheered for their sons, and the packs cheered for their cars. Marsha was right in the middle of it all. Her car was home on her dresser, but her heart was right in the middle of all this. She was excitingly pulling for G3 and for

Addison. Da and two other dads waited nervously by. In the end, it came down to G3 and Addison. Both had lost only one race. Those races had been lost to each other. The cars were very close to equal. This final race would declare the winner and champion of this year's derby.

Da felt terrible. He was torn over who to pull for. Would it be the young man he had helped who was carrying the burden of having a dad in prison or his own grandson? He stepped back and stood against the wall to watch the final race. He could not see very well, so he pulled up a chair and stood on it. From the chair he could see everything.

The command was given. "One at a time, you may place your cars. Step away three feet. Good luck and may the best car win." Da watched as Addison placed his car in position. G3 was next. Da noticed that he placed his car on the track at a slight angle. That angle would not allow his car to get a good start. G3 knew better. The plank was lifted, and Addison's car led the race and won. He was the new champ. Without the slightest emotion, G3 walked over to Addison. Using the Cub Scout handshake, he stuck his hand out with the two curled fingers. His simple and smiling words were, "Congratulations, champion." Addison beamed. It was the first time he had smiled like that since his father had been away.

That night, Da was as proud of his grandson as any grandfather could ever be. He never told a soul. Not even Aggie or Mama. He knew and G3 knew what had been done. Da wasn't sure but, by her reaction, he always believed that Marsha knew as well. Marsha knew G3 that well.

Both Marsha and G3 were growing up. They were no longer just little kids running around the neighborhood. They both had begun to realize how different their lives were becoming. Somewhere during this time, without ever discussing it and never having made any mention of it, the difference in their genders became evident to them both. Somehow, neither ever let that make any difference in their friendship.

As the years passed, G and G3 spent more and more time on the golf course. G3 had developed a reputation among the players at the course. He could hit the ball as far as any young man who had ever grown up playing there. He was excellent with his irons, and his putting improved every day. One thing he did do as often as possible was to play with G and his three friends on Saturday mornings. That had become a special game as it was his time with G. That group of guys all treated G3 like they would their own grandsons. He was special to them.

G and G3 got permission to enter the father-son tournament at the club. Since G was not G3's dad, it took a special ruling by the club's rules committee. They all agreed that G and G3 should be allowed to enter. It was a "best ball" tournament. It surprised everyone how many of the eleven-year-old Johnson kid's shots were used. Luck was with them, and they won that event.

As soon as the event ended, the group of three who played regularly with G and his grandson approached them. Joanus said, "Men, I have a suggestion. Your name, G3, is not a very good name for a golfer. You need a name like Arnold or Jack. I have a very good friend whose name, just like yours, is ended with the III. He is called 'Trip.' That is a good name and would be a really good name for a golf champion." They both said they would think about it.

On the way home, G3 asked his granddad what he thought about that change. Just like G's wife had always answered him about such issues, he said, "It's up to you."

G3 was about to enter the sixth grade. This would be a good time to make that change if he was going to do it. His name would not be the only thing that would change. He had grown much taller, and he was now beginning to look more like a teenager. He talked with Da and with Mama about his name. He also mentioned it to

Memaw. None of them seemed to have any problem with it but all indicated it would be his decision. He discussed it with Marsha. She told him that it was his decision but that she may still call him G3. Gus 3 did not mention it to his mom until he was ready to make his choice.

At dinner one night, he uttered that he was going to change the name he went by. That at the club and at school he wanted his name to be "Trip." Aggie's mom and dad were not the least bit surprised as they knew this would probably happen, and, in fact, they agreed with the change. Aggie did not respond positively but neither did she say no. He told his friends, who all agreed that was a great idea. His teachers, his friends at the club, even his grandparents—all but his mom and Marsha—began to call him Trip. To his mom, he was always Gus 3 and to Marsha, G3.

CHAPTER 6

THIRTY AND COUNTING

In a few days, Aggie would have a birthday. She would be thirty years old, and that must be a special year. Her mama and a number of her friends were planning a surprise party for her. Trip was told about it but that it was a big secret.

A group of her friends whom Aggie had been classmates with were all coming. Several were coming from out of town. The party would be at Aggie's house. When she got home on Friday night from work, they would all be hiding in the house and then surprise her when she got inside. Even Robert Neece and his wife had been invited. Robert would be sure Aggie did not leave the office until after 5:00.

On that Friday, Robert told her that he had to leave the office early to stop by a client's house. He told her to be sure to stay until 5:00 as he was expecting a call. After he left, he went home and picked up his wife and they returned to Aggie's home to wait for the party. Robert's wife was certainly not going to miss a party. Especially one like this with ladies coming in from out of town. Trip had helped his Mama get everything ready. Memaw and G were there and they helped too. The living room looked normal as you walked in but the dining room was full of balloons and a big sign that hung from the ceiling. It loudly proclaimed "Happy 30th Birthday!" The sign was black as a joke to signify she was getting old.

Aggie drove into the driveway in front of the house. Everything looked dark and quiet. That was the usual appearance for a Friday afternoon, so she suspected nothing. She walked up the sidewalk onto the porch and then into the living room. From there she turned to enter the dining room. When she did, the lights came on, and a great big group all shouted, "Happy birthday, old lady!"

She was surely surprised. Also, she became a little emotional. That did not last long, though. She was speaking to everyone. Some of them she had not seen since high school. They were hugging and laughing. She and that group of her friends acted no different than they had those twelve years ago. Each of them, for this night at least, was an eighteen-year-old, silly young girl again. Trip had no idea that anyone acted this way. Especially his mom!

After a little while, Memaw and G indicated they should get back home. Robert almost had to pull Mrs. Neece out of the house. She fit right in with that young group even though she was more than ten years their elder. Mama and Da said they thought they would go to bed as well. A stern look at Trip let him know that it was time for him to go into his room too. He did not mind that so much as he could hear everything that went on from his room. He went to the room, put on his pajamas, and got in the bed with the light out. He would listen to every word.

He heard them talking about the case of vino one of the friends had brought. Trip wasn't real sure what vino was but he heard one of the ladies ask, "Is it red or white?" The lady who had brought the "vino" answered, "Is there any color but white?" Whatever it was, it must have been good. They laughed and talked. Some of the things he was hearing he could not believe. If fact, some of the words he heard, he didn't even know what they meant. He tried to guess what the discussions were about. He knew they must all like big dogs as they talked a lot about heavy petting. He also figured out that it must have cost a lot of money to drive a car when they were in school. They discussed about how often their boyfriends would want to park. They also talked a lot about their "first time." He guessed they were talking about kissing. He remembered his first as he and Marsha had tried it once. He did not see much to it. In fact, he did not like the idea of putting his mouth on someone else's. Even Marsha's.

One of his mom's friends asked her what type of car she drove. She told them she had a station wagon. They laughed and agreed that most of them had station wagons also. One of the ladies spoke up and said, "Aggie, if I was as hot as you, I would be driving a red convertible. I would have a different man every week. One that would make every lady in this town jealous. I would go to every party and every nightclub I could find and I would live like there was no tomorrow." He had never imagined his mom doing anything like that, but he liked the part about the red convertible.

Each of them agreed. Aggie was lucky to be so pretty and well-built. And still be available. Each seemed to add something to that part of the conversation about how they knew all of the men must be chasing her. The party went on and soon those goings-on disappeared from Gus 3 as he fell asleep.

The next day, G3 made a beeline for Marsha's house. She was still his best friend, and he could talk with her about anything. She was much more knowledgeable about the stuff his mom and her friends were talking about last night than he was. He told her what they had said.

Later that afternoon, Marsha and G3 walked to the dime store. They walked past the lunch counter and then back into the area with the long counters full of things to sell. Mom's real birthday wasn't until the next day. It would be Sunday so no stores would be open. G3 went straight to the toy section. He found the cars and bought a red convertible. They stopped by the drug store that used to be G's and picked out a birthday card. He found one that was perfect.

It was in the section marked "humor." It had a picture of a red convertible on the outside and the writing inside just read, "Happy Birthday, Hot Stuff." Marsha wasn't sure if that was the right card but he was. After all, that is what they had talked and laughed about last night. Marsha and G3 wrapped the car with some of the paper left from the night before. He signed the card and wrote, "I love you," on the inside just under the other writing.

HOT STUFF

That night Gus 3 waited until they had finished their meal but were all still sitting at the table. He was anxious to give the present to her now. He told everyone to stay just where they were. He went into his room and got the package he and Marsha had wrapped and the card. He gave them to her, kissed her on the cheek, and said, "Happy birthday, Mom." She smiled and seemed so happy. First, she opened the card and read it to herself. She seemed a little surprised by it but said nothing. Maybe Marsha had been right. She then opened the package and saw the red convertible. When she saw the little red convertible, she knew exactly what the card meant. She looked at him with a sort of cross between a smile and a frown and said, "Somebody was listening last night, weren't they?" Gus 3 did not think Mama or Da ever saw the card. They did see the red convertible and they thought that was really cute. Mom let the conversation about the card and the present stop with that. He guessed that she did not want to talk about it so he never mentioned it again either.

Aggie had never really thought about dating. It was something that just had not entered her mind. Gus had died right at twelve years ago, but the time since had been full of making her way through a life without him and raising a young son. On the night after her birthday party, she stood in front of the mirror in her room.

She had not really looked at herself since she was pregnant with Gus 3. That was a long time ago. She was no longer a teenager. She was a young woman and she realized that as she looked into the mirror. It was hard to see beauty as she looked at herself, but privately, she admitted that she *was* attractive. She was tall, stylish, and confident, and her auburn hair caught the eye. All of this, but with an almost-twelve-year-old son depending on her for everything. Sure, he had his grandparents, but no one could be sure for how long. She knew that Gus 3 was her responsibility. Nothing would change that. Even though, time with an adult man might be fun. She longed to talk with such a partner.

HOW ABOUT A DATE?

Aggie had been asked out a number of times. She even went out with some of those guys who had asked her. Some were older, and some were younger. Those dates had been for dinner and a movie and even one time to dance at the country club. That date was the first time she had danced since high school. She was able to get back into her rhythm with no problem. It was fun and she was glad she had gone, but it was straight home, and, no, she did not dare let her date stop beside that bottom step.

She began to change a little. Nothing that was drastic or could be considered less than acceptable. She was a good mom and a good citizen. She went to church with her family every Sunday. Her son was at Sunday school and youth group, and any other events that called upon his attendance. She worked hard, saved her money, was involved with community events, and helped anyone she saw who may need her support. She did all of this without hesitation.

Aggie Johnson was a good example of a life lived well. It remained so even after she was made to carry the burden of widowhood and of being a single mom. She did it all. No one in their community could offer any criticism of her whatsoever. But at just over thirty, she knew that she had some living she needed to do. Her time and efforts to this point would allow her that latitude.

Robert could sense a change in her. He knew her well and could tell by small things that some of her focus was moving in a different direction than it had before. Minor things. Her lipstick color changed. Her dresses were just a bit shorter. (It was the mid-1980s, and almost all the ladies were wearing shorter dresses.) He was a keen interpreter of human nature. He knew what was going on in her life. One day it was just the two of them in his office. He walked out and sat on the chair that was just in front of her desk. She looked up at him and knew he had something he wanted to say.

He began, "Aggie, everyone knows what a wonderful mom and person you are. Everyone also knows that you are a young and attractive woman. Many have wondered for a long time why you did not have a man in your life. I understand why you do not. What I am about to say to you is none of my business, but I am going to say it anyway. You are a modern young woman, not a teenager, and men will treat you differently now than they did when you and Gus began dating. Because you are a widow, some may see you as an easy target. Be careful who you date. Not everyone is a good person. Don't get discouraged if the perfect guy does not come along right away. Every date does not have to be someone you want to marry. It is okay to go out and have fun. When that perfect guy comes along, you will know it. Be careful; be safe. I want you to know that other than my wife, you and Trip are the most important people in the world to me. I will always be here for you." With that, he got up and walked out of the room. He did not give her a chance to say a word. Nor did she want to say a word.

She was a little embarrassed. Embarrassed, but glad he had spoken. She held him in the same regard that he did her. After all, she would be just as quick to offer him personal advice as he had her. That was the nature of their relationship, and they both were happy that was true. She respected what he said.

THINGS CHANGE

Gus 3 was thirteen now and just like most thirteen-year-old boys felt he had the world all figured out. He listened closely as the older guys talked about girls. Just like most young men that age, he began to think about the opposite sex. It seemed to him, and he based it on those stories from those older guys, that he would soon have an opportunity to have a relationship of his own—but he wasn't sure with whom. Even though he and Marsha were still the very best of friends, it was something they did not discuss. Their relationship was still just as it had been for those eight or so years leading to this point. They saw each other every day. They walked into each other's houses almost at will. They had no secrets.

His golf continued to improve. On the Saturdays that he played with G and his three friends, all would brag on his shots. Each of them felt that through their instruction he had become the golfer that he was. He could hit the ball farther than any of them, and they had a hard time matching his score. He was barely a teenager now, but played golf like a man. He seemed to understand the way the lay of the land may come to his benefit. He could read the greens, judge distance as it related to which club should be used, and he could put backspin on the ball or hit it in a way that would cause it to bend around corners with a slice or a draw. He was, in the words of that Saturday group, a damn good golfer.

Some of the older guys who were members of the club and also of the high school team began to ask him to play along with them when they needed a fourth to fill out a team. He enjoyed that time as he still liked listening to some of those stories about the girls.

One thing, though, that he did not like was when they commented about his mom.

It was often mentioned that she was a real looker, and they would even use that word he had first heard a few years ago: hot. He did not like it when they said that. It sounded different coming from them than it had when the ladies had said it. In fact, one day when one of the older boys said it, he jumped from his cart and walked to the cart of the older player. He looked him straight in the eye and said, "You need to remember that is my mom you are talking about." The older boy knew in an instant that he should not have said it and he agreed that he would not say it again. Besides, Trip, even though several years younger, was a pretty big young man. The other kid did not want to give him a try. They all quit making those remarks about his mom.

G was really starting to show his seventy-five years. The loss of his son made him look and act much over eighty. In fact, often when they played golf on Saturday, he would not even take his clubs. His steps had shortened, he leaned forward, and his arms hung straight down by his side as he walked. He seemed to be looking downward as if he was looking for something. Very often when someone would speak to him, he would not respond. He talked a lot about Gus and how he missed him. It got so that his only few good moments would be when Trip sat with him on the porch. He could remember the exact details about a hunting trip he and Gus had taken thirty years ago, but had no idea what he had eaten for lunch. It did not surprise G3 when G had to be taken to the hospital.

The rescue squad truck was there as he passed on his way home from school. He had to walk right by Memaw and G's house to get home. He walked up the drive. When he got there, G was on a gurney and they were just about to roll him out of the house. Memaw spoke up and said, "The doctor and I feel he should spend some time at the hospital. He will get stronger there." The two attendants pushing the gurney stopped just as they came to where Trip was standing. G looked at him. Trip could tell by his eyes that he knew exactly what was happening. G looked up and smiled at Trip as he looked down at him. Both of them knew he would never come home again.

In a few weeks, G had continued to weaken, and it was only a matter of time before he would pass. G had left very strict orders that he was not to have his life prolonged needlessly. When it was his time, he should be allowed to go. In a few days, he developed pneumonia and slept as his heart stopped.

Memaw looked up at Trip and Aggie, who were sitting there. With a smile, she said, "He is with Gus now. G is where he has wanted to be for so long, and now he is." She went over to Trip and put her arms around him and spoke again, "What a wonderful job you did, always being there in place of your dad. You have been such a great blessing to us all, especially to G." With that, Aggie joined them, and the three of them stood with their arms around each other. Each of them had the strong sensation that all three Gusses were a part of that hug.

In less than a week after they had buried G, Memaw called Trip to come to her house. When he got there, he noticed that G's truck was sitting in front of the house, polished and cleaned. It had not been that way since G had bought it brand new several years earlier. When Trip walked up, she was sitting on the porch. Memaw looked at him and started, "You know, I asked G's friends, the ones you play golf with, what they thought I should do with G's truck. They all agreed with me that only you would appreciate it in the same way G did." She handed him the key and said, "It is yours now."

Soon, life moved forward again. Memaw had moved into an assisted living place about ten miles away. Aggie went to see her at least once a week. Trip less often, but he spoke with her several times each week on the phone. She seemed to love it there.

Several of her old friends were already living there when she moved in. She enjoyed them. She also enjoyed the card games, the bingo, and the special visits they got from church groups and choirs. Her life would soon end with her as happy as any person can be. Sometimes she wondered to herself, *Will I be with my two Gusses? I believe I will.*

Soon after she died, Trip learned that he would receive the Johnsons' estate. As Robert told him in that meeting, "Son, you and your mom are very wealthy. Your worth is now in excess of $7 million. Soon it will be up to you how you use it. Your mom has control of the entire estate until you reach the age of twenty-five. My advice to both of you is to use it wisely." They never wasted a penny.

OUT OF TOWN

Aggie had started dating more. The pharmacist at the drugstore and she seemed to get along very well. They had dated a number of times and had even spent some nights out of town. Trip liked him as he seemed a good guy. He did not try to tell Trip what to do or how to act. He was her friend, and Trip was not connected to that relationship in any way.

At dinner one night, Mom told Mama and Da that she was going to be out of town for five days. She and Skip Harrellson, the pharmacist at the drugstore, were going to the Bahamas. It was for a pharmacy convention and all their expenses were being paid. A lot of folks Skip knew would be there, and they were both really excited about going. Mama and Da did not seem to mind. As Trip got into the conversation, he really could not think of any reason that he should mind either. She deserved that trip. She began, "I will need to buy some new clothes. I don't have anything for a trip like this. I surely want to look good around all those friends of Skip's." Mama quickly jumped in and said she would like to help. Trip could tell that his mom would prefer to pick out those clothes herself, but she did not want to hurt Mama's feelings. "Sounds good," Mom replied.

On the day that Mom was to go shopping, she would be leaving early. It was to be an all-day event as they had to go to a town about thirty miles away to find a store that sold items like she would need. Trip certainly did not want to go shopping. That long day of shopping would also be too much for Mama. Who might be the right one to go with her? Happens that it was not one; it was two. Mrs. Neece was going as she was an expert in this endeavor. Even her husband had to admit that. Also, Marsha would be along. Her keen eye for fashion promised to be an asset to any decisions that had to be made. Saturday morning, Mom and Marsha left the house before 8:00. They would pick up Marylin Neece at her house and away they would go. Trip played golf.

TOURNAMENT TIME

Trip had been on his high school golf team for two years now. He was a junior in high school and had made the team both his sophomore and junior years. In fact, he was often the lead player. One of the other guys on the team was also pretty good. Raymond was also a member of the country club, and he and Trip had played golf many times. He was a year older, but they were good friends as well as being teammates. They split the lead golfer status fairly evenly. Trip would win one week and Raymond the other. They had won many of the school events in their district and in fact had become the district champions Trip's junior year. They would play in the state tournament. It was going to be at Eagle Perch, which was one of the nicest country clubs in their area. A club where a PGA tournament had been held a few years earlier. Each school would have two participants. About thirty of the state's schools had qualified for the tournament. Spectators were not to be allowed. This was all about golf in its purest form. Fifteen teams of four each began on a Thursday morning. By the end of the day, all the players would have completed thirty-six holes. The second day, only the top fifteen of those thirty schools would play. After an additional thirty-six holes, the scores for both days would be combined. The school with the lowest score would be the winner. If it was a tie for any of the top three spots, the scorecard hole handicaps would determine the winner. This was a typical way to determine the winner in non-PGA tournaments.

Trip's school did pretty well on the first day. Raymond and Trip had made the cut, and they would be in the playoff. They finished the first day in seventh place. Right in the middle. On the second day, each player was paired with someone from a different school. The golfer selected to play with Trip was a young man named Alan. His school had finished day one in third place. Each pair started at a different hole. A shotgun blast would let them know when it was time to tee off. They talked as they walked to the hole they were to begin from. Alan seemed to be a really great fellow. He told Trip of his plans. He had been accepted at the Naval Academy. Since his father had been killed in Vietnam, he was able to get special consideration in gaining that acceptance. Trip shared that was his history as well. Alan was excited because it meant he would receive one of the best educations available, at no cost. For that education, all he would have to do was to spend five years in the U.S. Navy. He was okay with that because he would be an officer. He went on to say that he had received a couple of offers from smaller schools for a golf scholarship, but the Academy was his choice.

Their conversation had opened Trip's eyes to a potential opportunity. The shotgun blasted. Alan's team had finished ahead of Trip's team the day before, so he got honors. By the end of the day, Trip and Alan had enjoyed the golf tournament, but more importantly, they had become good friends. Neither of their schools won, but that round was one of the best either of them had ever played. It was a perfect course. It was a perfect day. Trip had played well and had played with a new friend who had also played well.

YOU LOOK HOT

It took Aggie, along with Marsha and Mrs. Neece, about a week to accumulate the outfits she would need for her trip to the Bahamas. On the Tuesday night before she was to leave on Wednesday morning, everyone was to get together for a fashion show. It was Mama, Da, Mr. and Mrs. Neece, Marsha, and Trip. Trip was not at all sure Mom was as excited as were Marsha and Mrs. Neece. In fact, she seemed a little hesitant. Mrs. Neece and Marsha took full control of the night's show. They used Trip's bedroom as the changing room. It was the only bedroom downstairs and was close to the living room. Mrs. Neece would explain to everyone what the particular outfit Aggie was wearing was to be used for. The first part of it, they would not let Da, Mr. Neece, or Trip be present for. The men sat on the porch and wondered what the ladies were doing. Marsha later told them that Aggie was modeling her bathing suits and her nightgowns. Mom made it very clear that her dad nor her boss would be a part of that showing. Certainly, her son would not be. In a little while, they came to the door and called the guys in.

"Time now for the main show," is the way Mrs. Neece made her announcement. "First outfit will be worn on the day they go sightseeing." It was a yellow sundress, and while a little short, it was okay. That was followed by several outfits that included pants with matching tops, skirts, and dresses. All were pretty and Mom was pretty wearing them. She was a little embarrassed, but Mrs. Neece and Marsha were all aglow. Finally, as if it was a grand finale, Mrs. Neece announced again, "This is the outfit she will be wearing to the semi-formal gathering and dinner/dance on the last evening." It took a little longer for Mom to change this time. When she walked out and entered, it was as if the air had been sucked out of the room. There was total silence. Finally, Da smiled. He uttered his first words of the evening, "My God, my little girl grew up; you look beautiful." Mr. Neece made some comments but said very little. Maybe he was afraid that if he said too much, he may make Mrs. Neece jealous.

All looked at Trip as his mom turned so the admirers could see her whole outfit. He was going to have to state his judgment about how she looked, but was having a little trouble catching his breath. She looked as pretty as any girl he had ever seen. Aggie looked directly into Gus 3's eyes as she stood there. She wore black stockings and a pair of black high-heeled shoes. The shoes made her legs look long and lean. Her short black dress fit her closely. The top was cut very low in the back. In fact, it came down to the very bottom of her back, and it fit like a glove. It took Trip a minute to gather what he would say. This was the first time he had ever seen his mom in this way. She looked different. She wasn't Mom, but was a woman. She was just as good-looking, no, better-looking than many of the actresses he had admired in movies. He wanted to say exactly the right thing. Trip wanted her to know that he was not disappointed or ashamed of the way she looked. He now understood what all those guys meant when they commented about his mom's looks. Before he realized what he was saying, the words just came out with a slight nervous quiver, "You are hot!"

Not a single one of them said a word for what seemed like forever. Mom looked a little shocked and at the same time seemed to blush. It was as if she wanted to say, "You are my son." She did not.

First Marsha began to giggle. Then Mr. Neece burst into a full laugh. Mrs. Neece also smiled and laughed. In fact, she made a statement, "That is just the reaction we were looking for." Mama agreed that all the choices had been good ones. Da did not say any more than he had already. Mom walked over very slowly. Again, her son could not stop looking at her as she walked across the room. He could tell from her eyes that she saw his stare. When she got to him, she bent over, kissed him on the cheek, and then said, "Go finish your homework." She was Mom again.

The next morning, Skip picked her up and they headed for the airport. Her family would not see her again for five days. That was the longest they had ever been away from Aggie. They missed her and were anxious for her to return. And although they did not discuss it, they all wanted to see pictures of her wearing the black dress to the semi-formal event. Aggie and Skip were back home the following Sunday. She had a tan and that made her look even better. She looked as if she had received a much-needed rest from the world of raising a son and working in an office. And the tan made her look more like a college girl. She still looked much younger than her years.

CHAPTER 7

APPLICATIONS

Trip started asking his guidance counselor questions about college. He asked him if he thought he may be able to get into one of the military academies. He agreed that Trip's grades were certainly good enough and felt that his physical abilities were good. The counselor seemed to imply that Trip may be making a mistake by not going after a golf scholarship. Trip disagreed as he felt golf was a game to be enjoyed. He did not want to make it a duty, but instead wanted to enjoy the game just like he had on those Saturdays with G and his friends.

The counselor helped Trip gather applications to all three academies. Trip filled them out, wrote essays, and went to visit folks to ask them if they would be willing to write a recommendation for him. Soon they were completed and ready to mail. His counselor reviewed each one of them but changed nothing. Each one of them did have a place that asked if Trip had any family who had died in service of their country. That felt really good when he was able to mark yes. Perhaps if he had known his father, he would have felt differently. Since he had never known him except as a creation of those stories he had heard, more than anything else, it made him proud of what his father had done.

It was going to be several months before he would know if he had been accepted to any of the academies. He was anxious. It was about ninety days. Trip received a letter from West Point that they would like for him to come to the army recruiting station in Raleigh and to show them this letter. The soldiers at the station would know what to do.

He did just that. As his first road trip in the truck he had been given by Memaw, he would drive it to that meeting. Once in Raleigh, the first thing he had to do was find a parking place. That was no easy task. After parking, he found the recruiting station and went in.

The uniformed young man he gave the letter to asked him to wait right where he was. In just a minute, he came back to his desk and said, "Follow me, please." He took Trip to an office in the back. On the closed door was a sign that read, "Captain Young, Recruiting Officer." Trip was led into his office after the young soldier who had escorted him gave the door a knock.

"Enter," was the only answer after that knock.

Once they entered, the young soldier came to attention, looked directly at the captain, and said in a very stern voice, "Sir, reporting with candidate Johnson."

The captain appeared to be reading something and did not look up. He just said, "Have a seat, Johnson. PFC, you may be dismissed." With that, the young soldier left them alone.

He later found out that the captain was reading his "folder." Everything in the military has a folder. It was not his complete application, but was a list of instructions that the recruiting station must follow and send back to USMA. There was a test they referred as the USAT, and another that was the OCT. Both were easy tests and were followed by a medical exam. All together it took about a half a day. There were a bunch of other guys there also. Just after noon, he left, knowing nothing more than he had when he had arrived. Trip returned home disappointed that he could not share more information with his mom and his grandparents.

MAKE A FEW BUCKS

Golf was over for the year, so he had more time on his hands than usual. He looked around for a part-time job, but had to be very careful that it would not be a job that would interfere with his schoolwork.

Trip's good grades must be kept up if he was to have any luck getting into one of the academies. He stopped by the pro shop at the club to ask the manager there if he had heard any of his customers mention they may need a worker. The manager had not, but followed that he had been looking for someone to fill in at the pro shop on Saturdays. He went on to say that his son had become interested in a sport that was done only on Saturdays. It was an outgrowth of his high school wrestling. He had won the conference championship for his weight class, but could not compete in the state finals as he was only a sophomore. It had been recommended to his son that he could really enhance his wrestling abilities if he got into a weekend-only group that participated in something called "Greco-Roman wrestling." He made it very clear when he said, "If there is any way, I am going to be there with him on every one of those Saturdays."

Trip was interested, and it took only about five minutes for them to come to terms. Trip would work those Saturdays the manager of the pro shop was gone. It would be anywhere from a few hours to most of the day. It depended on where the match was held that day. He would make $30.00 for whatever time he was required to work. Plus, he would be able to buy all his golfing supplies at cost. Thirty dollars sounded good as he never spent that much in a week anyway. Trip was really excited about the "at cost" part of their agreement. He had his eye on a new set of clubs. It was time for a new set as he was just about to outgrow the ones he was using now. He was already over six feet tall and needed longer clubs. He did not know it then, but he would grow another four inches before he got to

West Point. He had found the perfect job and would start the next Saturday. Trip would go in on Friday so the manager could fill him in on what his duties would be.

He shared all of this with Marsha, and she was totally into it. She seemed to take as much interest in what he was doing as did his mom. He never really thought about it until later, but, even though he was around Marsha all the time, he knew very little about her plans. Trip mentioned that to Mama later, and she just laughed it off and said, "That is the way it usually is with a man." Even though their relationship seemed a little one-sided, in his favor, Marsha and he were still as close as any two could be.

A LITTLE BABY GIRL

Aggie had not gone out much since she had come back from her trip to the Bahamas with Skip. Trip did not understand why, but was afraid to ask her. She just stayed around the house most of the time. One evening Aggie and Trip decided to take a walk. Their conversation was about a lot of different things, and he felt it may be a good time for him to ask his mom about Skip. When he did, she first acted like she did not want to talk about it, so he let it drop. In a few minutes, she brought it up. She said, "You ask me why I'm not seeing Skip as much. We have been out only one time since the trip and that was a while ago. You deserve an answer, but I will ask that what I tell you be between just us." Trip nodded and she went on.

"While we were in the islands, at the dinner/dance, another lady joined us at our table. She was very attractive. The thing I remember most was her blond hair and blue eyes. She was about my age and was dressed very nicely. She introduced herself to me as a friend of Skip's. He seemed nervous about the whole thing, but he did ask her to join us. At first, I was angry at her for intruding, but after she began her conversation, I realized that she was probably doing it for my benefit. It became very obvious with the conversation that she and Skip had dated for quite a while. It was then I discovered that they had both been pharmacists at a drugstore in another part of the state. Then, wow, like a bomb going off, she took a picture from her purse and showed it to Skip. 'This is your daughter; she is almost four years old,' she stated. He did not seem surprised but did nothing that would make me believe it was not true. She excused herself and left the table. She laid the picture on the table and said, 'You should make contact.' Skip treated it as if it meant nothing.

"When I confronted him about it after we got back to our room, he apologized. He said that he had not known about the baby when he took the job at Medical Center Pharmacy in Cowan. When he later found out, even though he knew it could well be his child, he did nothing. He confessed that he had never told me anything about the possibility that he may have a child as he cared for me very much. All I could think about was you. The knowledge of that event would have followed Skip and it would have been just a matter of time before everyone in Cowan would know about it. He is not the kind of man I want you to be around and he is not the kind of guy I have any interest in. We were never 'in love,' but did have a lot of fun and good times. I decided later that the relationship was better ended then and there. I went out with him that one time just to tell him we would not be dating anymore."

She had just confided an innermost secret with her son. It made him feel like an adult. He imagined that is the way she saw him now. After all, he was only about a year younger than his dad was when he and Mom got married. It was about the time in his life that he and his mom became the closest of good friends.

Mom dated only a few more times while Trip finished high school. That was okay with him. She never went out with any of those guys more than two times. Their new bond of mutual trust seemed to bring them closer than ever.

GOOD DATES

Trip, on the other hand, was dating every weekend. During his sophomore year, he did not have to seek out a lot of girls because they would ask him. He liked that but it did make him wonder why. It was Marsha who helped him understand what was going on. He and Marsha had always been very open with each other. While they weren't interested in each other romantically, they were still best friends.

She explained, "To those girls, you are a trophy. You are good-looking, tall, athletic, and very smart. You represent everything most young women want. For them to be able to say that they went out with you is no different from you and I bragging about a picture of one of those big old bass you and I used to catch at the farm. You give them bragging rights. Now, here is my advice to you." She went on, "Act like you are not sure what you are doing. Let them take the lead. That way, you will have yourself a good time, and just remember, be careful and be safe. The last thing you want to find out is that you have gotten some girl pregnant." Marsha never minced her words.

He listened to her as he always had when she gave him advice about girls. He listened and he followed her instruction. She was right. His sophomore year and his junior year, he had a good time. Now, the Cowan Country Club pro shop proved a good place to find dates. Most of the girls who came in were really cute, had families with plenty of money, and as such did not expect him to spend much of his. Near the end of this near-perfect summer, Trip received a letter from the United States Military Academy. It was advising him that he had been accepted to enter the class that would begin just after his graduation from high school. Everyone in town learned about it when an article was printed in the *Cowan Chronicle*. It was his honor, but it was also the town's. His journey to this honor was one they all watched and rooted for as he grew up, the son of a fallen hero. Cowan's hero. And it didn't hurt that some of the girls he liked might now be even more interested in a young man who would soon be wearing a uniform.

NO BETTER DATE

Senior year seemed no more than a flash. Trip had to go to West Point, New York, for a week and spend it at the school. It was his "indoctrination." He knew he could take anything they handed out that first year. After seeing what life would be like at West Point, he began to have some second thoughts about why he was putting himself through that. That did not stop him from his determination to be the best student there. He later found out that with the caliber of young people who go to West Point, those who would be his classmates, being the best would be a hell of a reach. Like most of the other plebes, he was really excited about being there, but dreading all the hazing he would be put through that first year.

His senior year was very busy. First, it was golf season, and then in the spring, golf season again. He really enjoyed playing on the high school team. He was meeting people from all over the state. It was amazing how much he had in common with the other players, but at the same time, how different their lives were. The Christmas holiday was soon upon them all and just as quickly it was over. It was almost spring break. After spring break would be the Junior-Senior Prom. That dance, just like it had been every year before, was to be in the gym. It would be decorated and a live band would be playing. All this had to be done within the confines of a very low budget. It was not the dance, but the dancers who made proms special.

This would be his third prom. He had been invited the two years prior and enjoyed them pretty well. This year it was going to be different. Trip already had an idea of who he wanted his date to be. He had thought about it a lot. He weighed all the attributes of those girls he felt would have an interest in attending with him but had already settled on his choice. He realized how highly unusual it was for a young man to pick a prom date in whom he wasn't romantically interested. But he liked his choice.

Early during the customary time frame for prom date invitations to be made, Trip made his choice and issued his invitation. He did it by phone one night. Her mom answered the phone and seemed to have an unusual reaction. Marsha came to the phone and said, "Why don't you just come over? You don't usually call me. What's going on?"

In a very formal way, he said, "Marsha, it would be my great pleasure to have you attend this year's prom with me."

With no additional comments, her reply was, "We'll talk about it later." In a repay for the way he had made his invitation, she then stated, "Thanks so much for the call. Good-bye."

She hung up. In less time than he could think about what she had said, she was standing in his living room. She seemed very excited. "You know that I have never been to a prom and you also know this is my last chance. I want to be sure that is not why you are doing this."

His words to her were as true as any he had ever uttered. "My friend, please know this," Trip continued, "I would prefer your company to anyone I know. You are my first choice."

In less than a month, it was time. One night at dinner, Mom told Gus 3 that Mr. Neece would like for him to come by his office on that next Friday. He asked if she knew what he wanted, and she said she did not. It was the day of the prom. Trip had no idea what might be on Mr. Neece's mind. When he arrived, Mr. Neece was sitting in his office working on some papers. He looked up and saw Trip before his mom had even noticed he was there. He motioned Trip into his office. He seemed in a really great mood, and they exchanged some conversation about life in general and his mom in particular. In no more than a couple of minutes, he said, "I should get to the point. You have a lot of getting ready to do for the prom tonight."

"Marylin and your mom have discussed, at length, that you and Marsha will be attending the prom together. They both think the world of her." He went on to tell him, "Marylin decided that Marsha should not be attending the prom either in your truck or in your mom's minivan. So, here are the keys to her car. As I am sure you know, it is the black Mercedes sitting out front. She had it cleaned, and it is full of gas. She wants you to use it.

"On the console of the front seat, you will find a pre-paid card that can be used anywhere they accept Visa. You are to use it to purchase a corsage for Marsha. Marylin suggests that it would be best for you to order a white orchid. The balance remaining will be more than enough for both of you to enjoy a first-class meal anywhere you may choose. Just in case, she took the liberty of making a reservation for you at the "Angelina" French restaurant in Wilmington. Your reservation is for 6:00. That will give you time to have dinner and be at the prom shortly after 8:00. You can bring the car back anytime this weekend. I will need the key for your truck for me to drive as she is going to be using my car."

It was almost as if he had been made to rehearse his words to Trip. Knowing Mrs. Neece, he probably had.

G3 called Marsha and asked if she thought she could be ready by 5:00. Their original plans were to leave at 7:00. The plans were to eat in the restaurant downtown so they could make the prom about 8:00. She indicated that she had already been informed that she may need to be ready by 5:00. That would be no problem; she would be ready. G3 had his tux on and even though he did not have Marsha to check it out, he felt he looked okay. Since his mom was not there, Trip got Mama to give him her blessings as to how he looked. She agreed that he was just right. He drove the two doors down and pulled into Marsha's drive. Her dad's truck was not there.

As he walked onto the porch, flower box in hand, a flash near blinded him. It was Marylin and she was taking pictures of him. She and Mom were both there. He had to stand at the door for a picture. He had to have one made inside. It seemed that she and the two moms had taken over the whole ordeal. It was then that he heard Marsha's bedroom door shut and looked up to see her as she came down the steps.

The camera snapped and flashed as she started down. G3 could not believe what he saw. Marsha was a picture of beauty. He had never even imagined that she could look like this. Her sandy-colored hair was smooth and soft as it gently moved as she came down the steps. Her legs looked much like an advertisement as she took each step down. Her smile was that of the friend he had always known, but for the first time ever, Trip noticed that it was also the smile of a beautiful young woman. His mind raced to that time his mom had modeled that black dress. Marsha now wore it. Just like Mom, she wore it well. Marylin and Marsha had helped Mom as she had prepared. Now, his mom, Marylin, and Marsha's mom all had a hand with Marsha's entry. The black semi-formal ensemble was a somewhat unconventional choice for a young woman to wear to prom, but Marsha carried it off with poise and confidence.

Just like his mom had, Marsha turned as she entered the room where they stood. The dress had that same low-cut back. It fit Marsha just as well as it had his mom, but this time it had a completely new effect. Trip's mind was going in a direction it never had before—at least where Marsha was concerned. This time G3 was a little cooler in how he reacted. He looked at Marsha and said, "You are the most beautiful woman I have ever dated."

They all liked that, and Marylin even commented, "You did a little better tonight than when your mom modeled." They all laughed. Marsha glowed.

G3 tried to hand the flower to his mom so she could pin it on Marsha. She did not even reach her hands out as she said, "No, Son, that is your job."

He really began to fumble then as he knew that when he pinned that corsage to the front of that tight-fitting top, he would be flirting with embarrassing himself. He got it pinned on, though, and with no problem. It was easier than he had thought. He looked at them all and said in a sarcastic voice, "Can Marsha and I go and enjoy our prom now?" They all laughed and then continued to snap pictures as he escorted Marsha to the car and opened the door for her.

Trip closed the door of the Mercedes then went around to the driver's side and began their first and only date. When he looked over at Marsha, she smiled as if she was making fun of him for having been put through such an ordeal.

Again, he noticed, just as he had when she walked down those steps, what an attractive young woman was sharing the car with him. Her legs, with those black stockings, were gracefully crossed on the car's leather seat. And the seatbelt across Marsha's shoulder emphasized her form-fitting top. Trip's mind again raced to places it never had before. Marsha was as exciting as any young woman could be. She could tell just by looking at his stare what he was thinking. She even developed a little smirk of a smile. He wondered what that smile may mean.

Because she looked so good and because of the way she had looked with that little smirk, he made an awkward attempt to chart a different course than he had originally planned. G3 made a statement that he thought could either get him off the hook or, he half-wished, would open a door to a new opportunity. He spoke, "You will be my first."

She chuckled. Then, always having known how to keep him in his place, she responded very sternly, "My good friend, it just ain't gonna happen." She had settled it as easily as he had thought about it. He then fully understood the old saying as to how a good-looking woman could make the blood run out of your brain. They drove off.

Dinner was first class. Neither had ever been there, but G3 knew that his mom had. She had told them about it. There was a lady playing a harp near the front and white tablecloths on all the tables. A gentleman wearing a tuxedo stood at the front and had them follow him to their table. It was a table for four but he quickly took two of the chairs away. A waiter soon arrived and asked if they would like to see a wine list. Neither of them being old enough, G3 said, "No, thank you." They went on to order and decided after looking at the menu they would both just go with the night's special offering. First, they were served crackers and cheese. Next came a small bowl of soup, followed by a salad. It was then that the waiter brought out a small bowl with ice cream in it. When G3 saw what it was, he was concerned that the waiter had gotten confused and had given them their dessert prior to their having the main dish.

He did not want to embarrass the waiter so he motioned for the man in the tuxedo to come over. The gentleman did and leaned down to ask if there was a problem. G3 whispered that everything was really good but that the waiter had made a mistake. He had served them their dessert prior to their main entrée. The maître d' very quietly told him that the sorbet was to cleanse his palate prior to the main dish. He felt like an idiot, Marsha laughed, and both learned a valuable lesson in etiquette. Everything after that was just as you could imagine a fine restaurant would be.

The only thing that he could offer as a suggestion was that while the food was good, there just wasn't much of it. It would do well to serve bigger portions. When they finished, he gave the waiter the card. The waiter told him that the gratuity had already been added and he had to but sign the receipt. G3 thought that he could get accustomed to this kind of living but figured this was probably a little different lifestyle from the one he would be living at West Point.

They went on to the prom and got there later than they had expected. The dinner had taken longer than Mrs. Neece thought it would. No problem, though. Everyone was glad to see them and everyone raved about how gorgeous his date was. That was just what he wanted to hear. He knew it was just what Marsha needed to hear. She was the belle of the ball. They danced together and also danced with a lot of different people.

It was midnight, and the last song was about to play. The last song was announced and began. "Goodnight, Sweetheart, Goodnight" was the tradition. Tonight, it seemed much more than a tradition. It was a statement. G3 was not sure what he felt, but it was a special time. They went to the floor and he took Marsha into his arms. There was no doubt that each of them knew and respected the other's feelings. That all vanished as he pulled her close and she leaned her body into his. He held her softness against him as tightly as could be. His hands touched the skin of her open back. She lay her head on his chest and tightened their embrace even more than he had. This dance would be their way of saying to each other that the true friendship and love that they had shared these past thirteen years was more lasting than either of them could have shared with any other person. She had asked G3 those many years ago if he would be her friend, and he had never regretted that his answer had been yes. This night was confirmation of his decision. Neither of them had any way of knowing what the depth of their relationship may provide.

In less than a month, school would end with their graduation. He would be leaving in less than a week after that for West Point. Marsha had gotten a scholarship, and before he would be home again, she would be at Loyola with close to 20,000 others. Their paths would certainly cross, but probably not often. It really did not matter about the time or the miles; they would always be as close as a telephone call away.

CHAPTER 8

AN EXCELLENT ADVENTURE

In no time, Gus 3 was getting out of Marylin's Mercedes again. This time it was because she had let Trip and his mom drive it as they traveled to West Point for his entry. As close as Mom and Robert were, she and Marylin had become just as close. Different close, but just as close. Gus 3 was really glad about that as Mom would need a friend to fill his spot when he left. Marylin was perfect for that purpose. Gus 3 and his mom had spent two days in the car saying goodbye.

They both expected that when they parted at West Point it would be quick. It was, and she was gone. Trip did not have time to either feel sorry for himself or homesick. Neither did he have to wonder about where to go or what to do. Instruction is one thing that there is an abundance of at USMA. With just over 4,500 cadets, each wanting to be the best leader ever, there would always be someone who could tell him what to do.

They got fitted for uniforms, which had to fit perfectly. They were left with little to no hair. They were yelled at, made to do pushups, questioned by upper classmen about stuff to which there was no answer, and then yelled at again. They walked nowhere, and ran everywhere. For every minor infraction, they would be given demerits. Those demerits could be redeemed only by walking them off on the time during the weekend when they were "off." That meant mostly at night. Trip was not sure, but he believed that the courtyard in front of his barracks was the coldest place that ever existed.

The food was really good, and there were waiters to bring it to the table. It was on a rolling cart covered with a white tablecloth. The cart was rolled between the end seat and the first seat to the right of that end seat. A plebe would be placed in those two seats. Each table had two plebes. The plebes were those who were in their first year. There were also two yearlings, those who were now in their second year. Next were the two third-year cadets who were called cows. Finally, there were two in their last year who were known as firsties. One of them sat on the other end of the table with the second sitting on his right. Each item on the cart would be passed around the table. When it returned to the plebe who had first passed the item, he would look into it. He was sitting absolutely erect using only the three inches of his chair for his seat. That plebe would look into the serving dish and make a determination about how many servings of that item was left.

He would then announce, using the formal method, "Sir, there are approximately two-and-one-half servings of mashed potatoes remaining at this table. Would anyone care for more mashed potatoes, sir?" No matter what year they may be in, to the plebes, they were all addressed as "sir." In fact, anything that moved was a sir. If they called them anything different, they could plan to walk around and around the courtyard on Saturday night.

After Cadet Johnson had been at the Point for about three weeks, a regular army captain came into his room. He and his roomies were sure that they were in some grave trouble. When the captain walked in, he looked around as if he was about to bite all of their heads off. Instead, he just stated, "Cadet Johnson." Johnson stepped forward, having come to attention while making that step. "Yes, sir. That is I, sir," he stated in the most military voice he could muster.

"Come with me, Cadet," he followed. Cadet Johnson was not sure what he felt except numbness. The captain led Johnson to an area in the front entrance hall of the barracks. He then said, "At ease, Cadet."

Trip felt better right away. "Cadet, I have received a letter from a retired general who attended here a number of years ago. He indicates that he was a member of a country club your family belongs to back in your hometown. He speaks very highly of you, but that is not the reason for his letter. He knows that we have a golf team here at the Point. He believes you could be an asset to that team. I am here to ask if you have any interest in trying out for this team."

It did not take Trip but just a second to reply with a very strong, "Yes, sir."

The captain then followed, "Tryouts for the team are next week. If you make the team, you will not be able to participate in any match events until your cow year. You will, though, be considered on the team and will practice with the other players. Are you still interested?"

Again, "Yes, sir."

"Do you have a set of clubs that you prefer or would you like for us to let you use one of the Academy's sets?"

Cadet Johnson said, "Sir, I have a set I had acquired just prior to coming to the Point. If possible, I would prefer them, sir." The captain went on to tell him that he would handle getting his clubs to the Point and that they would be here in time for him to have a couple of practice rounds prior to the tryouts. Trip was not sure he understood how he could get them here that quickly, but the captain seemed to know that he could.

With that, he simply said, "Dismissed," then turned and left.

Cadet Johnson went back to his room where his roommates were anxious to know what that was about. After he told them about the conversation, one of them offered a very quick comment, "You lucky son of a bitch."

THE WOMAN IN THE JEEP

It was the very next morning. Aggie was sitting at her desk in Mr. Neece's office when there was a knock at the door. A knock was unusual, but she said in a loud voice, "Come in." Robert had heard the knock as well and had walked into the room. When the door opened, there was a young soldier standing there. Her first thought was of those two who had brought the news of Gus's death. A sudden panic was very quickly relieved by a, "Good morning, ma'am," from that soldier. That would not be the way bad news would come.

Her response was, "Good morning. How can we help you?"

"I am looking for Cadet Johnson's mom." When she acknowledged that she was his mom, he continued, "Ma'am, I have received orders from Captain Young, who is my commanding officer, to contact you and ask if you know the whereabouts of Cadet Johnson's golf clubs."

She said, "Indeed, I do."

"If you would allow, ma'am, I would like to pick them up as they will be sent to Cadet Johnson. That is all I know, ma'am." Robert told her she could go and get the clubs for him and then return. The soldier then indicated that he would be glad to drive her wherever they needed to go for the pickup. She accepted.

When they got downstairs, she saw a Jeep in one of the parking places right in front of the office. The canvas top was down. She got in, and they started for her house, which was only a few blocks away. In the Jeep, her dress seemed shorter than it was because the low seats caused her legs to bend at a sharper angle than normal. Her hair was blowing back across her shoulders. Aggie was looking "hot," as her birthday card from Gus 3 had said all those years ago. She noticed as the young soldier looked over at her with an admiring glance. She just smiled. It made her feel good about herself to think this young soldier would consider her attractive. It caused her to flush a little. He was cute, but about the same age as her son.

They got the clubs, and he drove Mrs. Johnson back to Robert's office. When she got out, he looked at her and said, "Ma'am, thank you for everything." She knew he was referring to the fact that he had admired her windblown appearance in the Jeep. Again, she felt funny, but she enjoyed the realization that she still had some of her youthful appeal.

The clubs were taken to the airport at Pope Air Force Base. It was located adjacent to Fort Bragg. Captain Young was on site to meet the Jeep. He had driven to Pope Air Force Base from the recruiting station in Raleigh. At the terminal, there were two lieutenants waiting in the lobby.

When the captain walked in, they stood and saluted and said at the same time, "Good morning, Captain."

He responded with a quick salute in return and with a chuckle he said, "I remember Cadet Johnson from his testing when attempting to enter the Point. I am not sure I understand why I am ensuring that a set of golf clubs is here for you to fly to West Point, but that is what I have been ordered to do, and here they are." Both of them responded that they had no idea what this was about either.

None of them would have any way of knowing what this was all about, but when a retired general of the U.S. Army, who was good friends with the current commandant of West Point, wanted to make something like this happen, it would. The clubs got there, and Trip was able to get his two practice rounds played prior to the tryouts. Cadet Johnson had no idea how or why all of this had taken place. He knew only that he was glad to have his clubs in his hands again.

When Aggie got back into the office, Robert laughed as he told her, "Well, you have stirred up a mess. Mrs. Becky Osgood has just gotten off the phone with Marylin. I guess by now she has called almost everyone in town. She is telling them that you have been 'sighted' riding around town in one of those 'army car' things that did not even have a top on it. And you were with a soldier who was no more than half your age. And you were wearing a dress that was entirely too short and anyone could plainly see your legs above your knees and that you did not even have a scarf on your hair. Apparently, it was a shock to all who saw and just plain tacky. I explained the truth of the story to Marylin, and she said she would call Mrs. Osgood and let her know what had really happened. It is like I have said, Aggie, you are on center stage. I will say, though, you are quite a star."

The whole episode about the Jeep and the young soldier had given Marylin Neece a great idea. She was on the local board of the USO (United Service Organizations). The board was for this entire area, but the only club nearby was in Wilmington. The USO did wonderful things for the young men who were serving their country. Marylin was explaining to Robert that there was no better way for Aggie to spend some of her time than by serving with her on that board. They could drive to meetings together, attend some of the functions, and help those who were serving their country. Besides, with her son soon to be in the military, she would have a very personal interest. Robert told Marylin right away that he was not going to get into that. That would be between her and Aggie and to keep him out of it. She almost did keep him out of it, but when she discussed it with Aggie, she was quick to point out that it would be no problem to get off early for those meetings. And certainly, Robert would not mind since he thought the USO was a wonderful organization. Aggie responded that she liked the idea but would need to think about it and would get back to her.

BACK ON THE GREEN

The golf course at West Point was just as perfect as the one where he had played in the state championships his junior year. Being late summer meant that everything about the course was manicured to perfection. The greens, the fairways, and the roughs could not have been any better maintained. Getting to play golf on a course where a lot of high-ranking military officers and politicians often played had its advantages.

A few minutes before he was to tee off, the commandant of the USMA walked up to him. Cadet Johnson was on the practice green putting. Only a select few of the cadets at the Point ever got close to this man, much less to speak to him.

"Cadet Johnson," was how the commandant hailed him as he walked onto the green. Johnson knew that he was not to salute the commandant while he was involved in a mission. The playing of a sport at the Academy was considered a mission. Even though he knew better than to salute, he did know to come to immediate attention and braced as the commandant spoke to him. "Cadet, I have a note for you from General Hrabal. He and I are friends. We were here at the Academy together years ago. He was a firstie when I was a plebe. He and I were both on the golf team then. He has asked that I give you this note and instruct that you remember that golf is just a game." He handed Cadet Johnson the note and walked away. In a few minutes, Johnson left the green and walked to an area where he could open and read the note. He still was not sure who General Hrabal was. The note read:

Cadet Johnson: I guess you think you are pretty special to have the commandant give you a note. I would bet you also get that same feeling having a letter from a general. Be assured, though, that not this, in fact nothing other than your hard work and dedication, will set you apart at the Point. I have had my eye on you for a number of years.

You did not know it at the time, but I was one of those who played golf with you and your granddad on those Saturdays. Your granddad was one of my best friends. You have made us all proud of you as we have watched you grow. Your potential is unlimited. My advice to you for your life in this man's army is to never underestimate yourself and never underestimate your enemy.

Best regards,

Your sincere friend,

Major General Joanus Hrabal, U.S. Army, Retired

Cadet Johnson would play golf well that day. He would become the newest member of the United States Military Academy at West Point's golf team.

Life at West Point fit him well. He liked the structure. He liked the routine. His fellow cadets represented every race, gender, and every background imaginable. They all shared in common that they were smart and they had great love for their country.

RACE AS A TEAM

He understood that every tradition and routine embraced by West Point was for a reason. That reason was to make them the world's best leaders. Whether it be sitting on the last three inches of your chair at meals and eating in block style or having to repeat, in detail, all the information that may be pertinent to a movie showing at the Academy's theater, everything had a purpose. He did all those things well. He was learning the importance of a good relationship with his fellow classmates.

His group was learning about how teamwork was a necessary component of military service. About how each must be dedicated to their team and that each team member had an obligation to the other. No matter the rank you may be, you are no more powerful than those you command. That point was essential to their mission as cadets. It would remain essential to their careers as military commanders. They could not forget it.

All of the cadets spent a great deal of time with various physical activities. The training was harsh and could take a toll on even the strongest cadet. Each cadet was to be responsible for one another, and the main point in all of this was that no man or woman should ever be left behind.

An event was planned for the coming Saturday. It would be an endurance race. There would be no specific distance but all would run until the last cadet on the track would be declared the winner. It would be an honor to prove yourself as the most enduring person in the class. This exercise sparked what Cadet Johnson thought may be a good idea. The cadets trained in squad-size units, and each squad would keep those same cadets for each segment of that training. They would then regroup into a different mix for subsequent training sessions. Each unit consisted mostly of males, but all units also had some females. His unit had two. The females could perform on a level very much equal to that of the male cadets. For this training cycle, he was his unit's squad leader.

The Friday night prior to the race, just after they had completed that afternoon's training, he asked his squad to all remain on the field a minute as he had an idea. They all listened intently as they respected his abilities. He was one of the emerging leaders of his class. He started, "We have been indoctrinated about teamwork and team singularity for a number of weeks. I propose that at the race tomorrow we will race together. By that I mean that when any one of us has reached a point where they think they can no longer participate, the others will help them. That way, our strength will be the strength of the squad, not of the individual. Once we do fall out, we will go back, as instructed, to the starting point on the track as a squad. If questioned, our responses should all be the same, no matter which of us is asked. If we are to fight as a team, we will race as a team." They all agreed.

The next day, they did just as planned. Because they helped each other, they were able to do well in the race. Many individuals had dropped out and taken the lonely walk back to the starting point. Well over half had fallen out. His team was doing everything they could to help every member continue. They finally came to the point when some of them could run no more. They must return to the start line. As they did, they did so as a team. After they had all had a chance to catch their breath and regather their strength, they formed a line, and in step, the squad marched back to the starting point.

The commandant was standing and talking with the officer in charge of physical education for the Academy. When he saw the group marching back as they were, the commandant questioned the officer, "What's the deal with them?" The training officer responded that he was not sure but would ask. He went to the very first person in that group and asked what they were doing.

The young cadet responded, "Sir, if we are to fight as a team, we will race as a team."

When the PE officer told the commandant what the answer was, the commandant responded that he would like to meet with them briefly. "Have them meet me at my table in the chow hall about ten minutes prior to the evening meal. I would like to see them as a unit." The PE officer passed that information to one of his staff who in turn went to the squad and passed on the orders as he had received them.

That evening all of Johnson's group made every effort to be in perfect form. They were standing at attention in front of the commandant's table when he arrived. None of them was sure why they were there, but guessed it must have something to do with today's race. The commandant spoke, "At ease, cadets."

He continued, "I would like to know what prompted your action at the endurance run today." He knew that no one would speak until addressed directly. He looked at the cadet who stood on the end. He nodded directly at her.

She responded, "Sir, Cadet Barnhill. Sir, we made that decision last evening. It was discussed and decided that based on our recent teaching about team responsibilities, that it may be a good idea, sir."

"Very good," he answered. "Can you be more specific about who brought this idea to the attention of the squad?"

"Yes, sir, it was squad leader Cadet Johnson."

"Well, Cadet Johnson, we meet again. Your unit today was the only one, to my knowledge, that has ever made a decision to do as yours did. I am not sure from the PE perspective of the race, if it was the best thing. I am sure that from a military perspective, it was brilliant." He told the rest of the cadets that they could be dismissed but asked Johnson to stand fast for just a minute. As the others were leaving, he told Cadet Johnson to give his regards to General Hrabal when he would be home a few weeks later during Christmas break.

Johnson was a little surprised that the commandant even remembered who he was but quickly responded, "Yes, sir."

The commandant then told him he could have a seat and to enjoy his meal. When he got to the table, all his tablemates wanted to know what that was about, and he just answered with, "He liked what our squad did today."

CHAPTER 9

FINALLY, CHRISTMAS AT HOME

Time passed more quickly than Trip would have thought possible. During his first year at West Point, Trip was not able to be home for Christmas. His duties and the fact he was a plebe made it impossible. He had missed being with his family, but they understood and so did he. This year, his second as a cadet, was going to be different. He would be home almost a week. Christmas was on Friday. He would get home on Tuesday and not have to be back until the following Monday at 0600 formation. He was looking forward to seeing them all.

He took a combination of the bus and Amtrak. He was allowed to leave after his last class on Monday. He caught the shuttle bus that left at 6:00 p.m. That put him into New York Grand Central Station in time to make the 9:00 train. He would be picked up at the Amtrak station in Fayetteville. From there, he would not be but about an hour from home. His arrival in Fayetteville was to be at 5:00 a.m.

When he got there, he was not the least bit surprised to be met by his mom and Mr. and Mrs. Neece. He was glad to see them, and they seemed just as glad to see him. He would get to ride in the Mercedes again. It was his third ride in it, and all those rides had ended with him being in a good place.

In a little over an hour, he was in bed. He slept for a couple of hours until just after 9:00 that morning. That was the latest he had slept in over a year. He got up, and Mom and Mama had breakfast ready. He had hoped they would have some of Mama's biscuits. He had not had such good biscuits since he left home. West Point food was good, but what he had grown up on at home was even better. After breakfast, his mom told him that he and she needed to talk just a minute.

Both of them with a cup of coffee in hand sat on the porch. It was warm for December and felt really good outside. She began, "Gus 3, I need a favor from you. You may not understand, but I need it anyway. Tonight they will be having the Christmas dance at the club. Everyone has pushed me to have you there." Gus 3's first thought, and question, was, "Can I bring Marsha?" Her reply as she smiled was that she knew that he would ask that. But Marsha would not be at home this Christmas. She was going to spend it with her roommate who was from California.

"Anyway," she continued, "that is not the only thing I would ask. If possible, I would like for you to wear your dress uniform. I want pictures and I especially want one of you and me with you decked out in that outfit."

He looked at her, and with a sort of wink and smile, he asked, "You gonna wear that black dress?"

"Absolutely not!" came quickly.

"Sure, Mom, I'll be glad to do that and I look forward to being there with you."

They then talked on about how she had been doing. She had one thing going on that she seemed very excited about and proceeded to tell him about it. "Just after that young fellow from the recruiting center had picked up your clubs, Marylin asked me if I may have an interest in joining her on the board of the USO. I researched the group and found that the main purpose for them is to serve soldiers away from home. They have about 160 locations around the world and have interest in building somewhere around here. I told her I would, and I have been involved for close to a year now. Seems like everything that gets proposed gets shot down, but we all feel we will hit upon the solution. Anyway, I am enjoying it, and it makes me think of you. That's why I like it."

Mama fixed a nice dinner for them that night. It was a little later than normal, and Da seemed to be having a hard time understanding why dinner was late. They tried to explain, but he never really got it. When they did sit down to eat, it was fantastic. Mama had cooked Trip's favorites. It was just as good as he remembered and then ended with pecan pie with ice cream, which was really a special treat that he had loved since he was a young boy. It was the dessert that reminded him the very most of home, and he ate way too much. After all of that, he hardly ate anything at the dance.

When they got to the dance and walked in, he recognized most of the faces. Having worked in the pro shop, and having dated a number of the players' daughters, Trip knew most of them. As he and his mom entered and almost as if on cue, the band stopped the song they were playing. They began playing a song he knew well. The singer started belting out the words: "Hail alma mater, dear, to us be ever near..." It was the West Point Alma Mater. By training and instinct, he started to sing along with her. In less than a moment, Major General Joanus Hrabal was standing by his side and singing along also. The band's singer let them have the floor. They finished the song, and the place went wild. It could not have been better if it had been rehearsed. The general took Cadet Johnson's hand, shook it, and then put his arm around Trip's shoulder and gently said, "How about a salute, cadet?" Trip stepped back, came to attention, and did the best salute he knew how. That was a hit too. He then gave the general his message from the commandant. The general shook his hand and said, "Let's talk later. Enjoy the dance and your mom now."

They shared a table with Robert and Marylin. His mom was on the dance floor constantly, be it fast or slow. As for Trip, he did not miss a single dance. Marylin was up and taking his hand before he ever got seated. All the ladies made it known that they wanted to dance with a cadet. At least one who had on his dress uniform. Old, young, married, and single, he danced with them all. He enjoyed every one of those dances. Some of the moms of the girls he had dated pointed out that their daughters would surely be sorry that they had not come to that dance. There were a couple of them who he wished had come as well, as he would love to see them again. One of that group of young ladies was there. Grace and Trip danced several times. The two of them planned to go out the next night.

The dance was ending, and the last song was about to play. Just as at the prom, that dance was for Trip and his date. His mom knew that was the way it was going to be. "Save the Last Dance for Me" began, and Aggie and Cadet Gus Johnson, III, took the floor. For a while, no one else got on the dance floor with them. It was just the two of them. It was as if every person there had waited until this night to acknowledge what his mother had gone through, and also what she had accomplished. Here she was. A young widow who had lost her husband in a war. She had successfully raised a son with no husband for support. She had taken part in every aspect of the community. Here Trip was having grown to adulthood. He had never had the advantages a dad provides. Wearing his West Point dress uniform confirmed the fact that she had done her task well and that he had grown up okay too.

The next night, Trip had a great time on his date. Grace was pretty, she was smart, and was about to graduate from Wake Forest University. Trip remembered the first date they had was while he was still a sophomore in high school. They had a good time then too. In fact, that one date had turned into several. Not much was said about those dates, but he remembered that they had a good time those nights also—even if Grace *had* asked him out so that he would be a "trophy" she could brag about to her friends.

The next night was Christmas Eve. Just as they had always done, his family went to their church. It would be a short service. After a quick sermon, they would sing a couple of songs, and would then take communion. There was always a special and somber ending to the Christmas Eve service as the congregation would exit with the lights out, each of them holding a candle while singing "Silent Night." The "somber" would come to a quick end as the kids were released from the confines of good behavior. They had nothing on their minds but Santa.

Christmas morning, they were all up early. He could remember those times that he would be up before the sun to check out what Santa had left. One Christmas that he especially remembered was the one that most of his friends and he all got bikes. Without prior planning, the entire group of them was outside on those bikes before daylight. On that day and in that small town, it was okay. In one way, Cadet Johnson dreaded having to return to the Point. In another, he was excited and looked forward to finishing his year. That summer he would be doing actual military training at a base that specialized in his chosen field. All the cadets looked forward to that as it would be their first taste of the "real army."

He had not committed yet to a choice but had thought about it very much. In fact, it was one of the things he had discussed with Gen. Hrabal when they had that chance to talk. He pointed out that it depended on Trip's career plans and goals. Most of the higher-ranking officers came from the infantry. Other choices could offer a more "enjoyable" career. What was he looking for? Cadet Johnson was leaning toward INSCOM (U.S. Army Intelligence and Security Command). He still had enough of a kid in him that the spy thing seemed enchanting. Besides that, who had a better career and life than Ian Fleming's "James Bond"? At the last moment, he followed his gut. Cadet Johnson picked INSCOM.

Early summer came, and it was time for his first "deployment." Even though it was just for training, it was treated as a mission deployment. He and one other cadet were picked up in a staff car and told they would be driving to Fort Belvoir, Virginia.

Later that same day, on arrival, they entered the base with no problem. Getting into the INSCOM center was a little harder. They would have to show their orders and their IDs, which were scanned, and their bags were also inspected and scanned. They were thinking this was their first lesson. When it comes to national security, nothing is left to chance.

This was all different from at the Point. The men who were in charge all seemed glad to have them there and treated them very well. They were taken to the officers' quarters, where they would spend the summer. At least that is what they thought. It was not correct. After a few days of basic instruction as to who and what INSCOM was, they were told they would get a chance to go on some practice missions. They were warned the missions would not all be on base. These missions may seem real, and their reactions would be noted. The men treat these situations as realistically as they would in real life. This was not a game; it was a life-and-death mission, and they would have more control than they could imagine over the way it would end.

The training area at Fort Belvoir was very impressive. There were realistic-looking towns and villages. There were car tracks for the purpose of teaching evasive driving. A mock-up airport and train station looked as real as had Grand Central Station when he was there last Christmas. And, the entire Alexandria area became part of their campus. Instructors in those training centers were dressed and spoke very much like they would in a foreign country. One thing they all shared was that each one of them took their role very seriously. For those two cadets to be successful, they must take their roles just as seriously.

Training varied among all the various departments. Many situations were simulated, and they had to make quick decisions on when and how to control them, such as whether or not it was okay to enter a location and when to shoot or when to run. They were taught how to deceive those who were trained to root out deceivers. They were taught that no one could be trusted. The good players would often be the bad ones and vice versa. Late in August, they were seeing and using some of the new electronic surveillance aids that were now being used.

A picture could be made of you and within seconds your identity would be available to those who may require it. There was a device that could pick up and identify your voice from a satellite. It would provide identifiable signatures, even if you may be thousands of miles away. A picture had been taken of the two cadets as they had entered the electronics lab that morning. From that picture, everything about them would be made available to those cleared for that information. In just a few minutes after those pictures were taken by a surveillance camera, the instructor was called away and actually left the room. When he got back, he began to offer some explanation as to what the last three months had provided. It was an ongoing study of that secretive segment of our country that is hidden so well. They were told they could not discuss what they had seen and learned even with their mates at the Point. The best way to handle those inquiries was to laugh them off as if they were a joke. As soon as he had finished that short summary, he instructed them that their training was now over and that they would be taken back to the Point that very day. Their personal items were being packed as they spoke, and a car was already at the entrance waiting to make that trip. They were then escorted to the entrance. Quickly they were gone.

The experience was fun, exciting, intriguing, and they learned a great deal from it. Cadet Johnson was pretty much convinced that he had chosen the right vocational field. He looked forward to joining that group again after his last two years at the Point. Turns out, he was wrong. It would not be that long.

Classes had begun in August, and they were getting into the full swing of being back at the Point. Classes this year included military tactics, military law, and a number of other classes that closely aligned with their soon-to-be army careers. They were now getting to what was required to be a vital part of the U.S. Army. They all loved it.

Toward the end of September, Johnson was put in front of the commandant for his third time. This time he was summoned to the commandant's office. He first told Cadet Johnson that the conversation he was to have was to be considered a military secret. Johnson could never mention the instructions that he was about to receive nor any information that may turn out to be a part of those instructions. He was going to be gone for a couple of days, and, as he had been instructed, he would be signed out on family leave. That leave was normally used in the case of the passing of a parent. He was very forceful in assuring that Cadet Johnson understood his orders. Johnson did and so acknowledged. The commandant took the opportunity to comment on how they had now been face-to-face on three occasions. He then said, "I, for instance, was never within twenty feet of my commandant."

CHAPTER 10

I'VE GOT A SECRET

That afternoon Johnson was picked up by an older lady driving a two-year-old green Chevrolet. She said very little and in fact offered nothing but very unmeaningful conversation. It took about five hours to get to Fort Belvoir, Virginia. He was not at all sure why he was going there. He thought to himself that he hoped that he had not done anything wrong or that he had in some way messed up that previous summer.

Cadet Johnson was let out of the car at the entrance of the INSCOM headquarters building. He went through the same drill of getting into the INSCOM headquarters as when he had gotten there the summer before. Once inside, he was taken into a conference room. He had not been in that room while in training. There were no windows, and the walls were padded. The room consisted of a conference table and chairs with a large television on the wall at the end. There was a phone on the table. His mind raced. Had he done something wrong? He had not discussed this summer with anyone. Only one thing he could do. He sat and waited.

A few minutes later, four gentlemen came in. He stood but they motioned that he should have a seat. He recognized only one of them. He was Major Hansen who had been one of his instructors. The other three sat but Major Hansen did not. He went on to say that these three gentlemen represented INSCOM, the CIA, and U.S. Foreign Service. He indicated that names would be shared if and when needed. However, he confirmed to them that it was Cadet Gus Johnson III with them at this moment. That he indeed had been one of the cadets who had spent the summer there. Major Hansen was told that he could leave by one of the three.

"Gus," one of the three gentlemen began, "Major Hansen's purpose was to assure us that you are in fact Cadet Johnson. He was also to make you comfortable with who we are." He then began to talk, and what Cadet Johnson heard would surely change his life forever. He started by pointing a remote at the screen. A film clip of a young man came on the screen. He was being filmed in various scenes around and near Yale University. They informed Gus that the young man on the screen had attended two years as a student. The camera closed in on the man's face. Gus thought that had he not known better, that young man could be him. No one had said a word. The gentleman clicked off the film and then turned and began to talk. "Gus, do you recognize that guy?"

"No, sir," said Gus 3.

"Your picture, when it was submitted to the ID process this summer, was incorrectly identified. That processor identified you as that young man, which triggered considerable distress. After identifying him, the computers then proposed that he had been in and out of INSCOM, that he had spent two years at West Point, and that he was the personal friend of a Major General Hrabal. As you can imagine, if all of that were true, it would have been a major security breach. Research quickly proved that the two of you are almost identical."

He continued, "Gus, this conversation is about to become very complicated, and it will put you in a situation that will be almost unbearable. If you decide to participate in a plan we are formulating, it will cause pain to those you love and to your many friends. Gus, this includes your family. It will even include the commandant, your general friend, and all but the few who are in this room. Only we three and you, along with a very few others, will know what is taking place. Understanding those conditions, do you want me to continue?"

Gus 3 could not imagine where this was going, but curiosity had gathered him in. He nodded in the affirmative. The man went on, "This incident caused havoc with our systems. At the same time, it has presented a significant opportunity. That adds to our problem. Your being a West Point cadet presents a hell of a conundrum. First, you would have to agree with this potential mission and agree to take part in it. A cadet has never been used for a mission such as this. You cannot be ordered to do it, and we are not sure if we can create a situation that will allow us to carry it out. Again, do you still want me to proceed?" Another nod.

"Gus, if we can get sign-off on this from the highest levels in our government, this is what will happen. But, before going to those powers, we need a commitment from you. If at any time we get to a point where the outcome appears to be anything less than perfect or in any way does not have your full support, the mission will be aborted. All you have to do to stop this conversation is to raise your hand.

"The young man you saw on the screen is Adjah Renede. His mother was an English citizen and died of natural causes a few years ago. He is the son of King Renede of Nagorno-Karabakh. Have you heard of it?"

Gus gave his first negative headshake along with a "no, sir."

"Most people have not. It is a small country, only a couple of thousand square miles in size, and is located in an area that is somewhat central to Iran, Armenia, Azerbaijan, Turkey, Russia, and others. It is just west of the Caspian Sea. There are about 150,000 people living there. It is a disputed country, but left alone to be run by King Renede as it is of little interest to its neighbors. Its greatest value is its location and a few oil wells. The king there lives a fairly uneventful life. He lives in luxury while most of his subjects also live fairly well. He has absolute control of them, but they do not have to serve in a military, pay taxes, or do anything other than live the life they choose. The country produces enough oil to allow them that lifestyle. You still with me, Gus?"

Gus 3 again nodded that he understood so far. "Our intelligence confirms that King Renede has a rare form of cancer and has only about a year to live. His son Adjah will replace him on that throne. Our interest in all of this is that we want a communications center and a landing strip there. It would provide a near perfect location in our efforts to have as much control in that area as possible. If we had such an air station, it would become very easy for us to install other deterrents at that same location. I will be very blunt and remind you that the information you are hearing is of the highest possible security classification. Only because we have done an extensive investigation into your life are we able to proceed with this conversation with you. For all purposes you now hold a Top Secret clearance classification. Any divulgence of this information would result in a shutdown of any military career you could ever pursue and in judicial actions. At this point, I will consider that unless you stop me, your interest in this mission is still viable." Gus 3 nodded again while the gentleman continued to talk.

"This, in basic form, is what we propose. Since Adjah has not been around his father or anyone else in the country for the last couple of years, he will have obviously changed. Also, with his mother gone, and no other family, it would be easy to insert someone who has his appearance and mannerisms as his substitute. That would be you. Adjah is in school now at Howard University studying international business. He will be there for up to two more years completing his degree.

"It would appear from our intelligence that his father will pass away prior to that time. Adjah will be called to Nagorno-Karabakh to take over as sole monarch of that country. For this plan to work, we must start now. The scheme would be to get you trained right away. For all purposes, you would become Adjah Renede. You would have to become well informed about every part of his life. His friends, his courses, his social life, and those lessons he has learned through the years on how to be a monarch.

"That is the easy part. You will need to be kept in a secret and secluded location during that training time. The time will be consistent with the king's lifespan. Almost assuredly less than two years. There would be a rush to train you as soon as possible, but your training would continue no matter what the length of time until the king's death. At that point, when Adjah is called to travel to attend his father's funeral, he will be replaced by you. Now comes the shitty part. For this mission to be successful, you must die. You must die in the sense that everyone thinks you are gone.

"As we have stated, this must include your family, even your mom. She must be convinced that you are dead. Your friends from home, your friends from the Point, and everybody you know will think you are gone. The good news is that this should take only three to five years. That will be somewhat dictated by the time of the king's natural death.

"After the mission is complete, we can extract you so that no one will know of your having been involved in any way. If you agree to all of this, I can promise the following. One, that upon completion of the mission, you could be reunited with your family, but the only explanation you could ever offer is that you are unable to discuss those years. At that time, you will be presented with three additional choices.

"You may go directly back into your current class level at the Point. If you do that and then graduate, you will be given the rank of captain within three months of your graduation. All of this time will be recorded as service time. Second, you could become immediately assigned to the army with the rank of captain. Third, and this depends on the successful completion of this mission, you would be offered the opportunity to join the diplomatic corps as a trained agent. Of course, there is a fourth option and that would be for you to walk away from all of this right now and return to your normal life, that is, the same life you were living yesterday. If that is your choice, there will be no record, either military or civilian, of this conversation. You will reassume your education at the Point or undertake other career options.

"If you do decide to complete this mission, your financial stability will be assured for the remainder of your life. It will be a very comfortable amount. A reasonable story will also be created to allow you to disavow any knowledge of any of the things that may be involved with this mission."

Another of the three men spoke up and followed, "There you have it, son. Should we proceed with our intention of gaining authorization for this mission? Before you answer, let me offer this. We have done many things just this complicated and important before. Most have succeeded. This will be the first time in the history of our country that a West Point student has been asked to participate in a clandestine operation. You can take that as either a compliment or that you have been put in one hell of a mess. I will tell you that this will gain your country a foothold that will provide security in the world for many years.

"You are the one person who can do this with this level of ease. If you want to serve your country, then you need to be advised that there is nothing you or any other soldier could accomplish, even in a long military career, that would produce the potential stability of peaceful world order any more so than this. The success of the mission is made possible by you. Only you can make it work. I hope you will accept, but the decision is yours. Understand that there are many details, but we have the resources to mold them into a workable plan. So, what's your answer?"

Gus 3 replied, "Sir, am I to understand that my family—most importantly, my mom—will think I am dead?"

He replied, "That is correct, son, and I know that is one of the worst things that could be done to her. We are well aware of your dad's death. We know when and how you fit into helping her through that loss. We understand that this is an unthinkable request for us to make of you. Here is the bottom line. If we do not attempt, and succeed, with this mission, our only alternative will be to take by force such an area for this purpose. If we must resort to using force, we risk extreme condemnation from our allies as well as those we do not consider friendly to us. It could even result in a war, which could cost many lives. If we do not attempt this mission or a suitable alternative, one that would give us some control of that area, we would set ourselves and our allies up to be attacked either overtly or through various terrorist-style atrocities. Either way, this plan, you, are the way to achieve our goal at what should be the most significant reduction or probability for any American casualties. That is our opinion, and it is that opinion upon which we must proceed. It is up to you, just you."

Cadet Johnson thought for a few minutes. For the first time, he became and thought like his dad. "Sir, I will do what I need to do for this country. After all, it is this country my dad died for before I was even born. I will accept this plan with one condition."

"Go ahead, Gus."

"My mom has given me her heart and soul, in fact, her total life. I do not see any way that I could perform on any level without knowing that she will be well taken care of and have at least some chance of being happy in her life. I want her protected in the same way I would do so. She has no husband to do that."

"Gus, that is an easy part; we have done it before. You will know all of the specifics prior to the launch of the operation."

The first of the three spoke up again, "I will take that as a yes, and we will meet you here at 0600 tomorrow to offer you more details of the plan. Wear your civvies. There is a full complement of clothes in your room. I can now tell you that this plan has already been approved at the very highest levels. From a review of your record, we were very certain what your response would be. We are already well into the planning stages. We will begin a full briefing beginning tomorrow at the 0600 meeting. You will be allowed input."

Trip was escorted to the same room he had used this past summer. As he had been told, there was a full set of civilian clothing laying on one of the two beds. It was all in his size. It was the style and selection that would be made by a young man attending Howard. Collegiate-style all the way.

Early the next afternoon, the commandant of West Point was visited by a young U.S. Army lieutenant colonel. The information he provided shook the very highest levels of that school. One of his cadets had been killed just before dawn on a trip returning from Ft. Belvoir. The car had been run off the road, flipped a number of times and burned. Fire had engulfed the car and very little remained. Positive identification was being confirmed about those remains. It was being done by INSCOM. They felt sure confirmation of this information would be available in a few hours. The young cadet was traveling with a driver assigned to INSCOM. Her identity was also to be confirmed by forensic ID. Everything was burned beyond recognition. He asked the commandant to please hold any announcement of the event until he had received notification of confirmation that all family had been notified.

That notification came just after lunch on that same day. At dinner that evening, the commandant stood and began speaking into the dining hall speaker system. "Cadets, this evening I must share with you news of a tragic event. Third-year cadet Gus Johnson III has died in an accident. He was killed this morning in a tragic car accident while on his way back to this institution. I will provide additional details as to the services as they are available. The West Point burial grounds and a full cadet service is being offered. I would assume, though, that his family will prefer burial at his home. There will be announcements regarding those services as information becomes available. Transportation will be provided for a group to attend that service."

AGAIN

When Aggie and Robert returned from a quick lunch at the drugstore, there were more cars than normal in front of the office. Neither of them paid particular attention to them. When they entered the office, that all changed. Aggie's preacher along with General Hrabal and his wife were sitting there with Marylin Neece. Marylin's eyes were red, and it was obvious she was doing everything she could to control herself. Gen. Hrabal was the first to stand and the first to speak.

"Aggie, I have just received a call from the commandant at West Point. He has asked that I tell you that Gus 3 has been in a horrible accident. It happened very early this morning as he was returning from Ft. Belvoir to West Point."

She did not cry, but seemed to take calm control of the conversation. "Where is he now? I need to be with him." When she looked into the eyes of the general, then over at her preacher and Marylin, she knew the answer. It was then that she softly began to cry, but tried to maintain control while asking questions about what had happened. She was given the details about the accident. Those who were standing with her at that moment were soon to be joined by a large group of more friends who would help her through this tragedy. Because her son had become a shining star of this community, he would be mourned by many.

Right now, she must go and share this news with her mom and dad and with those others not present who so loved her son, Gus 3. Marsha would be especially hard to tell. Marsha was completely devastated, but took control of her own emotions, and with a steady and compassionate composure, became Aggie's crutch through this horrible event.

THIS DAY'S REALITY NEVER GETS EASIER

All these events flashed through Aggie's mind as her thoughts gently flowed back to the reality of the funeral. "Taps" had ended, and the event was done. The only thing left was for her to mourn the loss of this, a second loved one. After this loss, she had nothing left to give.

A few months passed, and Aggie had gathered some of her strength and resolve. She was determined that she would not let this defeat her. It was a crippling blow, but no, it would not take away her ability to live her life and be able to provide for the many others she could help. Her belief in God demanded that, and she knew that is what Gus 3 would expect.

CHAPTER 11

LET'S DO IT

Aggie had gone back to work, which was creating a good distraction for her. A few months later, Marylin came into Robert's office one morning. She was chipper and very upbeat. "Aggie," said Marylin, "I really need you at the USO meeting tonight. Everyone on the board plans to be there, and it is my understanding that they will make some very hard decisions at this meeting."

Aggie reluctantly agreed. She had learned that to cope with the loss of her son, she must force herself toward activity. This meeting required that kind of force and she used it.

All of the attendees knew the details regarding her son and her husband. They were all glad she was there. The meeting always opened with a word of prayer followed by the minutes of the previous meeting. Those minutes were approved and the topic of new business opened for discussion. "It is time to either"—and the committee chairman used these words exactly—"either blank or get off the pot. I assume you all know what the blank means." A chuckle followed but indeed all understood. "Whatever we are going to do, it is now time to decide. We are in the perfect place at the perfect time to create something special. Can we do it?" They all agreed that bigger and better would be the way to go.

Marylin followed, "Why should we shackle ourselves with parameters? We can, no must, do something spectacular." No one seemed surprised by Marylin's words as they all knew her well.

They knew that she lived in a world of wondrous expectation. Even with that thought, they all agreed with what she said.

The topic then moved to funds and how much would be needed for a really first-class facility. Numbers were thrown out and ranged from a quarter of a million dollars to millions. Aggie sat there and took it all in. Her mind raced as she thought about all those service men who could be touched by a place where they and their families could be together. A place they could enjoy and where they could share quality time. Her late husband and her late son would have been able to take advantage of such a place had they lived to do so.

Aggie spoke, "In 1971 when my husband died, I was given $100,000 by the government for that loss. I put the money into an investment account for my unborn child. It has never been touched. The value of that investment is now over $700,000. I can think of no better use for those funds than for whatever we decide to create with them. I will pledge them for that purpose."

Everyone seemed to gasp as they could not believe what they had just heard.

The chairman spoke up, "That is one hell of a place to start. Aggie, there are no words that I or anyone on this committee can utter to follow that. Let's call it a night, try to absorb this information, and come back in a week with ideas."

With that, the meeting closed and everyone departed. Aggie was hugged by almost everyone. Some cried, some laughed, some never uttered a word. As they left the community building, all but Aggie already had an idea as to whose honor this USO center would be dedicated.

That meeting was on a Wednesday night. The next would be on the following Wednesday. On Friday morning, Robert called Aggie into the conference room. Marylin was there with them. Spread on the conference table was a large map of the county. It was a map used by the tax department and showed property lines of parcels.

A blown-up map of a particular area was also on the table. Robert called her to the side where he and Marylin stood and said, "Let me show you something." He pointed to an area and said, "This is the farm that G left to Trip. It is yours now. It is about 200 acres. On the east side is a 1,000-acre parcel that belongs to Benard Leonard from Raleigh. He uses it as a hunting preserve. It has a 100-acre pond on it and an upscale plantation-style home that has been fully remodeled.

"Just here, along Hwy. 53, is another 600 acres that belongs to Eve Lucas. She is the widow of Jack Lucas. He used his land as a hunting preserve and a family getaway. It also has a pond, but it is only about fifteen acres. The land to the north now belongs to Mr. Lucas's daughter. She inherited it from him. It is an inheritance that he received from his sister. In her will, she requested that he pass it along to his daughter. It is mostly wetland as a creek runs through it. It is about 200 acres and even though most of it is low, it has some beautiful ridges. It has little value except for hunting. His daughter does not hunt."

Aggie could tell exactly where this was going. "All this put together would create a tract of land of over 2,000 acres. Big enough for a tremendous undertaking. I know your finances very well, Aggie. Your farm produces very little in income. In fact, what it does produce is just about enough to pay the property taxes. If you were to donate that farm, say to the USO, it would be a write-off that could negate your requirement to pay income taxes for a number of years. It would be a good financial move. My gut feeling is that we could get a great deal of support, even to the point of full donations on these other properties surrounding your tract."

Aggie turned to Marylin and quickly indicated that she loved this plan. She said, "I think we should ask Robert to make this pitch at the meeting next Wednesday. If everyone is on board, it should be him who makes the inquiries into those other tracts. After all, he does most of the tax work for that group anyway."

Marylin beamed as she agreed. Marylin responded, "I bet I could talk him into doing all the legal work for nothing." She looked at him and gave him a real seductive grin.

He just put his hands up as if to say *tricked again*. It wasn't her first time to maneuver him using her charms. She was a master at it.

Robert, Marylin, and Aggie all spent time helping to prepare the presentation regarding that piece of property for the next Wednesday night meeting of the local USO committee. A great deal of information was gathered and made ready to be shared. It was now time for the meeting, and Marylin had made sure Robert was on the program for his presentation.

There were several others who had brought suggestions. One suggested a golf club. Another talked about how military guys loved the outdoors, including hunting. A tract of land would not require much spending beyond that of a lodge. A hunting preserve would be very doable. Another talked about a small resort that could include activities for the families of those soldiers. It was now Robert's turn to make his spiel.

Robert got up, flashed a big smile, and looked at them for a moment as if to ensure he had everyone's attention. He then followed, "How about we do them all?" Some of them nodded yes, some looked as if they were wondering how, and a couple even laughed. He then opened the maps, gathered the group around, and filled them in on the details of how to make it work. He went through his presentation. If they could acquire the land, then it could be used as collateral to gain enough funds to come close to finishing the project. As many funds as possible could be raised, and then they could proceed with other options. In the end, everybody was on board and talking ninety miles an hour.

The chairman then hushed all the chatter and said, "I need to make this presentation to the USO Board of Governors. They have a meeting scheduled for the eighteenth of this month, and I will get put on that agenda. If it is okay with everyone, I will ask that Robert travel with me to that meeting. We should have their answer by the, let's see, the twenty-eighth, when our next meeting is scheduled. Let's don't even vote; let's just do it." All agreed.

Marylin and Aggie talked Robert's head off on the way home. They were so excited about this project. And all of this excitement was helping Aggie recover. She was beginning to become her old self again, and everybody welcomed that. Even her mom and dad noticed the change. Robert felt that he should calm them down a bit, but he could see how the new project was helping Aggie so he avoided saying a negative word. There was a lot to be done before this would all be put together. When they got home that night, Robert talked to Marylin about that. She did not disagree.

KEEP THE FIRE BURNING

Robert was very surprised when Marylin seemed to be getting quite flirty with him. She had not acted this way in a long time. He was beginning to enjoy all of her sultry attention. And she was enjoying watching his reaction to her. He was some years older than fifty, and she was only about five years behind him. For her actions to have this effect on him excited her almost as much as they did him. That night ended on a very high note for Robert and Marylin. The next morning as soon as Robert left the house, Marylin called Aggie. She could not wait to give Aggie the details.

Aggie was a little embarrassed when Marylin gave more details of her evening than might be necessary. This is the kind of information two middle-aged women did not normally share. But Marylin was special and so was her relationship with Aggie. Very few women were as close as Marylin and Aggie. Aggie certainly did not want to create any problem between Marylin and Robert. Still, she just could not let her knowledge of the details from last night fall to no good use. Since she and Robert didn't have a typical boss-employee relationship where each keeps their personal lives private, many times he would tease about her previous night's date. He would always make some remark as to how she may feel the following morning or how she may seem all aglow. It would be a shot that would imply that he knew more than he really did about her previous night's activities. This time, Aggie was the one loaded and she did have details.

That morning, Robert parked and went straight into his office. Aggie knew that the events from the previous night were something he would not want to talk about. It had been a long time since he and his wife had a night like that. After a little while, Aggie made him a cup of coffee and took it into his office. "My God, Robert," she stated as if in shock, "you are all flushed. It looks like your blood pressure must be through the roof. Are you all right? Do you think we need to call the doctor? A person your age needs to be really careful not to overexert himself. What in the world have you been doing? We should call EMS or do something!"

He had a very concerned look on his face. He reached down and took his wrist as if he was going to take his own pulse. Before he could answer, she got up and went back into her office. "I am right here if you need me. I think it's best if you take it easy this morning."

A few minutes later, he walked into her office, looked at her as if he could shoot her, and asked, "Has my wife called you this morning?" Aggie blushed a little as she knew the answer would reveal that she had some very personal knowledge of what went on last night.

The only answer she could think of that may save her was, "Why, what do you think she could have said?"

The conversation ended there with both of them knowing that the other knew. One good thing that did come from it all was that Robert kept Marylin on his mind all day. He got home that night with a bottle of wine and roses. He wanted to keep this fire kindled as long as his fuel would hold out.

WE CAN MAKE IT WORK

Robert arrived at the meeting of the national USO committee along with Arley Blossom. Arley was the chairman of the Cowan-area USO committee. They were both impressed by the facility that housed the national headquarters in Arlington. Arley and Robert were ready to make their pitch to the national committee. Considerable preparation had been done for their presentation, such as estimated cost, preliminary conversations with the land owners involved, and other information they felt would help them win the national USO support they needed for their project. They were using a computerized projector program that could show on any wall, but in this case, a screen was available.

Arley was a little nervous but stood tall as he took the floor and quickly explained to that committee who Robert was and that it would be him discussing their concept plan along with visual aids. Robert took the floor and began.

He had often argued a client's case before a review board of the IRS. That experience served him well in this presentation. He began with an explanation of geography and location. He had a map of the eastern United States on the screen. He was using a laser pointer. First, he swept it up and down the entire East Coast. He made his point that the location they had picked was almost exactly in the center. It was close to several major highways and was a short distance to either the mountains or the coast. He then pointed to Washington, to Norfolk, and right on down the East Coast. He stopped the laser at Fort Bragg and at Camp Lejeune, both in North Carolina. He put that little dot of light on every major military base up and down the coast. He even highlighted a number of those that were inland. This group all understood the purpose of this slide. The area they were drawing attention to was centrally located to the largest number of military personnel in this country. He went on with the remaining details of the potential facility. In the end, all those in attendance stood and clapped. Arley and Robert had not expected that kind of acceptance, but they had it. Now, the hard work must begin.

LOOKING OUT FOR MOM

Aggie did not know it, but she was safer than she had ever been in her life. Almost everything she did was being monitored. There were two different programs that had been put into place for her protection. One was an individual who would keep close tabs on her. It was done in a way that would not invade her privacy. The second was an electronic surveillance program. The surveillance was designed to be private and protective. She was part of a fairly new program that was in place at the CIA. Cameras were planted in a number of places that she frequented. Her work, her home, and others.

These special cameras were supported by the other public cameras being used for safety purposes. The purpose of this program was just to keep up with her and assure she was safe. No one she had any connection with knew anything about it. The program that monitored those concealed cameras was all on computer. No person would see them unless something out of the ordinary triggered a special application. It was all brand new.

The program had been written for this specific personal surveillance purpose. It was a babysitter (in fact, the nickname for the new program was "BS"). The program had the ability to activate if anything other than activities it had been programed to accept as normal took place. One day, Da was walking from his work shed back to the house. He tripped and fell. A notification indicator was activated. It was on a computer screen at the CIA office in Langley, Virginia. The operator pushed that alert and a live picture of Da on the ground was immediately on the screen. All that was required was for him to click on "activate response" and the required notifications to address the incident would be made. It was all done by computer except for the operator having to make a quick decision as to whether or not the incident needed intervention. Under normal conditions, no one would have known he had fallen and it would not have been for several hours that he would have been found. The analyst in Langley quickly clicked the appropriate icon to begin immediate response.

In less than six minutes, the local rescue squad was there. They went straight into the backyard and helped him up. They tried their best to get him to go to the local emergency room to be checked out, but he would not. He wondered who had called them, but they had no access to that information. He never mentioned it to Mama or Aggie as he did not want them to make a big deal out of his falling. The analyst was notified the incident was successfully ended and he released that "live alert notification" with a simple press of his mouse.

The computer program known to the agency as PSAN (Protective Surveillance and Notification) was being used on a number of subjects. Aggie was new on the list and no one was sure why. The fact was, it really did not matter why.

GIVE ME YOUR PROPERTY

Robert had already begun negotiations with those property owners who may be involved with the potential new USO facility. He would gain a commitment from an owner and then go to the others using those commitments as an enticement to get them on board. He started with Aggie. She was all in. Next was Jack Lucas's daughter. She was the one with the less-valuable piece of that property. She agreed as well.

Using Aggie's and the Lucases' daughter's agreements as his lure, he was able to explain to Jack Lucas's widow the value of the tax deduction she could receive. Mrs. Lucas agreed. That left only the 1,000-acre tract owned by Benard Leonard up in Raleigh. He called to see if he could set up a meeting with Mr. Leonard to discuss this issue. He did not tell him the specifics but did tell him that it was a national issue. Benard invited Robert to stop by his "playhouse" on the following Friday for lunch. Lunch would be about 12:30.

He left the office a little before noon and told Aggie to wish him luck. He was about to tackle the last of the property donors, but it was the one who would be the most difficult. He arrived, and as he drove up, Benard walked out of the door to meet him. "Welcome, Robert," was his cheerful greeting as he stuck his hand out for Robert to shake. He was an older man, but had a handshake like a vice. Robert had always been told you could judge a man by his handshake. He was not sure how this would fit into his efforts as an indicator for this deal. Based on the shake, Benard may be a hard nut to crack. He went in and they walked directly into the dining room where they were joined by Mrs. Leonard and Robert's preserve manager. A few pleasantries were exchanged. In a moment, Mrs. Leonard said in an almost passing way, "Robert, what brings you to the playhouse?"

Robert began his pitch. His assurance that all the other land owners had agreed seemed to make a difference. While Benard had never served in the military, his wife's first husband had. After the pitch was made, Mrs. Leonard spoke. Nothing she could have said could have better fit with Robert's attempts.

"Well, I will declare," she said, stopping for a moment to gain her composure, "my first husband and I met at a USO club. It was in Wilmington and was during the Second World War. I was raised up there with my family, and I volunteered to help out at the USO during that time. I had just finished high school. It was lucky for me. I got my first husband there, and had it not been for him, I would not have been able to hook Benard. Raymond and Benard were close friends." All chuckled. They finished their lunch and nothing else about the property was mentioned until Robert started to leave. Benard walked him to his car and then said, "Robert, I think what you are doing has merit. Certainly appears that Mrs. Leonard thinks so. I will be back with you in a couple of days with a reply."

Those days did not go by quickly. They all waited anxiously for Benard Leonard's reply. His was the only one needed to set them in motion. The lunch meeting at the "playhouse" had been on Friday. It was Tuesday when Aggie answered the phone and nervously announced to Robert that he had a call from Mr. Leonard. She walked to the door of Robert's office and blatantly tried to listen to every word. When it was done, Robert did not say a word. He just looked down at his desk and went back to work. Aggie was about to go nuts. "Are you not going to tell me what he said?"

His response was, "Why? What do you think he could have said?" She laughed; he had gotten her back for her answer when he had asked her what Marylin had told her. Robert continued, "He said, 'I think I can make it work. It is going to require some wiggling, though.'"

Robert put together a proposal for the Leonards. He met with them and their attorney, Gene McCrackin, a couple of weeks later. That meeting took place in Raleigh. Arley went with him as the

USO representative and Robert presented the offer. "I think this is in line with everything you requested. Your attorney will want to review the documents but in basic terms here is what they say. You will deed the entire tract of the 'playhouse' properties to the USO nonprofit. For that you can take a full tax deduction. You and your wife will have lifetime rights to your house on the property, complete with a separate entrance. It will be fenced off from the other areas. You will also both have special deeded privilege to use the preserve area for your personal recreational requirements. That includes the pool, golf, fishing, trails, etc." He stuck all of those in just to remind Benard of the scope of the project. "You may use a guide of your choice and your own personal hunting dogs. At your death, it will all revert to the control of the USO."

Benard flipped the typed agreement to his lawyer who already had his own copy. "That sounds perfect. Let Gene review it, and if all is acceptable, you can draw the deeds," Benard said. Less than a week later, Robert got a call from the McCrackin Law Firm. The message was that everything seemed in place and for Robert to go ahead and create the documents needed to complete the transaction. As soon as he heard those words, he called for Aggie to come in. She was delighted as he explained that she should go ahead and prepare all the paperwork needed to complete the transfer of ownership on all those tracts. None of the land had been transferred yet as each was contingent on the other. The land deal was done.

A TREMENDOUS WINDFALL

Quick calls were made to all of the members of the USO board and everyone was ready to run. The national board members were just as excited as were the locals. Aggie's first call had been to Marylin. Aggie told her that Robert had worked his magic, and that the deal was done. Marylin answered back that she had a little magic of her own and that she would see that he was "well paid" for his efforts when he got home. "I just bought an outfit that is going to drive him crazy." Aggie laughed, and was a bit surprised to find herself thinking that she too might enjoy buying a new outfit to wear on a date. That was the first time that she had even thought such a thing since Gus 3's death. She did not tell Robert what Marylin had said, but let him wade through it on his own.

The next morning as Robert came into the office, she looked at him and just said with her most innocent smile, "You okay, old man?"

Having known she and Marylin had talked, he suspected some such remark from her this morning. He simply looked back at her and responded, "I am just fine, Aggie. Marylin is the one you should be checking on; she is exhausted." It took her a minute, but then she knew she had just been gotten, again. Robert was slick.

The land deals had all been done and signed. It was time to move forward. Funds needed to be raised. The national committee had taken a great deal of interest in this project. They had members at the subsequent local meetings. It seemed they were working on a number of financial opportunities and should have information soon. Advertising was being done for the new "Disneyland for our Soldiers," as it was being pegged. Donations of monies and donations in kind were pouring in. Corporations were jumping aboard, especially those that may have military contracts. Well over $2 million, not counting Aggie's pledge, had been committed and such needed equipment as computers, tractors, various building supplies, and even food preparation equipment had been promised. The national USO had asked for a special meeting and it was to be next week.

It was not a formal meeting but instead a conversation. The national USO chairman began, "What has been put together here is beyond belief. It brings with it the potential to be one of the most important recruiting tools and one of the biggest enlistment perks the armed services has ever had. As such, each of the services is willing to fund a portion of this project with part of their recruitment budgets. All of the branches have agreed. They are putting $2.5 million of their combined budgets in this plan. The only request from them is that they be allowed a project representative to participate in this building project and then a seat on the governing board."

No one could have imagined such a windfall. Also, having such a professional on board may negate the expense of the many dollars required for them to hire a project manager. "There is one more thing the national committee would like to ask," the chairman continued. "We would like for there to be an official ribbon-cutting ceremony. This thing has reached into the highest levels of our government. Any number of military officials as well as politicians would like to attend. Everyone wants to be identified with this thing." How could the local group oppose? All were in agreement.

Aggie, Robert, and Marylin were almost in disbelief as to how this project had taken off. From his small office on the day that the three of them had looked at those maps until now, for such a thing as this to have been born was a miracle. What a wonderful time and how much fun it would be to watch this creation manifest itself. They would just sit back and enjoy every minute.

CHAPTER 12

HERE WE GO

And enjoy they did. Imagine the interest that a multi-million-dollar project would create in a small, poor county in the southeastern portion of North Carolina. Nothing of this magnitude had ever been attempted in this area before. The project had developed a life of its own and now proceeded without a hitch. It seemed there would be a group, some private and some government, that would provide service to almost every particular segment. The county, the state, and even the national departments of this or that all wanted to participate.

Local corporations came to the table with many offers of financial assistance as well as those that could donate services. The list was endless. It may be the electric company or the gas company. Internet providers and cell providers all came to the table.

A project manager had been put in place and he seemed to be well in control. It was, in fact, the guy the military had proposed as their representative. He was a well-known project manager and brought a staff with him. The project was estimated to take almost two years, front to back. All of this was a boon to the local economy. From the largest to the smallest, all were the benefactors of this project. The equipment being used to clear and prepare the area required fuel and maintenance. The people working required a place to live and eat. The diner had never been busier. Even Aggie had profited as she had rented Memaw and G's house to the project manager. She had not had the heart to do anything with it before as it had been Gus 3's. Now, it seemed that because of this project, it included Gus 3. Robert had never had as much going on. His business was booming. He had hired two new assistants just to help Aggie. Aggie was now managing people. Their world was changing, and so far, the changes had been good.

One morning just after Robert had come in, the manager for the project stopped in. He needed to see Aggie and Mrs. Neece. He had called Mrs. Neece and she was to meet the two of them at Mr. Neece's office. In a few minutes, she came in. They sat in Robert's conference room. He was immediately bombarded by questions from Marylin and Aggie about how and what was going on with construction.

His reply was much the same as it always was, "Just fine. In fact, that is why I am here. I was told that at the appropriate time we needed to plan to have a ribbon-cutting ceremony for our project. We are within about 120 days of that point. We need to establish the plans that will make this event as stellar as it can possibly be. Planning an event like that is a little out of my wheelhouse, so I will give you and Mrs. Neece some details about where and how, and then you can plan the ceremony." He broke out a drawing of the facility. Using a red marker, he indicated a couple of spots that could be used for that ribbon cutting.

His first choice was that it be at the entrance. That would make it easier on workers as they would not have to stop their work projects on the inner areas. Also, it would provide a much safer and more easily accessible site for the attendees. Aggie and Marylin agreed with his suggestion and now the planning and an exact date was all that remained. He had done his part and needed to get back to the worksite, so he departed. There would be many issues awaiting a decision from him at the site.

NOTHING BUT THE GOOD THINGS

Aggie and Marylin contacted Arley to set up a meeting of the USO committee. He contacted everyone, and they could all be at the meeting on Wednesday night. It would have to be either before or after the Wednesday church services. They chose after. That way, the meeting could take place in the sanctuary of the church just after that service. All but two would be at the Presbyterian service and those two could stop by on the way from their churches.

Aggie was caught by the minister's sermon Wednesday night. She usually enjoyed those mid-week meetings. They were a little less formal than the Sunday morning service and it seemed to her the sermon was more conversational than instructional. She liked that as it seemed to make for easier listening. Easier and more understandable.

Tonight, it was all about dwelling on the good things and letting the bad ones fade away. If anyone had a reason to ponder the bad things that had happened to them, it was her. Seemed this sermon may have been written for her. She listened intently as he began.

"You, all of you, need to know and understand just how much God has given you," the pastor began. "It may or may not be exactly what you have wanted. I am not talking about gifts of material things, but gifts of life and of the heart. You may have had your heart broken, and you may think whatever caused it had no good reason. Sorry, people, but you do not have the ability to understand what the reasons could be. You may think you are as smart as God, but we are not." His sermon continued. Soon after the service, the USO board began their meeting.

The meeting was quick and a time was picked for the ribbon cutting. One of the men on the board was adamant that the ceremony not be on a Friday or Saturday. That is when the locals liked to hunt and fish. He was right. He argued that a Tuesday afternoon would accommodate most everybody he knew. Few people hunted or fished on Tuesdays. Businesspeople would have put the first-of-the-week issues behind them. Politicians did not seem to care as they could put off anything to gain a little public exposure. A Tuesday almost exactly four months away was picked. The time was set for 4:00 p.m., which would give them two hours before dark.

The committee was quick to appoint Arley, Marylin, and Aggie to make the appropriate plans. "We'll meet on Thursday at 5:00 and begin—that is, if it is okay with you two," Arley said to them. Both were okay with that. Besides, that would give each of them an opportunity to do some research and then be able to discuss this thing with more of a realistic idea of what it should be.

When Aggie got home, she found Mama and Da sitting in the living room fast asleep. The Braves were playing ball on TV. They loved their Atlanta Braves. It was after 10:00 p.m. and she was tired. She did not wake either of them. She was darn sure that she did not want to watch a baseball game. She was going to go upstairs and take herself a long bath. That had become much easier now as Mama and Da had moved into the bedroom that was Gus 3's. It was downstairs and so was much easier for them now as it did not require them to climb the stairs.

The three bedrooms that were upstairs had been small and had only one bathroom. Because it was just the three of them now, Da made some changes to the upstairs for Aggie's benefit. He had left her room intact; it would become the spare. He took out the wall between the main bedroom and the guest bedroom. It was now one large suite with a sitting area and much more closet space. He was not a plumber, so the bath was the only thing he had to hire someone to do. He had moved forward with the renovations despite Aggie's reluctance. It was for a purpose.

He knew she would be very hesitant to spend the kind of money involved with the project. Aggie was financially well-off due to her own savings and Gus 3's inheritance from the Johnsons, but she was reluctant to spend the money. In her mind, her financial portfolio was tied to her son. Spending such a relatively large sum was an upsetting reminder that Gus 3 would never receive or enjoy his inheritance.

Da knew all this, and was still determined to create something much nicer for his daughter. A small second bath with a shower was added on the end. A larger master bath was then rebuilt using some of the space they had gained from opening the two bedrooms. It was a nice upfit. She now had a large shower with overhead and wall mounts on both ends. There were temperature controls on the knobs. A Jacuzzi had been added and it was a nice one. Larger than normal. All of the other amenities were modernized and were appropriately secluded. She deserved it, he wanted to do it, so he just did.

She did keep her same bedroom furniture. It almost seemed too small for the bedroom, but it was the same furniture that she and Gus had shared those two weeks that they had together before she lost him to the war. That bed was her security blanket.

Before she went upstairs, she walked into the kitchen. She knew there would be some wine in the refrigerator as Mama and Da had a glass every night just before dinner. That may be some of the reason they slept during those games.

She poured herself a glass and went upstairs to crash. Before the Jacuzzi was full, she added some special bath oil. It had become one of her luxuries, and this night she wanted luxury. The water was hot, so hot, in fact, that the mirrors were becoming covered with fog. She was about to get into the tub as she turned and looked into the mirror. There was not much detail as the fog had robbed the reflective surface of that. Still, she felt good about what she saw. She had been blessed with good health and, yes, an attractive figure. Maybe she *should* buy that new outfit and re-enter the dating scene.

When she sank into the bath, it was wonderful. The almost-too-hot water, the contour of the perfectly shaped tub, and the gentle circulation of the water around her created the sensation of floating on a perfect summer day among the clouds. She had dreamed of being able to sit on a cloud since she was a small girl. This was about as close as a person could come.

Her mind drifted, but soon settled on that night's sermon at her church. She thought back to the two basic happenings that had controlled her life. First was the death of her beloved Gus. The only thing that had gotten her through that horror was waiting for and then raising her son. Now, without anything to keep her focus away from her current loss, she must focus only on Gus 3's death. Almost as a blessing, she began to remember more of the preacher's words: "Do not allow your heart to be filled with the things that you cannot control. Those are the things that will drag you into a place of depression or create a delusion of non-releasable and unbearable grief. You must instead seize your thoughts, take control of them. In a way, put them into your pocket. Let your mind be filled with things that provide you with pleasure. Force yourself to push those things to the front. Keep pushing to keep them there. It is the good things that will bring joy and completeness to your life. It is them that will help you be all that you can be. They are the fuel that will propel you to that good end. The heaviest of all of your bad memories become but a feather when placed on the scale to be balanced by those memories from which you derived joy and pleasure. If you do not believe what I tell you tonight, what do you have to lose by trying it? When those other horrors must be called upon, you can take them from your pocket as you decide, not as they dictate. It will become easy for you to control them, to repocket them. In the end, that is where they will stay. Stored near you but far from controlling you. God wants you to be happy!" It had been a good sermon.

Aggie thought about that night Gus had asked if he could join her on the school bus seat. She also thought about standing just beside that bottom step and looking into his eyes. Staring at the stars on a warm July night. Holding Gus 3 for the first time and feeling the warmth and love that becomes a part of that moment. Watching as he grew into a fine young man. Things like a small girl walking up and saying, "Can I be your friend?" A toy red convertible and a card that read, "Happy birthday, hot stuff." Long walks and endless conversations. Wide eyes peering as she turned in her short black dress. Those same eyes as Marsha walked down her stairs in that same dress. The wonders of having a near-perfect son in your life. The love and security of a mom and dad who provided unconditional love. And, one of her fondest memories, that dance at the Christmas party with a tall, good-looking young man who was her own blood. The words of that song, "Save the Last Dance for Me," would not be put in her pocket. That perfect dance had become the most valuable of all good memories. Now she would focus on the joy in those eyes as he stood tall and proud and held his mom for those moments.

As she got out of the tub and again looked into the mirror, the fog was gone. It was she, and she was smiling but had tears in her eyes. This time they were tears of joy. She was so very lucky. What she had been given and enjoyed was more than most people could even dream about. Perfect love is a snapshot of nothing less than God's promise of an eternal heaven.

That night, she did not need a security blanket. Her sleep was quick and sound. That preacher had gotten ahold of her, and between him and God, they had led her to this place.

Early the next morning, she was up. She felt great. As she went into her celebrity-style bathroom to put on makeup, she noticed the glass of wine sitting on the side of the tub. She had not even taken a sip. She poured it down the drain and then left for work.

Marylin came to the office the next morning with Robert. You could tell that he was a little put out with this change of routine. He, like most men, was a creature of habit. Her continuous talking was not his norm for the ride to the office. It was obvious to Aggie when he pawned Marylin off to her. She probably noticed, but it certainly did not seem to bother her. She was just that sure of him.

The planning began. It did not take long to get it done. The ribbon cutting was going to be somewhere between Marylin's extravagant musings and Aggie's more simplistic style. Everyone would be in place by 4:00 p.m. That is when the opening prayer would be made by the chaplain the military would provide. There would be a few words from a representative of each of the four major branches and then the ribbon cutting. It would be done by whoever was the highest-ranking politician in attendance. None of them had any concept of who that was going to be. That was the program, and now the logistics to make it all happen began to take shape.

RIDE THE BUS

Military buses from Fort Bragg, Camp Lejeune, and Seymour Johnson AFB would shuttle people from their small town to the site. Parking would be at the ball fields and schools in town, and the buses would transport them from there. Each bus would have a "host" who would talk about the areas they passed through, the various crops and livestock they raised, and a little of the history of Cowan. The thirty-minute trip would be as much a part of the event as the more formal portions. Large tents complete with places to sit were to be erected in the area. The roads would be blocked by the state highway patrol and traffic would be rerouted. Ushers would be military men from all of the various services. After the cutting, refreshments were to be offered in one of those large tents.

The food was being provided by the companies who had the food contracts for the USO clubs. The event could go beyond sunset as lighting would be plenty. The local electric membership co-op was going to see to that. Liaisons between all the different factions of this event began to come together and synchronize their plans. The local VFW post building had been turned into a busy office. It was the downtown headquarters for the event.

A group of six administrative assistants had been sent by the Department of State to help sort through all the details. This was not their first event. Casual discussion with them led the group to the reality that this was the staff who had directly coordinated with the White House to set up the president's inauguration. As obvious as it should have been, none of them had even dreamed who might be attending.

During all of this, life for the locals must go on. There was church, social events at the club, and all those regular activities that are the cornerstone of social life in a small town. Seemed that there was a multitude of folks about town who were in and out. It was one of those, maybe a businessman, who would catch her eye. He was well dressed. He always wore a dark suit. He also was one of the most confident men she had ever noticed. She could tell by the way he carried himself that he was sure. And he was about as nice as any one such good-looking guy could be.

CHAPTER 13

IN THE HEAT OF THE NIGHT

They had spoken but never had a real conversation. One afternoon he came into her office and asked to speak with Robert. She showed him to Robert's office and within a few minutes Robert called for her to come in. He introduced them. "This gentleman is Chuck Greely. He is a land acquisition specialist and does contract work for a number of major companies. One of his clients is Marriott. He is here on their behalf looking at potential sites for them to build a facility. They have interest in finding a location that would put them near the new USO facility. Since he has already identified several sites and determined that I was legal counsel for at least a couple of them, he has stopped by.

"My reason for involving you in this is that one of the sites, and the one I am pushing him toward, is yours. It is twelve acres that belonged to G. It is that parcel that is just south of Highway 53 on 421." Aggie knew it well. "As you know, it is less than five miles from the site of the center. One, do you think you may have interest in hearing an offer from him, and two, would you have time to ride out to the parcel with him and talk about what his interest may be in all or part of that site?" Aggie was a little frustrated that Robert had thrown her into a situation like this. He could sense that and added very quickly that he would go, but had one of the other property owners in the area coming in on another matter. She agreed, but with some concern for being cast into this pairing.

She got her coat and joined Chuck as they walked out to the street. He was driving a very nice, and new, Land Rover. He had to move papers from the front seat prior to letting her sit down. She wasn't sure if that was the reason he got her door. Either way, it seemed to fit his demeanor. On the twelve-mile trip to the intersection of 421, they exchanged what would be no more than trivial chitchat. A couple of times, she glanced over at him looking at her. A memory flashed of how that young soldier had looked at her in the Jeep as they went to get Gus 3's clubs. She was checking him out as well. When they got to the 421/53 intersection, she instructed him to go south onto Highway 421.

Aggie explained about the proximity to Wilmington, the new developments planned for the area, the industrial parks taking a foothold in that part of the world, and other things that area could provide. He seemed interested, but she suspected he knew those things anyway.

After a few minutes, she told him to pull off the road as she indicated that the land began right along there. "It goes down this road for close to 800 feet and is just shy of 1,000 feet deep," she explained. She also included that if she were to divide the property, she would have no interest in developing more than two parcels.

He understood and commented, "It is a larger piece of land than we need for just the Marriott unit. It is possible that I could find a use for the other portion of it. Let me talk to the hotel real estate folks and see what their thoughts may be."

He asked, "Is there an access road on the property that may take us to the back portion? I would like to see if the majority of the land is usable."

"Yes, there is a road right up here about a hundred yards. It is not a very good road, though," Aggie responded. Working with Robert had given her a good background in what the transference of real estate could entail so she had no hesitation going down that road with him. He eased ahead, staying on the shoulder of the road. He was looking at the property as he drove. They quickly came upon the access road. Turning in, he found a gate crossing the entrance. It was locked. She was able to give him the combination for the lock. All of G's land had locked gates. He used combination padlocks, and all had the same combination. It was Gus's birthdate, and Aggie knew that well. "The combination is 5 3 5 3," she said.

The gate was quickly opened, and he got back into the car. He looked over at her and said, "I really appreciate your doing this for me. It makes my job much easier. This is a great-looking location." It had been a long time since anyone had gone down this road. Especially long for her. After a few minutes of bouncing along, they came to the end of the road. She told him that from here on, it would be on foot. They could walk to the creek that marked the boundary if he so desired. He did. It was not far at all, and there was an old log path. After a couple of minutes, they came to an opening near the edge of the creek. She smiled to herself as she remembered that special night, the one when she and Gus had first shared themselves with each other. It was this spot.

"Used to be a swimming hole right down here," Aggie said as she turned to move closer and point it out. She was closer than she anticipated, and as she stepped on the slick clay, she slipped. Before she could react, she was in the creek. Just like a prince in a novel, he was right behind her and quickly took her hand and helped her out of the water. They were both soaked. She was embarrassed, but he laughed. "I am soaked; I hate to get in your new car," she said.

He laughed again and replied, "Both of us are. Don't you dare worry about the car; this is what it is for, and besides, it's a rental." She was cold from the water and muddy from the climb out. So was he.

They looked at each other, and both knew a solution would have to follow. He quickly offered that solution. "I am staying at the 'playhouse,' the one that belongs to Benard Leonard, while I am here. He has been a client for a number of years, and he and I have become good friends. I was asking him about potential sites for the Marriott, and he offered his house for me to stay in. It sounded perfect, so I took it. It is only a couple of miles from here, so let's go over there and dry off. It is still early, and we have time." She agreed, but like so many things that were changing in her life, she thought this time she might be off on a whole new adventure. She was right.

When they got there, he showed her to a bedroom that had a private bath. He told her to go in and get herself a hot bath. And if she would throw her clothes out, he would stick them in the washer with his. It would not take long at all to wash and dry them. She went in and began to undress. The house felt warm to her bare skin as she removed all that she wore. She cracked the door and put her wet clothes on the floor just in front of it. Before she could get to the shower, she heard him speak through the door: "I am getting your clothes now. I put a highball by the door. It will warm you up."

THE MOON AND STARS AND BIRDS AND BEES

Wow, she was in uncharted territory now! She cracked the door again, peeking to make sure he was no longer there, and then she picked up the drink. With drink in hand, she went into the bathroom. The door in the old house did not shut as it should and was left slightly open. He was right; the drink was perfect. She was not at all accustomed to any of this, and the idea of where she was and the situation she was in caused her to smile. The drink also had an effect on her. "I guess I am thoroughly modern Aggie now," she giggled to herself. The shower hit the spot, and soon she was out and drying. She heard him call her name.

"Aggie, I have a refill for that drink," he called. She pulled the long towel around her, tucked it in just under her arm, and leaned around the bathroom door. She could see him through the slightly opened door. He was also clad in just a towel. She could see his strong, slim shoulders and flat stomach. He looked just as she had thought he would. She was excited by him. It also occurred to her that he could have seen her before she covered with the towel. That also felt different. That feeling added even more excitement. The drink, the room, the afternoon, and his good looks all worked a magical spell on Aggie. What she was feeling was different from anything she had ever felt before. Her body began to tingle. In fact, she had never had this sensation before. The only thing that guided her now was instinct. The instinct of a woman who secretly longed for such a moment. Her breath was rapid. She knew what was happening as she found herself hoping he would come in. This was the first time that she had ever felt this kind of anticipation.

Unlike Aggie, Chuck was in a place that he had enjoyed many times before. He knew exactly what to do. Here he was with a beautiful woman who was obviously as attracted to him as he was to her. He slipped through the door and stepped toward her as if to hand her the drink. Instead, he set the drink on the counter and reached out and took her into his arms. From there, she gave in to passion. The next while was fierce and it was physical. There was no soft and tender moment, but an intense session unlike any she had ever had before.

Now, they lay on the bed staring into each other's eyes. Neither said a word; the moment spoke for itself. A few minutes later, she was asleep. She awoke to see that it had turned dark outside. She was alone, but there was the gentle glow of a fire burning in the bedroom's fireplace. She sat up and looked around to see if she could find Chuck. He was standing on the deck that was just outside of the bedroom. He was wrapped in a blanket and looking out into the night. She got up carefully and pulled a blanket around her. She walked onto the deck and stood beside him. He looked at her and without any hesitation said, "Spend the night." She had just been in a place she had never even known existed. She liked it and wanted to stay.

"Let me use your phone," she responded. First, she dialed Marylin. Her words were simple and quick: "If anyone calls or needs to know, I am spending tonight with you and we are working late."

Marylin knew where she was and who she was with, so it did not take her long to imagine what was going on. She replied, "Done."

Aggie then called Mama and told her that she was involved with some issues regarding the project. She would be "working" very late and would not see her until tomorrow. Mama was fine with that. In fact, she would have been fine if Aggie had said exactly where she was and what she was doing. Aggie felt guilty because she had misled her mom. She had not lied but had quibbled.

Aggie handed the phone back to Chuck, smiled, and said, "Okay."

"Are you hungry?" he asked her.

"Not a bit," was her reply. "I will take another of those drinks, though."

He went inside and fixed it for her. She could tell that the warm and good feeling from the alcohol was part of this night's adventure. After a big sip, she realized that she liked this and did not want it to end. He stepped toward her, reached, and pushed the blanket down from her shoulders, and it fell. The cold night air affected her but not in a negative way. All these new sensations she was feeling made her feel alive. She opened his blanket and wrapped it around them both. He took her into his arms. They stood there, not moving, for a few minutes. Then he gently picked her up, carried her into the bedroom, and laid her on the bed.

The world melted away into the warm glow of the fire and the warm glow of their embrace. She had visited that special place again. This time was no less than the first. It was not long before she awoke again. Again, the bed was empty, and it was still dark. Her clothes were laying on the end of her bed, dry and folded. So were his. She took his t-shirt and put it on. She walked into the kitchen where she could hear him moving. He was standing in a pair of pajama pants and was cooking. The aroma of bacon filled the air. She realized she was hungry. They talked while they ate and quickly became friends. He was a master at getting her to talk, so she opened up as he listened intently.

He told her he would be thirty years old soon. She did not give him her age. She could not help but think that when she was a senior in high school, he was only in kindergarten. That was a scary thought, but this night had worked in spite of that difference. Besides, if she had told him her age, he probably would not have believed her. She surely did not look it, and on this night, she had certainly not acted like it. None of that would have mattered anyway. Both of them understood that this night was about nothing beyond just this night.

Soon he reached and took her hand across the table. "Come with me," he said in a confident tone. She did just as he said, as he steered her back to the bedroom for a third time. He walked behind with his hands on her hips. Anticipation was her only feeling. She had done things tonight that before she could have imagined in only the wildest of her fantasies. Those, each of them, would provide her with fond memories, and she would recall them for the rest of her life. It was this night that she stepped into her identity not as a widow or as a mother, but as a woman focused on her own desires and future.

Early the next morning, Chuck dropped Aggie off at her car, which was still in front of Robert's office. She went home, showered, and dressed to begin a new day. Chuck had said goodbye and would be flying back to his home in Pueblo, Colorado, that afternoon. He assured her that she would see her again and that last night was one of his best memories. They would never forget each other. It was a perfect night and neither could rewrite it in a way that could make it any better.

Aggie had hardly gotten into the office when the phone rang. It was Marylin. "I want to hear every detail, and I mean every detail," she said. Aggie promised she would share all about it, but not now. Marylin seemed satisfied with that answer. Aggie thought about the "every detail" aspect of their future conversation. Before this day, she would have never considered doing something like she had the night before, much less talking about it. Somehow on this day, it felt different. There had been no violation of trust or even expectation of secrecy between her and Chuck. She felt sure he would share that night with his friends. She did not care if he did. She wanted her friend to know the details too.

A few days later, Robert came to Aggie's desk and said, "I got you an offer from Marriott." He looked at her with his innocent face but knowing eyes. "I will admit," he said, "I am not surprised." Those were the only words he ever spoke that would indicate he had any idea about that night. She and Marylin had talked, in detail, about it. By telling Marylin, she relived some of those moments. And they both enjoyed the details.

In fact, the conversation had ended as Marylin commented, "I am going to do that with Robert. All I have to do is to figure out how to get him to try it, though."

Aggie thought almost constantly about that night. She had very mixed feelings about it. Was she embarrassed, or was she just happy it happened? What would her mom or the preacher think? What did God think? Those thoughts were not an issue she could discuss with anyone. She needed to work out those issues in her own mind. No one had been violated and no had one had been hurt or taken advantage of. Perhaps she allowed her determination to be dictated by what she wanted. Using those determinations, she decided that this was one of those good things that the preacher had talked about. She would dwell on it often.

GETTING CLOSE

Everything was happening in a rapid manner. Thank goodness for so much help and so many folks working toward the end of a perfect ribbon cutting. It was a little less than a week away. It had finally been announced that the vice president would attend. To her knowledge, there had never been such a high-ranking government official in their county before. Eleanor Roosevelt was here during the time her husband was president. She came when they opened Penderlea. It was just a few miles up the road from the new compound and was one of the first government settlements built during the Depression. It was from its success that others followed.

All members of the committee were working overtime to ensure that everything would fall into place as expected. The Secret Service had joined in the task, as they needed to ensure the safety of the vice president. The one thing that everyone found out pretty quickly was that those guys who were a part of the Secret Service did not play. It was obvious that their job was a serious undertaking. So much of what they did was not even visible. This entire thing was exciting; its end would create a really wonderful space and a special addition to this area. It was a win-win for all concerned but was starting to get a little old to those who had to live with it. Normal routine was a thing of history. The routine now was whatever seemed to be the issue of the day. Just four more days and it would be over.

The big day was to be Tuesday. On Saturday everyone involved was busy making all of the last-minute adjustments needed and ensuring everything was in its place. Aggie was home and going through some final details that were a part of her place in the ribbon cutting. Marylin was doing the same thing. All those involved would be glad when Tuesday had come and gone.

Mama and Da were watching the football game that afternoon. It seemed like the only thing on TV that would keep their interest anymore was ball games. Most of the other shows just did not seem to interest them. They were watching an NC State football game downstairs when Aggie heard the phone ring. They could not hear the phone as the TV was blasting. She answered and it was Arley. He was about to cry. It seemed the king of some small country in the Middle East had passed away and the vice president was going to have to attend that funeral. The U.S. needed to send someone, and he was the chosen one. Arley was more than disappointed as he had never even heard of the country. It was Nagorno-Karabakh. He couldn't even say it. The notification from the State Department had named it and indicated that it was a country that could be an important ally of the U.S. The vice president and a group of other dignitaries would attend. He was assured, though, that someone would be at the ribbon cutting in the vice president's place. They would just have to wait and see who it was. Arley wanted her to call Marylin and let her know, so she did.

THE SWITCH

On a Tuesday evening, Adjah got the call he had been anticipating. His father had passed away peacefully. It would now fall on him to take over as monarch of his country. Adjah responded to the caller, "I will get a flight out immediately. I will call you back and let you know when I will arrive. That way you can have the plane waiting for me to take me on home." That call was monitored, as were all the calls made to and from Adjah. Adjah made his reservations and then called his staff back in Nagorno-Karabakh to give them the details. He would arrive in Armenia at 11:20 their time on Thursday morning. They acknowledged that the plane would be waiting. He then called and reserved a limo to pick him up at 6:00 a.m. the next day for his 11:30 flight. The drive to New York City would take about four and a half hours, but it would save him travel time as he would not have a layover.

The next morning, a limo was waiting just as he had requested. He and his luggage began the trip to New York. The driver indicated that he needed to stop for just one minute in a small town in Connecticut to pick up a package. Adjah did not mind so long as he made his flight. He was assured that was no problem. As the black limo pulled into the parking lot of a small strip center, an envelope containing the papers and wallet of Adjah was handed to another limo identical to it.

Adjah never had any knowledge of the transfer as he had fallen into a deep sleep. The other limo carried the soon-to-be new King of Nagorno-Karabakh to the airport in New York for his flight home. In a few days, he would be in place as that country's new leader. In the parking lot, the other Adjah, who was no longer essential, would never wake up.

CHAPTER 14

AIR FORCE ONE

Sunday passed, Monday arrived, and all the final preparations were put into place. Not being sure who was coming did not seem to bother anyone but the committee. The workers and military seemed oblivious to it all. It was a little strange that the Secret Service stayed in place. On Tuesday morning, everyone was excited beyond control. What a day this would be! This would be the kind of day they could tell their grandchildren about. It was just what the local history books would speak of often.

Arley called Aggie again. This time he seemed out of breath. Trying to sound cool and collected, but talking very rapidly, he said, "I have just been instructed who will be attending this evening's event. In fact, he will be arriving about 3:00 p.m. to review the facility and to go over the schedule for the event. All of the committee is to be at the site by around 2:00. That way if any last-minute issues come up, they can address them."

"Arley, are you going to tell me who is coming or not?" Aggie continued speaking very slowly, "Who…is…it?" He laughed as he replied in a very flippant rebuttal to her slow speech, "OH, IT IS JUST THE PRESIDENT!"

Aggie could not get the phone hung up quickly enough to dial Marylin. "Have you heard?" she almost shouted as she heard the phone being picked up on the other end.

"He tried it; he tried it," was Marylin's announcement as she knew it was Aggie calling. Neither was sure the other had heard.

Aggie simply came back with a, "What?"

"I said he tried it, that thing you told me about from your 'sex-capade' the other night," said Marylin. She put a great deal of emphasis on that word.

Aggie was somewhere between embarrassed and laughing. She did remember what Marylin was talking about. Somehow, Robert and Marylin in that particular embrace seemed less romantic than was her memory of her and Chuck.

"Let's talk about that later," said Aggie. "Did you hear what I said? The president of the United States is going to be here today!"

Marylin gasped and was silent. For the first time ever, Marylin was silent. Aggie intently waited just to see how long it would take her to respond. After Marylin's pause, she just responded in a tone that was very matter-of-fact, "I guess today will be special. I will have gotten all excited twice."

Aggie knew again just what she meant. Marylin thought the president was a real hunk. "I'll pick you up at 9:00. We will come back home just after noon and change. I want to be looking my best when the big guy cruises in." With that, Marylin just hung up.

Aggie was left standing there holding the phone. She smiled as she thought, *I am going to have to watch her like a hawk if she gets around him.*

She was ready as Marylin honked the horn on the Mercedes. Aggie went out to the car. Once inside, she looked over at Marylin, who was gazing back at her as well. The reality of all that had gone on over the last six months, the change that was taking place in their hometown, and the magnitude of this day's events flashed before them both. It was almost as if they spoke at the same time. "What have we done?" Both laughed. This thing was on the two of them, and they knew it.

When they got to the site, it was as busy as a stirred-up anthill. People going everywhere, but with a purpose. Everything from guys raking leaves to the grass being watered. The place looked good and could not be a disappointment to anyone, no matter how important or discerning. Aggie and Marylin, along with the other members of the local board, had a very specific role to play in this event. They were the welcome committee. In fact, Arley was going to do just that: welcome the crowd from the podium. They both knew he had been agonizing over his words, but they were sure he would do well. The others on the team would just "work the crowd" and ensure everyone was spoken to by the host committee. After several hours had passed, it was time for Marylin and Aggie to drive back home and change into something for the big event.

As much as Marylin would have liked to wear something like that little black dress that Aggie and Marsha had made famous, she knew better. It would be enough fun to see just how the president reacted to her. That is if she was even able to get close enough to him to speak. *How do you act when you meet the president?* she wondered. *Do I curtsy, do I smile, do I let him speak first?* She just wasn't sure. Anyone else who knew Marylin would have had no such thought. She was a natural at this kind of thing and she would have it going her way in quick order.

Aggie, on the other hand, had bittersweet thoughts going through her head. All of this was so wonderful, such a tribute to her two loves. But with that pride, the memories intermingled the sadness of their death and the warmth of this reward. She put that sadness in her pocket. The bus for her and the other hosts left the American Legion building just after 1:00 p.m. When they arrived, their work was completely done.

For the first time, Aggie could see the reality of what the pictures and plans had created. There were signs all along the way. The Department of Transportation had done their part. That was made even more evident as they merged into the turn lanes, both off of Highway 53 onto Point Caswell Road and then again at the main entrance. What she saw, and this was the first time she had really looked at the completed entryway, was as perfect as the drawings had indicated it would be. In fact, she could hear the reaction of those on the bus as they watched. Theirs was the same as hers. This place was truly a wonderful dream become reality. Arches covered the road with a statue in the center under the arch. The statue had just been installed and was covered. That would be part of the ribbon cutting, she assumed.

There was nothing to do now but wait. Reporters and photographers were everywhere. There was even a press tent. The press had already started interviewing workers and arriving dignitaries. The constant blink of the flash of cameras was all around them. Stage lights for the purpose of recording the whole event were in place. Cameras were in a bunch a few feet in front of the stage. All the major networks were there. Much of this event would be telecast live. Newspaper reporters by the dozen. Many more than Aggie even knew existed. Even cameras from foreign countries. Their reporters speaking in languages that they had never heard. Marylin commented to Aggie, "Where the hell are all these people going to sit?"

Someone shouted, "There he is! There he is!" They were pointing to the sky. All looked up. Marine One was above and was maneuvering in a way that would let the passengers get a good view of this place. Up considerably higher were a number of other planes of every description. One of the onlookers pointed at them and indicated that they were security. After about two or three minutes of hovering, the chopper left. It was headed to wherever the secret landing spot was to be. In a moment, another chopper, just like the first, did the same thing. The same person who had spoken about security spoke up again. "That one, or the one in front, is a decoy. Whichever one the president is in is a guess."

The selection of the landing site for the president was an important issue. It had to be an area that would easily accommodate the weight of those choppers as well as the weight of the many vehicles that would be in his convoy. All of this had been done by those Secret Service guys. They were tight-lipped—no, they were closed-lipped.

Just a little over ten miles away, the choppers landed at a new complex, which was an industrial park. There were a number of new small manufacturing facilities there and a fairly large warehouse distributor. The truck parking lot of that distributor was the perfect place. A group of black SUVs awaited the president's arrival. Also in the group were two black Cadillac limousines. The limo the president would ride in was dubbed "The Beast" by the Secret Service detail. Just like with the choppers, one of the limos was a decoy. Snipers on top of buildings, planes flying overhead, twenty or more vehicles all in a row, police escorts, and the highway patrol were all there. A group of people waving signs were also a part of this extravagant spectacle. They were protesting something. How could they have possibly known where he was going to land?

The response to that question would be pretty simple. First, it did not take a brilliant mind to determine the better options for the location of the landing. The crowd could then gather as soon as they witnessed where the choppers were descending. They could rush to that spot in a few minutes and then get as close as security would allow. This was all normal procedure. As smart as all of those protest organizers may think they are, the Secret Service is just a little quicker. They had undercover agents embedded with those protest groups and organizers for weeks. Slick as the organizers and leaders may think they are, it is hard to get ahead of the reach of the United States of America. In fact, another group of protestors had gathered at the airport in Wilmington. They had received a "secret tip" that the president would be arriving there on Air Force One. It circled the area but never landed. Their group on 421 was much smaller than it could have been.

As the presidential convoy turned on Highway 421 North, it accelerated quickly. It did not seem like they were bound by any speed limit. The patrol had strict instruction. About eighty miles an hour was the preferred gait for their travel. The patrol guys loved that. This was a first for most of them too. This day was farther reaching than any one person or group could imagine. The tentacles were everywhere and near impossible to trace.

Traffic was being held or diverted away from Highway 421 and Highway 53 in that area. Announcements had been made a number of days in advance so the detours would not disrupt the locals. The locals seemed not to care, though, since most of them would be at the event.

In a surprise move, the convoy slowed and turned left onto Highway 210 a few miles prior to the Highway 53 intersection. They followed that route through the country and then soon took a left onto Highway 53. Looking from the window, the president commented to one of his staff, "Oh look, there is Silver." A life-size cutout of a white horse, with its front two hooves high in the air, was against the woods just behind a hayfield. All laughed as the president added, "Surely they did not make the Lone Ranger park his horse this far away. That is a hell of a walk for a man dressed like he does."

It was just a little after 3:00 when the announcement was made over the speaker system that the president of the United States of America would be here in about ten minutes. Most folks were already there and had enjoyed looking at what this complex would look like. One large tent held nothing but displays and pictures of what the completed USO mega center would be. All were impressed.

The entrance, where they were now, would be as-is. The road would travel straight into the main building. It would be very visible from the entrance. It would be white and have the appearance of a grand home. The flag of the United States would fly high above those flags of each of the services. A large circle complete with a covered departure area would be in front of that "big ol' home," as it was dubbed. The idea was to provide a home away from home for those who visited. That building would house the welcome center and the staff offices for the complex. From that circle you could bear to the right and follow a short road to the golf course and pro shop. A snack bar would be built there along with everything needed to provide a first-class, no, a fantastic round of golf. Eighteen holes designed by the best of the best was as high end as golf could be.

Just past the covered entry/exit from the circle was another road. The sign to it would be much more extensive, listing a variety of destinations including Hunting Lodge, Fishing Area, ATV Trails, Nature Trails, and Restaurant. These things were all brand-new endeavors for the USO, but a staff was already in place, and each of these venues was taking on a life of its own. They would be utilized at capacity.

The hunting lodge would resemble a large log cabin complete with a huge fireplace. Game trophy mounts would hang from every wall. The only requirement for those mounts was that they be locally taken. A main desk and information center would be at the center of the large room. It had everything imaginable that a hunting lodge should have. The only firearms allowed on this site would be shotguns. The same paperwork was required to borrow as there was to buy, but the concept was that if a soldier was to have an issued military weapon, surely they could be trusted with a shotgun. There was also plenty of free ammo given by those who were in that business. Most had government contracts; these donations would be a write-off, so it did not take any brains to see the advantages.

In the back were the dog pens. These pens would be as upscale as most homes. There would also be a cleaning area and even a refrigerated holding area for dressed wild game. Bulletin boards would advertise local taxidermists for hunters who might want a trophy for their wall. Seasons did apply, so there would also be a large and modern shooting range and a number of different types of skeet ranges also on-site. These would be used mostly in the off-season.

The fishing lodge would be more of a large bait shop. One could get every type of lure or bait known for this type of fishing. Again, no fishing rod, no worry. Some of the best equipment made, just as it had been with the guns, had been donated by the manufacturers. The walls of the bait shop would also be covered with mounts, mostly replicas. The only difference was that a number of those mounts were of fish caught in the nearby Atlantic Ocean. If one so desired, a fishing trip at one of the local beaches could be arranged by lodge staff.

The ATV trails were to be long and varied. Riders would find just about any type of terrain they may want. The equipment was all first-class and, again, donated. In fact, five different brands of ATVs would be available. If a rider had a preference, they could pick their favorite.

The nature trail was unusual in that a lot of it was over the wetlands. In fact, it was more of a swamp. The trails would be elevated above those areas and were safe and dry. Hikers might see almost any type of wildlife as they walked along the length of the trail. Alligators and snakes were in abundance. They may not be for the faint of heart, but were in areas that provided safety, as much for them as for the hikers.

The restaurant was also to be decorated in a very rustic and country style. Guests would be able to order about anything imaginable there, from an early morning hunting breakfast, a first-class lunch, or an evening meal. It was all delicious. One could order wild game, or they could, in fact, have some of the game they had taken to be prepared. The same was true of the fish. Steaks and seafood would also be available. A special section of the menu highlighted "Local Favorites" included everything from fried chicken to collards. A guest may want to try the crackling bread or even brave an appetizer that was called "souse." (Souse is a pickled mixture of meats from around the head of the pig.) Prices were very low as all of this was being subsidized by donations and free products.

The president and his crowd had offloaded at the administrative tent just behind the main event area in front of the gate. He had toured the tent with the models and the drawings. He had done this with a group of high-ranking military officials and his staff. The national chairman of the USO committee had been their only guide.

CHAPTER 15

A CHICKEN LEG

The president was to come back into the administrative tent where some of the local dignitaries could meet him. He did, but he didn't stay very long. No one seemed sure where he was. Aggie and Marylin had not had a chance to meet him. They were not too disappointed, though; after all, he was the president. They needed to go into the food preparation tent and check on the status of the food to be served after the ribbon cutting. When they did, they walked into a dream. The president of the United States was sitting on one of the prep tables. He had a chicken leg in his hand and was entertaining the ten or so food prep employees standing before him. He looked over and saw Aggie and Marylin.

He flashed a great big smile and motioned with the chicken leg as he said, "Why don't you two cute young ladies come over here and allow me the pleasure of introducing myself to you." Almost in a daze, they walked up to him. He stuck out a dry hand as if to shake theirs. He did not. As he introduced himself to each of them, he took their hand and just held it in his. It was obvious to Aggie and Marylin that he was enjoying the touching. He had no concern about who saw or what they thought. In this specific moment, it was he and the pretty ladies. Yes, he was just like his reputation. An absolute master at being everyone's best friend and the life of the party. All of this was done while providing a very specific but unspoken message to Aggie and Marylin that he found them both very cute. His eyes flirted in a masterful way. He was good, and it was easy to see why he stayed in so much trouble with the ladies. Marylin was just as good as he was. Neither had any expectation from this meeting, but both knew what it could have been. His staff quickly gathered him up and whisked him off. It was now time to begin the ribbon cutting. So much had been put into what would take only a few minutes to complete.

Aggie and the other members of the local board had reserved seats near the front. The official count was that there were over 4,200 in attendance. Aggie was not sure how anyone could even guess. Everyone could see the stage as they crowded all the way back to the edge of Point Caswell Road. Arley began by asking everyone to stand and face the flag of our great nation. When the band played "The Star Spangled Banner," all stood and sang. Next the "Pledge of Allegiance" was recited as all continued to stand with hand over heart or military salute. It was one of those times that flip somewhere between tears and joy. To some it may be the somber remembering of a battle fought on a faraway shore. To others no more than the symbol of that nation they love. To all, the song and pledge should mean something. To Aggie, they meant everything. To those who are unmoved by our national anthem or the pledge to our flag, Aggie felt only pity. Arley began again by thanking everybody, welcoming everybody, and then passing the master of ceremonies task to the chairman of the Joint Chiefs of Staff. Since the president was here, the chairman's remarks would be short, and the four chiefs of staff would not make any comment. Fleet Admiral Palenta commented about the success of this event and the undertaking of it. He even indicated that he looked very much forward to visiting during quail and duck season. He went on and talked about how his soldiers were the best in the world and how they would enjoy this exciting new facility.

He proceeded, "Now, before I have the high honor of introducing the commander in chief of our armed forces, it is my great pleasure to introduce Captain Lewis Morgan. He is the chaplain for the Joint Chiefs and will lead us in an opening prayer." Aggie nearly fainted. Why had she not been warned, and how could she not have known?

This was the man who had led her through one of the darkest periods of her life. He had been her friend, her crutch, her advisor, and above all else, the most understanding and obliging person she had ever known. Her eyes filled with tears, and as they did, Aggie felt Marylin's hand reach over, squeeze, and hold tightly to hers. Marylin knew this was to happen but this was all part of this special day for Aggie. He looked very much like Aggie remembered. He was tall, stood erect and proud in his uniform, and had the air of accomplishment written all over him. Aggie looked over and Marylin was looking directly at her. "Don't hate me for not telling you. I was sworn to secrecy. Today, you must be strong."

He began with a short message. "This is not my first time here," he said. "I was here a number of years ago as young lieutenant. It was my first task as a military officer. That time helped me to learn the greatest lesson of my career, which is that no matter the darkness of the hour, the light of God will guide you to a new dawn. Faith is the greatest remedy for any ailment, be it of the mind or the body. Now, let us pray. Heavenly Father, how do we have any right to be here at a time like this? This beautiful place, these beautiful people, and You among us. This is a time when we come together to celebrate all that is right and good in this fair land. The things You provide are manifested in all that is around us. Give us the strength and the courage to stand fast against any enemy, be it small or large, in the protection of these, Your gifts. Allow us to be the best of caretakers in Your kingdom. Dedicate these grounds to a purpose that supports all those things that create Your end. Especially stand with and guide our armed forces as they attempt to protect the very principles that You have taught us. Help them to be enriched by this place, that they will find pleasure in this, just one more of Your gracious blessings. You are our heavenly Father and to You we are forever thankful. Amen."

He turned and sat as Admiral Palenta retook the mic. "For a meager sailor to have come to a facility such as this on this day is a miracle. It is a path that only the luckiest could have hoped to travel. Today, I am that lucky one. So now, it gives me the highest honor of my career, and life, to introduce my commander in chief, the president of the United States of America." He signaled for all to stand, and they did. The military band played "Hail to the Chief." The president walked to the mic with all the confidence and ability that his office demanded.

He began, "First, let me say thank you to all of those who have had a hand in this grand undertaking. It is obvious that the result is and will be a wonderful achievement. To you, the local folk who have sacrificed so much to allow this to take place, to the many donors, to the military personnel who have worked so hard, and to any and all who may have touched this end, I say job well done. There is nothing I would rather do than to stand here and speak. I do so love a crowd, and even more so, I love the opportunity to make a speech. But today is not about me or my office. It is about this place. It is about how and why it is here. I would now like to ask Mrs. Aggie Johnson to come up and join me on the platform."

REACH

Aggie gasped and felt as though she would faint. Again, Marylin leaned to her and said, "I said for you to stay strong; do it." Aggie somehow gathered her strength, and with the help of a military usher, made her way to the president's side. She was in shock, as any person in this situation would be. The president took her hand again.

Again, he gave it a little squeeze. This time it was not a romantic one, but a squeeze of comfort and support. He began to speak, "I will now share some details that many of you may know at least in part. This story may even be one that Aggie does not know fully. It has been created at my request through interviews and research. Interviews of those who witnessed and were involved. Research into once-classified documents that have since been declassified.

"On an early morning just over twenty years ago, some ten miles off the coast of South Vietnam, the USS *Sanctuary* sailed in support of those soldiers fighting that war. It was a secret mission. Petty Officer Gus Johnson was aboard. Aggie, this young wife, did not even know where her husband was or what he was doing. Wounded soldiers would be flown by Army helicopter to that ship so they could receive hospital-level care. A nineteen-year-old petty officer named Gus Johnson met those helicopters and helped the wounded find their way to the right care. On this morning, he had done that when he discovered that the normal medic for that chopper had been injured by gunfire. At Petty Officer Johnson's insistence, that medic was moved into the care unit and so survived.

"A call came over the radio that the chopper was needed to help evacuate a number of civilians, including children, who had been injured by a bomb explosion of unknown origin. Defying what he knew was correct protocol, Petty Officer Johnson was able to board that craft and travel with it in an attempt to help those civilians. Once there, the chopper was loaded with the injured and just about to take off. In that moment, another child rushed to gain a way to find help and join with other members of her family aboard this craft. As she approached, Petty Officer Johnson reached out for her. As she reached up to take his hand, the chopper exploded. All were lost. I can tell you that a monument to that tragedy is now located at the spot of that explosion. It depicts that event. Today we honor

Petty Officer Johnson and all those like him who gave so unselfishly of their lives." He motioned to the covered statue in the circle.

"Men, please unveil the statue," he said. They did so. It was a bronze work and was beautiful in the fading light of the late-afternoon sun. A young naval petty officer stood with his arm reaching down. A small girl reached up as if to take his hand. "FOR ANY WHO MAY NEED A HAND, REACH" was carved into the base of the statue, and under that were the words "Petty Officer Gus Johnson." On the base of the young girl was carved "The World." Many of the attendees knew the Johnson family. They knew Aggie and they had known Gus 3. They began to applaud. The applause continued until the president began to speak again. "Aggie, I will now ask that you help me cut this ribbon to celebrate the official beginning of this important new place. Ladies and Gentlemen," he said as they cut the ribbon, "REACH." The president of the United States had named this facility by his use of this one word he used during the cutting of the ribbon.

After the ribbon cutting, the president said a few more words. He then smiled, waved, and turned to walk away. As he turned, he again took Aggie's hand and placed a small note in her palm. Her thoughts were, *Where in the heck is this going?* As he left the stage, reporters by the dozen dashed toward his exit. His escorts simply held them away while he got back into "The Beast" and drove away. The band was playing while the large crowd mingled and enjoyed the food and drink. The other dignitaries hung around.

A large crowd now gathered near the warehouse where the two presidential choppers waited. They were sure they would get his attention this time. But this time he took a little different route. In a few moments, he was pulling into the private terminal at the Wilmington Airport. Air Force One had been "practicing" touch-and-goes and just happened to complete a landing and pull up to the terminal just long enough to take aboard the president and his entourage. He was off again to be in the White House in a couple of hours. The protesters were duped again as they all waited in the area of Marine One. Imagine the surprise of that radical group when the choppers simply cranked and then took off with no one having boarded.

The first to approach Aggie was General Hrabal. He opened his arms with his palms up as if to say, *I have no excuse.* He went on to tell her that he had known what the events were to be. He could not tell her as he had agreed to its secrecy. He had also gotten to know Lt. Morgan when he was here for Gus's funeral all those years ago. He had avoided her these last few weeks as he knew that if he was around her, he would probably blab it out. She hugged his neck, and followed that she could never be mad with him. His relationship with Gus 3 had cemented that. She smiled, but in a very sad way, she said, "After all, you and he sang a duet."

They both smiled at that comment even though they both felt the hurt it reminded them of. Just like the sermon had instructed, she was trying to focus on the good things.

THE NOTE

Marylin joined Aggie and General Hrabal and their discussion. She added that she had the same knowledge of what was going to happen but had been sworn to silence. It was all she could do, but she had held her tongue. As the general walked away, Aggie took the opportunity to glance at the note the president had placed in her hand. After all, she certainly had no secrets from Marylin. When she looked, she was surprised to see that it was folded and had "Marylin" written on it.

Handing it to Marylin, she smiled and said, "This is going to be fun to read." At first Marylin acted as if she was going to conceal its contents from Aggie. Marylin looked at her with that devious smile and responded, "We share almost everything don't we?" The "almost" was a confirmation that Aggie and Robert were purely business associates. She opened it and read it aloud, "If you are ever in D.C., give this number a call: 202-555-1969." It was not signed and was done in the handwriting of a lady. He had everyone helping him keep his antics under wraps, even the females on his staff. Both looked at each other and with a great big grin and a girlish giggle, both laughed. Marylin spoke, "Guess I'll need to see that new 'birds and bees' display at the Smithsonian." Both knew that her comment was no more than victorious nonsense. She had won her battle just by getting him to acknowledge her.

A number of the locals had begun to gather around Aggie just to shake her hand or to get a hug. All were so proud of her and of Gus. They all commented about Gus 3 and how proud Gus would have been of him. This place was a showcase to all three of the Gusses. It was their glory, but all knew it was her efforts that made it possible. She was still in a cloud of shock from the events, but was about to regain her place in reality. Aggie was chatting with those in the crowd when Mama and Da walked up. Mama spoke, "We told you we weren't coming today because we weren't sure we would feel up to it but we wanted to surprise you. Robert picked us up and brought us. He had a special parking pass and we were able to drive right up to the tent. We are so very proud of you and of what you have done. Our little girl standing up there with the president. Two parents have never had more to brag about. Somewhere, Gus and Trip are watching; they are proud too. Don't consider us rude, but we are going to get Robert to take us home."

"I think he is ready to go anyway," added her dad.

Not one of the three had any idea that the comment "somewhere they are watching" could be so true. Trip had followed the dedication closely on the international news network. He watched it alone from his office in a faraway land. He had seen his mom standing hand-in-hand with the president of the United States of America. It saddened him, but affirmed that she was okay and doing well. He had learned very quickly that being a sovereign was a lonely job.

CHAPTER 16

ANOTHER FELLOW

As Aggie started to walk toward the food tent, she heard someone call her name. "Mrs. Johnson, can I have just a minute?" She turned, and approaching her was Captain Morgan. He just smiled as he walked up to her. He maintained that same professionalism he displayed those twenty-plus years ago as he had helped her through her ordeal. This time was a little different; he was no longer Lieutenant Morgan. His demeanor fit his rank.

He started the conversation, "Mrs. Johnson, it is so very nice to see you again. I hope you remember me. I probably know more about you than you know about me. I have kept up with you since our time together those years ago. In fact, I was at Cadet Johnson's, your son's, funeral. I wore civilian clothing and stayed in the background as I did not want to add fuel to your tragic situation. I would like to praise you and the things you have done. You are a remarkable woman."

It took Aggie a few moments to respond. She just looked at him as she tried to draw the line that led from Lieutenant Morgan to Captain Morgan. Also, she wondered why he would have kept up with her. "Thank you so much. I do remember. I remember you very well. You were my biggest support during that time. I wish I had known you were at Gus 3's funeral. It would have been like attaching myself to the same solid foundation that had supported me before. It is so great to see you, and, please, from now on, I am Aggie." With that, she reached up and gave him a hug as if she wanted their talk to feel less formal, then continued, "It is so good to see you again." He knew what she meant and was happy for the conversation to have gotten off on that good foot. They walked together to the tent, enjoyed the food, and then soon hugged again as a soldier told him that the Joint Chiefs were ready to leave. He had a special place in her heart. She was glad to have seen him but wished they had more time to catch up. So did he.

Later on, Aggie and Marylin boarded a bus to take them back to the departure location and their car. The bus was much quieter on the trip back to town. They arrived and did a lot of backslapping and handshaking with others on the committee as they split up. It was an end to a major part of the undertaking. It had gone well, and all had every right to be proud of the entire process.

When they got into Marylin's car, Aggie let out a "Whew!" Before she could say that she was tired, Marylin piped up, "Don't even go there. We are going to stop by my house and have a drink and talk about all of this before you sleep tonight. After all," she continued, "you should be used to drinking and running all night."

Aggie only grinned as she rebutted, "Good thing that's not tonight. I am not sure if I would wake up for those second and third times." Both laughed. The enjoyment of the things they shared blended perfectly into their close relationship.

Once inside Marylin's house, both of them kicked off their shoes. Aggie sat on the couch as Marylin made them both a drink. It was a drink of the South, bourbon and Sun Drop. The Sun Drop made it just sweet enough to help it go down easy. They enjoyed several, and before long, the drinks were going down pretty easily. Tired, tipsy, and already being a little teenage-silly, they were really talking about things that may have been better left unsaid. Robert was fast asleep, and with no one else there, it really did not matter. It was just the two of them, and that night nothing was off-limits. They talked about the note from the president. And yes, both of them agreed, at least the way they felt this minute, yes, they would indeed give in to his seductive charms. They even got into a conversation about how many he may have seduced. The night went on, the conversation went on, and the sun rose. During that night, if there was any gap in their relationship, it was closed. Friends bound as tightly as if they were joined at the hip. Neither had a secret from the other.

Robert woke up, dressed, and started to the office the next morning. He saw Aggie and Marylin sprawled out on the couch. He also saw the empty fifth of Jim Beam on the coffee table. He knew it had been almost full earlier. They had drunk it all and were totally wasted. His first thought was that if it had been him and Marylin with that bottle instead of Marylin and Aggie, he would have had one hell of a memorable night. He just passed it off and thought to himself, *They deserve it.* When he got to the office, he announced to her two assistants that he did not think Aggie would make it in today because she didn't feel well.

AN UNEXPECTED PHONE CALL

Wednesday was a long day. Aggie and Marylin slept until after lunch. They agreed very quickly that either sleep or death would have to take them now. Headaches of this magnitude were bound to be deadly. Also, the nausea and the all over sickness that kept them running to the bathroom lingered. Marylin finally got Aggie home late on Wednesday afternoon. One look at her and Mama knew that condition. She had seen it before when Da would return hungover from an occasional fishing trip. Mama's reaction was, "Umph!"

Marriott bought Aggie's twelve acres. Because she had plenty to live on already, those funds were placed into another investment account like the one she had opened with Gus's insurance payout. The only difference was that this time the amount was just over six times as much. Soon it would be a Marriott facility and a restaurant. These would be the first of a quickly growing private industry sector in their local economy. It was all made possible by "Reach."

On Friday Aggie got a call at her desk in Robert's office. "Good morning," was the quick greeting. She knew at once who it was. It was Captain Morgan. This time he said, "Aggie, this is Lewis Morgan. I have a long weekend and hoped you may allow me to visit. We could go to dinner on Saturday night if that would work for you. General Hrabal has offered me the use of his guest house and I would like to take him up on it. How about it?"

This was a little bit quick. She knew this is what she wanted, but she hadn't had time to work it all out in her head. She certainly knew she could enjoy being with him. She wanted to be very careful that this was not just a call that may relate to some pity or concerns of that time when Gus was killed. He sensed her hesitation and quickly offered, "If you are busy, I certainly understand." He had given her the perfect out, and she knew it. That is just how nice a guy he was. That was just one of the attributes that made him attractive to her. She quickly thought that she should say yes; it would be better not to miss this opportunity. It may not present itself again. "No, no, I think that would be perfect. We really need to catch up anyway."

"Great," he said, "I'll see you about 7:00 on Saturday."

CUTE IS FOR PUPPY DOGS

Well, Aggie thought, *here I am headed into uncharted territory again. Until earlier this week, this was a man I had not seen in over twenty years. I know nothing about him except that he is a captain in the U.S. Navy. He may even be married. I just don't know. But then on the other hand, he is good-looking, very successful, and quite a charmer. My best bet is to bounce this off Marylin and see what she thinks.*

It doesn't make sense for me to do that because she will definitely be in favor of my going to this dinner and probably anything else the captain may want to do that night. Anyway, I will see what she says.

She went by Marylin's on the way home and popped in. Marylin was right there and glad to see her. After all, they were drinking buddies. When Marylin answered the door, her first words were, "I am having a glass of wine. Do you want one?"

A quick reply, "I guess I better." They sat on the couch and Aggie gave her the details of the call. "I hope I am doing the right thing by saying yes."

Marylin looked over at her and said, "What are you talking about? Don't come in here and ask me if I think you should go. Damn right, I do! The question is what you are going to wear? Do you still have that little black dress? No, I am just joking. Really, what do you plan to wear?"

Responding, Aggie noted, "I was thinking about just a dress with a sweater."

Without hesitation, Marylin said, "No. I will pick you up tomorrow about 10:00 a.m., and we will run to Wilmington and pick you up something."

With that, Aggie threw up her hands as if to say, "I give up!" She finished her wine and then with one last question she asked, "Do you think he is cute?"

Marylin responded, "Aggie, you are over forty years old. This is a man five years your senior. Cute is not an appropriate question. Your list needs to include things like common interests, a good sense of humor, similar values, and possibly others that may pertain to his physical characteristics and financial standing. Those qualities are what is important. Cute is for a puppy dog or a teen. You, my lady, are neither!"

With that assessment, Aggie set her glass down and walked to her car. On the way out, she looked back and said, "See you at about

10:00." As she walked into her house, she could not help but pause by that bottom step again. She wondered if everyone had such a spot.

It was right here that she realized her first love. It was here that she had spent many hours with the person she had loved most and longest, Gus 3. And now it was here that a seed had been planted by Lewis. As her thoughts darted, her wish was that this seed would grow into the kind of love that she had found before. In her innermost self, those thoughts raced as she bound those memories into a package. That package would hold many different forms of love, each woven together to create this wonderful new gift she had been given. When it was opened, it would include the passion and wide-eyed attraction that was felt when two young people enjoyed their first embrace. It would be the never-ending and unquestioned love that she had shared with her son. A love that could never be doubted. And, she felt a little guilty about this one, it would be full of passion and unbridled pleasures shared as those she had enjoyed with Chuck. It would bundle all things love into a single magical star that would provide her guidance through her life.

She went in, sat, and talked with Mama and Da a few minutes before saying, "I am off to bed. I am going shopping with Marylin in the morning, and by the way, I have a date tomorrow night."

When Marylin honked it was just a few minutes before 10:00. Aggie jumped in and off they went. Another great adventure for these two "pioneers of love." Aggie made it quite clear that she was not going to do a modeling thing after this trip. "On this date, it will not be a short, skintight, backless dress that makes me feel almost naked. Tonight, it will be an appropriate and modest dress."

Marylin did say, almost as if she were whispering, "Well, at least wear sexy underwear. I'll help you pick them out." Aggie gave a one-word response: "Bull!"

Aggie found a dress that she thought just fit the bill. It was less formal than a cocktail outfit, but more formal than office clothes. Marylin thought she needed something more provocative, but did say that Aggie looked really good in the one she had picked out. With that, Marylin started showing Aggie what she thought may be the appropriate undergarments for this night's adventure. It was certainly not what Aggie had in mind. "I am not going to wear a thong, and it would be like wearing nothing at all if I wore that bra. Marylin, he is a preacher! I have underwear that will be just fine. Besides, he certainly does not expect to see any of that on this, our first date."

Marylin rolled her eyes and said straight out, "Is that what Chuck thought on your first time out with him?"

"Marylin, I tell you too much." They both smiled.

She got back home with just enough time to take a bath and get ready. As she was dressing, just before she put on the new dress, she did look at herself in the mirror. She wanted to check and make sure her underwear was okay. Now she felt like a hypocrite. That thought made her look away quickly even before she had a chance to make that determination. "Damn," she murmured to herself as she turned again and looked into the mirror at those garments. They were plenty good, and she did not look at all shabby in them. The dress slipped on easily and fit her perfectly. She heard the doorbell ring and started down the steps. Lewis was already inside the door. When he looked at her, she could see Gus 3's eyes as he had looked at Marsha the night of the prom. That made her feel good.

Lewis had spoken with Mama and Da. They both remembered him. He assured them he would have their daughter home at a respectful time. As they walked off the porch, they passed that step. Lewis got the car door for her and then got in as she buckled up. Looking over with his fascinating blue eyes, he asked, "Do you have a preference as to where you want to eat?"

"Tonight, I am with you," Aggie replied. "I have not been out like this in so long. In fact, I am looking forward to not making any decisions."

"Well," he said, "General Hrabal said that there are a lot of good restaurants in Wilmington, but that the officers' club at the air force base in Goldsboro was just fantastic. Let's go there."

"Fine by me."

They talked a lot as they drove. She was starting to gain a little knowledge about him. He did know an awful lot about her, as he had indicated. Nothing real personal, just about how she was getting along, and that she had not remarried. He filled her in on the fact that he had never married. When she asked him if he had not met the right woman, he seemed embarrassed a little. In short time, they had traveled the hour trip to Goldsboro and were going through the gate of the Seymour Johnson Air Force Base.

The front gate guard stopped him and asked for his ID. When the guard looked at it, he stepped back and came to attention. He then gave a salute and said loudly, "Welcome to Seymour Johnson, sir. Can I offer directions or ask for a lead car to escort you?"

"No, Airman, just give me directions to the officers' club," said Captain Morgan. He did and they were on their way. It was just a couple of blocks. The guard quickly notified both the officers' club and the commander of his watch that a member of the Joint Chiefs was on base. When they pulled in front of the officers' club, they were met by two young airmen. Each one opened a door on either side of the car. The one on Lewis's side saluted him, and this time he returned the salute. They went inside and walked up to the maître d'. He very quickly said, "Welcome to the Seymour Johnson officers' club, Captain Morgan. Can I escort you and Mrs. Morgan to a table?"

"Thank you for the compliment, young man, but this young lady is not Mrs. Morgan. This is Mrs. Johnson, and she is my date," responded Lewis.

"Then, sir, let me compliment you on this night's date. Captain, you and Mrs. Johnson this way, please."

When they sat down, Aggie wondered out loud, "What in the world was that all about?"

He laughed and told her that his ID showed that he was on the Staff of the Joint Chiefs. In the military, that is a powerful association for him to have. He was used to this; it was one of the perks of the job. She felt as though she was among royalty. The dinner proved to be just what General Hrabal had suggested. He reached out and took her hand as they blessed it before they ate. The meal was fantastic. It took a long time for them to eat as they spent as much time talking as eating.

After they left, they both agreed that it had been a wonderful dinner. The ride back home was as full of conversation, about each other, as had been the ride over. It was after midnight when they pulled in front of her house. They talked a few more minutes. He then opened her car door, and they walked to the steps. They stopped at the bottom one just like she and Gus had done those many years before. This time she made no effort to move from that spot. He looked straight into her eyes, but did not take her hand. Her mind could only think, *I have been here before, and my heart is about to explode*. He spoke and said, "I have had a really great time tonight. It is the first time I have enjoyed anything this much. I do not have to leave until mid-afternoon tomorrow, so with your permission, I would like to join you at church tomorrow morning." She started to pinch herself to see if this was real. He bent and kissed her gently on the cheek. Aggie was breathless as that kiss took all of it away. She turned and walked into her house. First thing she thought was, *I did not tell him church would be fine*.

Then she noticed Mama and Da both asleep in front of the TV. She turned it off and left them. When upstairs, she called Marylin. Marylin said, "I was waiting for your call. Tell me every detail." Aggie just responded, "I think I am going to get married again!"

Outside, Lewis walked to his car and wondered why she had not answered him. It did not matter, though; he was going to be at her church tomorrow.

CHAPTER 17

OUT OF THE MOUTHS OF BABES

It was Sunday and a beautiful morning. Aggie was teaching her usual Sunday School class. It was the twelve-year-old group. They were still just their moms' babies, but had begun to know and even understand stuff that was way ahead of their time. The media made sure of that. That media caused them to be several years ahead of their parents at the same age. Some of the parents did not understand that. To those parents, they were still just sweet and innocent little people with toy trucks and dolls. The reality was that they were full of all the things they had seen on the TV. Both good and bad. A show about an angel and the wonders of good he was able to create. The excitement of a bikini-clad lifeguard as she ran "bouncing" down the beach. Young men who were way ahead of their years, both in mind and body. And, examples offered by those whose antics were displayed on that same TV as news. Sexual encounters in every segment of their lives, even in the Oval Office.

They sat in her class, giggling one moment and then asking unbelievably complex questions about almost every aspect of life the next. This was tomorrow's society. They were the parents and leaders of the future. It took a special hand to keep them focused and in line. She had that talent; they respected and loved her. She was perfect for the task.

Just after Sunday School, one of those young ladies, one who was way ahead of her years, walked up to her. "You okay, Mrs. Aggie? You seem different today. I hope nothing is wrong."

"No, Beth, it just couldn't be any better." She left the classroom to go into the sanctuary and found Lewis standing there waiting for her. He had on his uniform and looked like that same "recruitment poster" he had over twenty years ago. Tall, square and erect, good-looking, and most of all, those blue eyes. He reached for her hand as he said, "Good morning; you look perfect again."

Most of her class had gathered just up the sidewalk from where Mrs. Aggie and the soldier stood. They were smiling as they whispered and watched her.

As she and Lewis walked by the group, one of the young men spoke up and said, "Enjoy church, Mrs. Aggie."

She looked and pointed at him, then smiled and returned, "Oh, I will." Oddly enough, they all seemed to beam at her plight. They really cared about her. That sailor and Mrs. Aggie together, they understood.

The preacher's sermon was just as good as the one he had preached on that Wednesday night. The one that had made her see life a little differently. Definitely for the better. This was a different subject, but would offer her the same comforts as did that other service. It was as if he had written it for her. The timing and subject made it perfect for this day. It was about new beginnings and how God would always provide a perfect dawn following the darkest part of the night. That our part in this was to recognize the brightness of that dawn and use it to find our way through that day. To remember the light provided was for the purpose of seeing those things that God had given us. A wonderful trail for life to travel. Those paths that violated His wishes would remain dark. In that darkness a clear and easy path would not lay ahead. During this sermon, Lewis again reached over and took her hand and held it. Why, how, did God pick her to be so blessed? It was those dark spots that made this, a bright place, possible. She should never question God's plan again.

After the service and still at the church, Mama quickly cornered Aggie and Lewis. She would accept no plan except that he was to have lunch with them. She had already prepared it and, with a little of that devious attitude that was still Mama's, flatly stated, "Besides, we need to know a little about who our little girl is seeing."

He laughed and replied, "This will be a good day for that. I will be open to anything you want to know. Especially if you have the ballgame on. The Redskins are playing the Falcons, and I do love my 'Skins."

Da then spoke and said, "You'll be the only one pulling for the 'Skins. It will be good to see just what kind of loser you are."

They finished lunch and the 3:00 p.m. game was just starting when they cut the TV on. Da spoke again, "Preacher, if it won't offend you, I am going to have a cold beer."

Lewis replied, "How about if I have one with you? It may calm me down when the Falcons get about two touchdowns ahead."

Da said right back, "Huh, ain't enough beer in the fridge to make that happen."

That exchange solidified Da and Lewis's relationship. They were now friends. Lewis smiled at Aggie as if to say, *Now I need to work on your mom.* Aggie smiled back as she had a good idea of his plan. Mama would not be such an easy target. She was a pretty slick lady. She had been around this world long enough to read a personality pretty quickly. It would be interesting to watch him make those efforts.

Halftime had come, and Mama commented that she was going to finish the dishes and make some popcorn for the second half. Before Aggie could get up, Lewis was on his feet and spoke directly to Aggie, "You sit right there with your dad and I'll give your mom a hand." Oh, he was another slick one! No doubt that he would soon have Mama eating from his hand. And he did.

Just before the second half kickoff, Aggie mentioned to Lewis that she had thought he had to drive back to Washington that afternoon. He responded that the general had told him there was no problem if he wanted to stay over another night. No problem about work as he could leave about 6:00 a.m. and still be there by lunch. Aggie wondered if General Hrabal was trying to push this romance on his own or if Marylin had gotten to him. It was probably both. Honestly it was a moot point. Right now she was still in neutral. However, she knew it wouldn't take much for her to put this relationship in gear and ride it wildly into the future.

The game ended with the 'Skins winning on a last-minute field goal. It was a good sermon, a good lunch, and a good game. It was time to say goodbye and Aggie walked onto the porch with Lewis to do so. They stepped down those same steps. Those steps that always seemed to insert themselves into every important thing in her life. On the bottom step, she sat and patted the place just beside her. He also sat.

She began, "I have a question I would like to ask. You made the statement that you probably knew more about me than I did you. I have wondered, since you said that, just what you meant by it. How, or, more importantly, why, do you have that knowledge about me?"

Lewis responded, "Aggie, I guess that is a fair question, but it puts me in somewhat of a pickle. To answer I will have to say some things that may cause you to think I am trying to advance our relationship too quickly. To be honest, it began as concern and my wanting to confirm I had done the right things in the right ways when I helped you through the time of Gus's death. I was brand new at my position, and you were my very first assignment. I was young, just starting a career that I believed deeply in. It was all about you and your well-being. How would you take care of yourself and a child? I could only hope that in some way, I played a positive part in that. That is why I began to follow and keep up with you. At first it was easy. I could ask soldiers who were also from this area about you and then also about little Gus 3. General Hrabal was my best source. Just like any other small town, that info was easily available. Later it became more difficult. I could not find out as much as I wanted to know.

"I had been very lucky in my career and found myself in an elite group of leaders as a result of a mutual family friend. One of my mom's neighbors was very close to Admiral Palenta when he became Chief of Staff of the U.S. Navy. Through that connection, he brought me on as a staff member. Just a couple of years later, he became chairman of the Joint Chiefs, and I was offered the job as chaplain to the Joint Chiefs and with that a promotion to captain. It was a fairy tale of good luck. I am talking too much; do you want me to continue?"

Aggie quickly nodded, "Yes, I want the whole story."

"Okay, you asked for it." He went on, "General Hrabal contacted me with the news about your son's death. The story about the death of a young West Point cadet also made its way to the Joint Chiefs. I decided I must come to his funeral. I was torn about whether to speak to you or not, but I guess I was a coward. No, not a coward, I was afraid you either may not even remember me or may find fault in my having reappeared under that circumstance. All of those years, I thought my inability to get you off my mind was based upon the fact that you were my first assignment. Anyway, I came but did not make myself known. In fact, no one knew I was even there until General Hrabal recognized me, even though I was wearing civvies. I shared the details with him, and he has since been my ally in this, whatever this is. I knew through him that you would be involved with the presentations at the ribbon-cutting at the new USO facility and felt that may provide an opportunity for me to speak to you in a casual setting. When I approached you and stood beside you at that ceremony, I knew that I could accept nothing less than getting to know you as I do now. Neither of us have any idea where this may go, but there is nothing I would like better than to find out. Either way, at the very least, I would like to believe we are now good friends.

"You can respond to me in the best way your heart directs. I will respect whatever you say, and I do apologize if I have put you in a bad place. If you ask, I will walk away and remember this time fondly. You wondered why I had never married. I will share an absolute truth, even though it may scare you away. I think that you are the reason, I want to be sure, and I want you to feel the same way I do."

Aggie did not speak; she could not speak. She stood up and still held his hand as she walked with him to the car. He opened the door and got in. She simply leaned over, planted a kiss very firmly on his cheek, and said, "I want to see you again." He started the engine, and that was a good thing. If not, the thump from both of their heartbeats would have become obvious, each to the other.

She called Marylin. Aggie gave her the details of what Lewis had said. "Marylin," she continued, "I don't know what to do or say. In one way, I feel as if I am on top of the world. And the best thing that could happen in my life happened. At the same time, my heart is broken. Am I cheated or am I rewarded? Marylin, I need you to help me decide."

"Nope," came as a quick reply from Marylin. "This is not about a dress to wear or what kind of shoes may work. This is not even about sharing a steamy moment. This is a matter of the heart, a matter of *your* heart. You must decide, and the only thing I can offer is that no matter what you decide, I will be your strongest supporter. But he sure does have pretty eyes."

That brought Aggie down a little from her unrealistic peak. "You know what," Aggie answered, "you seem to always have the right answer for me. You are right. I am going to give this thing a try and let those eyes work their wonder." Marylin had given Aggie a new perspective. It was just what she needed.

DUTY IN DC

Lewis was in town now almost every weekend. He would be on duty one weekend out of every six. The six highest-ranking officers on the Joint Chiefs of Staff were required to rotate for weekend duty. It was almost never that they got called on. The whole thing was more of a traditional formality than a usable military tool. That officer was there to make a quick decision about when and if that group should be notified in case of a national military emergency. It would be the on-duty officer who made that decision.

It was several months before Lewis could talk her into joining him for a weekend at his apartment in Washington, D.C. She was still a little old-fashioned, and as such, she certainly did not want them to create the appearance that they were "shacking up." After all, she was the Sunday School teacher of students who could be heavily influenced by that choice if they found out.

It was the weekend of the National Cherry Blossom Festival in Washington. Even though he could not stray from his apartment to attend any of those festivities, Aggie would at least have a good excuse about being there. No one would know they must stay right there.

Marylin picked up the ringing phone, and it was Aggie who began, "Well, I have done it. I told Lewis I would spend the weekend with him next week. It is the Cherry Blossom Festival, and I am excited about going."

In typical Marylin fashion, she came back with, "I am sure you are excited about going, but I am also pretty damn sure it has nothing to do with the Cherry Blossom Festival."

"Marylin," Aggie replied, "it certainly does, in one way or another." The chitchat continued. Marylin wanted to know what kind of clothes she was going to take. Just casual walking around stuff was her answer.

"This is the point where I must intercede. Your clothes for an occasion such as this are extremely important. It is the impression you make on him, and even more importantly, the impression you make on his friends, that is important."

Aggie thought it may be better not to tell her they would not be around any other folks, and he must stay close to home for duty purposes. "I have some things that will be just perfect; it is just for two days."

"Aggie, you just don't get it," said Marylin. "You are my best friend and I must live part of my magical life through you. So much of my enjoyment and anticipation for certain things in my life become alive to me as you live them. Please, for the sake of my enjoyment and sensual anticipation, go to Wilmington with me tomorrow night and do some shopping. Each time I pick out something for you, I live, at least in my mind, with the vision of what kind of response it will create. That gives me a target."

Aggie followed, "Somehow that makes sense, weird sense, but sense still. I think we are at a point in our relationship that I will accept that premise on one condition."

"What is that condition?" asked Marylin.

"Just this: If I give you those pleasures, then you owe me the same," Aggie replied. "I want to be involved in helping you create those same pleasures as they relate to you and Robert. I have to admit, it will be a little strange with Robert being involved. It will be more like I am helping to set up my brother. I guess that is okay, though, as I assume it is acceptable to set up a brother. Marsha sure looked after Gus 3 in that way, and they were certainly like brother and sister. And I think it worked well for Gus 3." Aggie thought out loud, "I am really coming out of a shell now. Where am I going? I am turning into you, or maybe worse!"

Marylin laughed as she responded, "I am not sure you are ready or capable of jumping in that deep. Some of my escapades are much more advanced than your level of expertise will allow. Although, I must admit that your round with Chuck set a little fire in my fireplace too. Anyway, I am all in. I will pick you up at 5:00 at Robert's office and we will have dinner down there."

By 4:30, Marylin was sitting in the office with Robert. "What is the deal?" he asked.

"Aggie and I are going to Wilmington shopping. Your dinner is on the stove. We probably will not be back until late as we will shop until the stores close."

"Well, in that case, you and Aggie just go ahead and leave. I can't get anything done with you sitting here, and Aggie is probably thinking more about shopping than my business anyway. Have fun and bring me something." Marylin almost laughed out loud at his last request. She thought to herself, *I am sure I will, but it will be something we can enjoy together.*

Marylin and Aggie decided just to get a bite in the food court at the shopping center. It was just okay, but gave them time for more shopping. Marylin suggested that they first go to a dress shop and pick up a couple of things for her to wear during the day at the Cherry Blossom Festival. Aggie squirmed as she said, "I've got to make a confession before we waste our time. We really are not going to be spending any of our time at the festival. Lewis is on duty and has to stay at his apartment. That is the only place we will be spending any time other than my trip up and back."

Marylin replied quickly, "Don't guess you will need any clothes at all then."

Aggie remembered, "The only thing he mentioned was that they do have an indoor pool and a club room where a lot of his friends hang out."

"All right, now we are getting somewhere. Are his friends married? Will they have dates? Surely you are not going to be the only woman among a bunch of military guys. If that's true, I think I will go in your place," was Marylin's next directive.

Aggie followed, "Not sure," cocking her head, "but I bet there will be wives and probably dates there. I hope so."

"Honey, don't hope that. There isn't anything like not having any competition. I have always wanted to be in that spot," Marylin answered, but Aggie knew that Marylin was just sharing those wild fantasies of hers when she made such statements.

They walked into a couple of different stores, but none of them looked promising so they moved on. The third store they went into Marylin spied a swimsuit cover that was sharp as could be. "Look at that," she said, "and I see a bunch of suits over on that rack. We can fix this part up right here."

"Okay, but I am not going to buy any tiny bikini. I would not wear it even if I was not already too old. Remember, I am over forty, and he is a preacher, not even to mention me still being a Sunday School teacher," finished Aggie. They both giggled like two teenagers. They did end up with a two-piece, maybe even one a little on the skimpier side.

Shopping was fun that day. Two good friends and a mutually appreciated adventure set the stage for that play. It ended late that night as the stores closed. Aggie had everything she needed for her trip, and Marylin had everything she needed for her weekend too. Both would have fun, and they both hoped the men in their lives would too. After all, Marylin had bought something "for Robert."

CHAPTER 18

THE GOOD KING

Over 6,000 miles away, the new young king of Nagorno-Karabakh was starting to become just that, a king. It had been a year since his father had died and he had taken the throne. It would not be an easy pair of shoes to fill. King Renede had been loved by his subjects. They lived in a world that had not yet found its way into the twenty-first century. The people had warmth and food and an easy and safe life. That seemed to keep them well satisfied. The old king had made sure that his people were treated well. He genuinely cared for them and they for him. The mourning time had passed, and his son had taken his place. No one knew the son very well as he had been gone for a number of years. He had been groomed for this role for the several years prior to traveling the world to earn a formal education. His studies carried him to many countries, but the U.S. seemed to be the one that he was most fond of. It placed him in a bit of a dilemma as his home neighbors were staunch Muslim countries. His country was much more liberal, and this king, just like his father, was also.

King Adjah, as he had become known, was learning as he went along. Everyone was excited as he took full control. They felt he would do it well and keep his father's better policies in place. He was beginning to travel away from his palace and to be among his country's people. It was obvious that he had been in America for a while as he had picked up an accent. That was okay with most of his country's citizens. Most of them thought America must be a good land. Maybe a little self-righteous and too sure of themselves, but a good country and good people.

The new king had begun to pick his priorities. On the top of his list was the health of his subjects. He began recruiting doctors from other countries and also providing scholarships to the brightest students so they could study medicine. He had begun a program of building health centers around the country so everyone would have access to professional care when needed. Another of his priorities was education. Teachers and facilities were all getting an uplift. He had little problem with financing all the improvements. His studies and his policies had created a very good relationship between his country and the U.S. They were eager to provide funds for such improvements. Teachers were required to take online classes that would help in their educational efforts. Facilities were upgraded to provide warm and healthy food along with many new books and other educational tools. A full stomach and a good book create a perfect venue from which to gain knowledge. The path that carries a good country to a great one.

The king had also set out a growth program for the next several years. The country needed more roads and it needed more of an infrastructure. Its citizens needed easier access and communications with the world around them. His goals and dreams were very obviously aligned with those who called him their king. King Adjah much preferred being with a group in a non-formal setting, one that would allow him to hear and learn the needs and thoughts of those he had taken an oath to protect. His preference was to hear them. He would listen to what they had to say and he would respond with truth and respect. His reign was certainly off on the right foot.

Most of his subjects also viewed him as a very available young bachelor. Especially those who had daughters who wanted to pursue him as a potential mate. He was introduced to a constant stream of young women, some very beautiful. He did not allow himself any of the pleasure of that pursuit as the last thing he needed right now was a queen. More important things lay ahead of that choice. He respected and understood their ambitions, but this was just not the right time, and he made that known. One day he would pick one of them for his queen. Not yet.

When alone, he kept serious his ambitions and at the same time developed a new quest that would make these people secure in their lives. Both now and in the future. Other issues were on his mind. His family, his home, and his country. The information he could receive was somewhat limited. All correspondence came to him through a staff who reviewed it, which limited what he knew. He could gather only bits and pieces from the newspapers he read and from the TV. There was a message code in the classifieds of his country's weekly newspaper. It was in Farsi, but he could write and speak it perfectly. An international news channel provided information about issues of the world and many of those issues involved the U.S.

Information from his small hometown and his family was rare. He did have assurance from his superiors that if anything was less than wonderful for his mom or his grandparents, they would find a way to let him know. Life was good for him, and he never missed an opportunity to talk with God. He prayed for his country and for this one that he now ruled. He prayed for many, but the prayer he made stronger than any other was for his mom.

MARYLIN IS JUST MARYLIN

Marylin took Aggie to the airport for her early flight out on Friday morning. Marylin continued to quiz her about every detail. "Do you have that swimsuit cover? How about the new suit? I still think you looked good in that yellow one. Don't forget to flip your hair back like I showed you; it enhances your sexy eyes. You get your sexy eyes looking into those blue sexy eyes of Lewis's, and there's just no telling what might happen."

Aggie had to respond, "Yes, and if you will burn that candle, open the bottle of red wine, and wear that new outfit, you will have all you can handle, too. I also want to hear every detail when I get back."

Marylin pulled into the departure lane at the Wilmington Airport, let Aggie and her bags out, and was soon on her way back home. She was working on all the details as they related to the red wine and candles. This was fun, it felt good, and she reflected on how wonderful her life had turned out. Her husband and all that he provided, her friends, and especially Aggie, enriched her beyond anything she could have dreamed of.

GOLDEN DUSK

Aggie's plane landed on time and she quickly made her way to pick up her luggage. Lewis was waiting in the luggage claim area as they had planned. He pulled her bags from the carousel. Soon he was throwing them onto the back seat of his car. She had been to Washington before, but it was a church trip. She was along as a youth advisor and chaperone. This weekend would certainly have a different set of rules from those she had enforced during that trip. They had been driving only a few minutes when he pulled into the parking lot of his apartment complex. It was not as she had imagined.

It was a tall building. It had a lobby with an attendant who must unlock the doors as they attempted to enter. He saw Lewis, smiled, and said, "Come on in Captain. Welcome, Aggie, most of us already know your name. Lewis talks about you a lot."

Lewis gave him a quick look and said, "Maybe some talk too much." The attendant laughed as he told them to have a nice weekend. They took the elevator to the twenty-fourth floor. He pointed out that the pool and deck were on the top floor, which was the twenty-fifth. The club and bar were also on the twenty-fifth. He punched in his code and entered. His apartment was fantastic. It had two large bedrooms and each had its own bath. He took her into one of the two and said, "This is the guest bedroom. A private bath is right over there, and you can hang your things in this closet. Make yourself at home and comfortable. I apologize that we are restricted to this building. I have to be within range of a private phone intercom that hooks me directly to my office. From tonight at 5:00 until Monday morning at 6:00, I am bound here. I have made arrangements for one of my friends to get you to your plane Sunday evening.

"It is just about the right time for lunch so I thought we would go out and have something," he continued. "From there we can walk to the store and pick up whatever we may want for our next few meals. I can cook pretty well, though not as well as you and your mom. Steak and spaghetti are my specialties."

"That all sounds good to me," said Aggie. "I would be hard-pressed to find fault with anything in this beautiful place. Just look at your view."

"Take whatever time you need before we go," said Lewis. "We don't have to be back here until 5:00."

Soon they were exiting the elevator and walking through the lobby. Everyone they passed waved and smiled, and most spoke to them. Most of the men shouted something along the lines of, "What's up, Captain; who is your friend?" while the ladies all seemed to offer a more formal, "How about introducing me to your friend." They stopped and made the introductions to each inquirer. Most of the ladies ended with the comment, "I'll probably see you tomorrow." Lewis could tell that she did not understand so he offered the following explanation, "Most of the time, a group of us guys play golf on Saturday. The ladies all hang out on the deck and sun. They don't realize that I won't be able to go tomorrow so they assume you will probably be joining them on the sun deck."

"I might like to do that anyway," Aggie said. "I could use some sun, and I might be able to gather a little more info on just who you are."

He smiled, she smiled, and with those smiles was a silent acknowledgment that their relationship was gaining strength, quickly.

Lunch was at a deli nearby and was really good. Sandwiches were about three times larger than they should have been so carryout boxes went with them as they left. The grocery store was different from what she was accustomed to back home. It had a lot more stuff and it was a lot of different stuff. Most of the things in this store were either ready to be put into the microwave and heated or required little to no preparation. He commented that most folks did very little "home cooking." It was all about quick and easy, so long as it was good. They picked up some items from a section with signs reading "gourmet," "restaurant quality," "ready to eat," etc. She wondered what Mama and Da would think about this. Da probably would not like this store. She had not seen a single biscuit among all those meals. Mama may enjoy the less-cooking concept.

They got back to his apartment and put the food away. It was close to 5:00 and the sun had just started to go down. Lewis took Aggie's hand and said, "Walk with me." She felt a little funny as he walked into his bedroom, but quickly felt relieved as he opened a double glass door and they stepped out onto a balcony. The sun was setting behind Georgetown. All of the monuments were cloaked with the faint remains of the day's light. In fact, they were framed by the setting sun. It was a beautiful sight and a different look from this twenty-fourth floor than when she toured with the church youth group. The setting sun provided a golden screen for the nation's capital. She could see the sun move as it sank into the area behind the city. It was big and it was beautiful. She had seen the sun rise on the ocean many times, but this time she saw it as it went the other way. Not the beginning of a new and exciting day, but the beginning of a new and exciting evening. As she began to wonder what was next, he put his arm around her shoulder and pulled her close to him. He never said a word; he did not need to. Aggie could not imagine a more perfect place, a place that could provide the absolute safety and warmth than did his embrace. A perfect moment in a perfect place!

A loud beep shook them back to reality. It was the duty phone, and he must answer it. She heard him give some type of code and then hang up. It was just a couple of minutes after 5:00, and this was a very young night. They talked on for a while sitting across the bar from each other.

"I will offer you a drink or some wine, but I cannot join you," said Lewis.

She said, "No, I am fine. Why don't I go in and take a shower and change?"

She did and the entire time she was in the shower he was a part of her every thought. She was pretty sure this relationship could not have been written any better than its reality made it seem. She even felt that certain tingle of anticipation, that reminder that she was all woman.

He was in his bathroom and showering as well. Many of the same thoughts raced through his mind. He thought, *With all my heart, I love her. I have never said it, but it is true. Does she know? Is this the right time?* He now felt so inadequate to meet this task. He was no stranger to passion, but was an absolute novice when it came to this, his first and only love.

They both came back out at about the same time. It was almost funny how they both avoided any suggestive wear. Respect and a need for a perfect prelude were the way the evening would move forward. It flashed in her mind, *I bet Marylin is not following this script*. She was right.

RED WINE AND LITTLE BLUE PILLS

Marylin had cooked Robert's favorite dinner and served it with the red wine she bought. The wine glowed in the soft light of a candle. Robert was taking the bait, hook, line, and sinker. She was going to slip into "something a little different" and join him. "You wait right here; do not move," she told him. She could tell that the wine had his mind going where she wanted it. Her outfit would do the rest. *Boy, I am good*, she thought. *I still have it*.

Robert had his own thoughts as well. This night was working out just like he had hoped. He worked hard in a profession that required that he be able to bring his clients to an appropriate level of closure. This was no different. He and Marylin had done this before and he loved it. She was doing those exact things he had worked so hard to lead her to. He had her just where he wanted her. While she was out of the room, and this was a first, he reached into his pocket and took out a light blue pill shaped like a triangle. He took it with a sip of the wine, and wondered if it would make a difference in his abilities. His friends certainly lauded this tiny pill's attributes. In fact, one of them had insisted he use this one just to prove a point.

In a minute, Marylin walked out into the candlelit room. She was beaming and had a look about her that was craving an appropriate response. Sort of a *How do I look?* look in her eyes. His response, "Wow, you are hot!" She smiled as she remembered those words. She had heard them before. When Gus 3 had said them to Aggie, she had blushed. But this was a different situation. Marylin did not blush. The words just accelerated her already-adventurous imagination.

Their night was a perfect blend of all that could be right in a marriage. Both thought they had control, each of the other. Both were as filled with passion as they had been all those years ago, that night they had shared their love with each other for the first time. Later, as they lay exhausted in each other's arms, she imagined that the wonder that created this night was candles, red wine, and a skimpy nightgown. Robert was thinking about how he had maneuvered to create a lifestyle and place that could manifest a night like this. They were both young again, and felt that same love that had drawn them together as college kids. It was that love, nothing either of them had conjured, that made this night. Robert rolled onto his side and began to stroke her face. His hands wandered. His touch was like a million tiny feathers whose very purpose was to arouse. It worked, and, again, they enjoyed an encounter that only mutual experience could create. An end that left the sultry anticipation of the next beginning. Robert smiled as he fell asleep wondering how he might be able to get a bottle of those pills.

FIRST TIME IN THE LIGHT

Up in Washington, it was late as well. Lewis stepped up from the bar and said, "I want you to see something else." This time he simply reached over and turned off the lights. When he did, the city before them spread like a romantic poem. It was a mosaic of blinking, sparkling lights against a black sky. It was not unlike looking at the stars. Her thoughts wandered to those stars from that first night that she and Gus had made love. She was not sad, but instead the memories made her smile as she knew this night would be forever remembered as well. He reached over and turned on the radio.

It was a soft and slow song that played as he took her hand and said, "Can I have this dance?" It was very formal as she placed one hand on his shoulder and held the other out for him to take into his. Lewis took her right hand into his left as his right hand reached around her and gently pulled against the small of her back. They lost all concept of time. It was them and the music. She reached up and put both hands around his neck and laid her head against his chest. His hands nearly touched as he placed both of them on her back. This was done as they both pulled to a closeness they had never enjoyed. And enjoy they did. It was different from that first time with Gus. It was different as well from that night she so enjoyed with Chuck. This was not like either of those, but was instead a combination of them both and this time with a difference. No questions, no nervousness, and no awareness that a world existed beyond right here, right now. This was love, and this night they would enjoy it in its purest form. It was more than she had ever dreamed it could be. It was perfection. This would be forever. He felt the same. Those simple three words finally came, as both of them uttered, "I love you." For the first time since he met Aggie, he listened as he heard those words he had so longed for. For the first time in over twenty years, she was hearing them directed to her from someone other than a family member. A long time can seem so short when anticipation becomes reality.

The next morning, she awoke in his arms. They had slept as if one. He was awake and looking at her. She smiled as he took her face into both hands and brought her to his lips. That kiss created a new wave of passion that would again confirm the soft "I love you" they shared. About an hour later, close to 10:00, she got up and put on her bathing suit. He thought he may be dreaming as he saw her standing in that suit. She was wearing a cover over it that provided little cover. It did not hide the realities of what lay beneath. She was a beautiful woman, and he felt blessed that she had chosen to be there with him.

LOTION HERE AND THERE

Aggie smiled as she told him she had made coffee and handed him a cup. She went on, "If you don't mind, I think I will join those ladies on the sun deck. I do need the sun, and, again, I will be listening for any information they may have about you."

It caused her to wonder a little if he'd had any relationships like the one she had with Chuck. It would probably be better if she never knew. Still, she wondered.

He smiled, "Okay by me, as I have some work I need to do. I will be right here when you come back. I have my cell if you need me." She got on the elevator and punched the button for the twenty-fifth floor. Soon she was joining a group of women on the sun deck who were laid out and working on their tans.

One of them jumped up and told her, "Come lay right here on this chaise. That way, we can all ask you all about yourself. We need to know if everything about you is as perfect as Lewis has told us." They all laughed. She took off the thin cover-up and lay with the warm sun stroking her. They had not lied. They started asking questions by the dozen about every conceivable aspect of her life. Her life was an open book, and she shared it with this group. It was unlike any group she had ever bonded with before. They were mostly her age and younger. None of them had children at home as this was an "adult living complex."

After she had given them about an hour of unhindered responses, she belted out, "Now, guys, I need a few answers too."

"Shoot," was the quick response.

"How long have you known Lewis?" Aggie asked. "I cannot imagine that he has never been married. What are his favorite things? Have his other girlfriends been cute?" Her list was almost as endless as theirs had been.

They began to answer as they all contributed with their conversational response. "I have known Lewis the longest," said one of the ladies. "In fact, he and I dated a couple of times. He introduced me to my husband. Your man has always been considered a prize. Lots of girls, most of them beautiful young women, have tried to hook him. He was always a confirmed bachelor. All of us got the idea, when he started speaking of you, that he may be in for defeat.

"Seems that he was," she continued. "You are the first lady to spend the weekend in that apartment. I am not implying anything, but you are the first to be more than a 'one-nighter.'" It was said as a joke and they all laughed. Aggie did not find it as humorous as did the other ladies. "We would know as we watched carefully," she added. "Lewis is like a big brother to us all." Before she knew it, it was afternoon and the crowd started to thin. The sun had taken a toll, and they all were quite pink. It snuck up on them.

She tapped on the door as she punched in the code and opened it and went in. He was sitting at the bar and had taken out the doggie bags from the deli the day before. He had the sandwiches served up on plates. "What do you want to drink?" he asked as he walked up to her and kissed her cheek. "A little burned, aren't we?"

"Yeah, I think so," Aggie replied.

"Let's have lunch and then you can take a shower and I will put some lotion on your back," said Lewis.

The sandwich was just as good as it was the day before. He asked her if she had enjoyed the ladies and said he hoped they had not talked her head off.

She said she did enjoy them and they had not talked too much. "It was very pleasant and quite informative," she said, as she rolled her eyes in an attempt to make him think she may know something that she did not.

Not to be outdone, he answered, "Easy to find out all kinds of stuff about other people isn't it?" With that, they finished their lunch with nothing else but normal and unimportant chitchat. When finished, she said, "I think I will get that shower now."

The water was cold against her pink skin. The two-piece suit was modest as bikinis go, but still left more of her uncovered than she was accustomed to. None of that had bothered her as she sunned. All of those wives and girlfriends wore suits much the same or even much less. She wondered just how pink they must be and some probably so in a lot more places than was she. After the shower, she dried off as well as she could, but the tenderness of the burn made it difficult. She heard Lewis say, "Lie on the bed, cover up, and I will come in and put some lotion on you. I have some that is really good. We use it when we play golf."

Aggie was a little uneasy as to how this was going to work out. They had made love several times, but this time it was as if she was about to be on display. In fact, this would be the very first time she had ever made love, and she assumed they would, with anyone other than in the dark or under the covers. She lay a dry towel on the unused bed. She was totally nude and had never begun an encounter with nothing on before. This was to be a first and did cause her to feel quite aroused. It made her blush at her own daring. Her mind raced as she tried to figure the best way to cover herself. She needed to feel seductive and appealing, but also wanted to leave some mystery for Lewis to uncover. *Fine line*, she thought. She finally decided to pull back the covers, put the towel down, then cover herself up with the sheet. She was back under the covers. She called out, "I'm ready. Come on in."

As soon as he came in, he moved the lower portion of the sheet away and gently began to apply the lotion to her legs. Next, he pulled it down a little from the top and applied lotion to her shoulders, and she realized just how ready she was. It was all she could do to keep her muscles from tightening at his every touch. She stayed silent, but she knew he could feel her body respond as he applied the cool lotion. It was just her back, but she felt bare. He applied the lotion there, then he covered her back up. His hands never touched a forbidden place, but she had begun to realize that she would not resist if they did.

Once he had finished her back, he lightly tapped her on the butt and said, "Roll over." Even that brief touch excited her. He held the sheet in a way that kept her covered as she turned. This time, as she looked into his eyes, they both knew where this was going and she was just fine with that. He must be as well, because he never hesitated. He applied lotion to every part of her that had been burned. He may have even extended that boundary a tiny bit. As he finished, he reached down to kiss her, as if to say, "We are done."

She put her hand to his lips and said, "No, first, you must swap places with me. It is my turn to rub your back like you rubbed mine." She had never said, much less done, anything that aggressive before. She could not believe she had said it but the prospect of her having this control of him seemed a fairy tale. "Once upon a time" became "this time." The guest bedroom bed was now well used. It was late afternoon.

The rest of the weekend followed that same pattern of adventure. Not an adventure of just passion but also an adventure of the exploration of love and closeness. By Sunday afternoon, just before one of the neighbor couples would drive her to the airport, Aggie and Lewis hugged for a long time, they kissed, and simply looked into each other's eyes as they parted. Not a single word needed to be said. Their eyes explained that this was the way it should be. He had finally caught the woman he had longed for all those years. She had become a grateful catch.

The plane ride home was a replay of the weekend's events. The memories were wonderful. The trip ended as she stepped into the car with Marylin, who was wearing her devious smile. "Okay," she said, "let me hear."

"I will," said Aggie, "but first you need to tell me all about your Friday night and the wine. You do remember our deal?"

"Oh my," Marylin said as she let out a breath. "It was wonderful. I can remember older ladies laughing as they told stories about their love life. They indicated that it got better with age. I did not believe it then, but I do now. I did play a little trick on Robert, though. I had heard Lisa talk about the way Viagra had perked up her and Johnathan's love life. I got her to have Johnathan give Robert one of those pills. I can tell you; it worked a long time, and in fact, several times. I am hoping he'll get a whole bottle. Now, it's your turn."

Aggie began, "Well it was kind of like a fairy tale. Everything you can imagine was easy. It was like a dream or a fantasy from a romance novel. This is one detail that is special. It was something I had never even thought about, but I must tell you." She went on to explain about the session with the lotion. Marylin listened intently to every word. When she let Aggie out at her home, Aggie knew she would get the same inquiries from Mama and Da, but she also knew her answers this time would provide a whole different set of details.

Marylin got home and was watching TV with Robert when she looked over at him and said, "By the way, I am going to lie out on the deck tomorrow. I have been needing some sun. How about bringing a bottle of sunburn lotion home just in case I get too much." He just nodded.

CHAPTER 19

CONSTRUCTION WORKERS

The construction out on Highway 53 was progressing. Aggie and Marylin did not go out too much as it was mostly heavy equipment and construction workers. In her usual way, Marylin said it well: "The only thing interesting out there right now is the workers with their shirts off." There was only about one year left before they would be done. Most of the buildings had been built and were now being finished inside. The most important thing ever to happen in this area's history was about to be complete. Every report the committee got was upbeat, and everything was on schedule. They would have their opening just as planned. It would work out well too, as Christmas decorations would make the whole thing magical. It would be several months before opening, but those lights would be the best advertisement available. Final plans for the grand opening would begin in about a month. Everyone needed to begin thinking about it. Everyone wondered if the president would come back.

APPROVAL

King Adjah was being well discussed at CIA headquarters in Langley. It was a very small group who was discussing him as only a handful of top staff knew what was going on in Nagorno-Karabakh.

It was more of an open conversation that had begun as to the need for an airport in the area near the Caspian Sea. All agreed that such an airport would provide a very strong deterrent to aggression from those "rogue countries" in the area. Also, it could be a vital asset in the war that was ramping up against terrorism. A small delegation was going to "attempt" an audience with King Adjah Renede of Nagorno-Karabakh to discuss the possibility that some of that country's land could be acquired to make such a project a reality.

All agreed that the king seemed to be open to such talks. His actions in the areas of humanitarian projects and human rights indicated a potential alignment with the U.S. This whole project would be framed as a joint effort to provide a much-needed air hub for that area, and the U.S. would require only a small area that it could utilize purely for transportation services. Agreement was close on a time and place for that event. This was a big deal and was high on the priority list. It would be a big win for the States if it could be pulled off.

ENGAGED

Things could not have been going better for Aggie and Lewis. Each visit seemed to cement them into an even closer relationship. They were a couple now. They had talked about marriage and agreed that a good time to make it formal would be in late summer when he was to retire. He had put the word out that he may have interest in starting another career. But a job was not the highest thing on his list. His retirement income was going to be more than some people made. He would have all the benefits that went with it. He also knew he would get any number of offers to be on boards of companies that did work with and for the government. He was just letting word get around that he was going to be available and open to opportunities. Also, he was an ordained minister and had a degree from UVA and from Union Presbyterian Seminary. Aggie and he both were well positioned financially. It would be a strong union from that point of view. From the perspective of love and compatibility, there would be none stronger. Storybook all the way.

THE CALL

One Sunday after the service, Aggie's preacher told Lewis that, if possible, he would like to chat with him that afternoon. Lewis agreed. They would meet and talk during the afternoon golf tournament on TV. It was just before March. After lunch with Aggie and her folks, Lewis walked to the minister's residence. The minister and his wife were waiting for Lewis. The wife got him a glass of tea and left the two of them to talk.

The local minister began, "Lewis, I have been approached by another church. They would like to offer me a call to take over as pastor of their church. It is not a better position, but it is my home. My wife and I have always wanted to return there. Many of our lifelong friends are still in the area. It would be like a dream if we could make that happen. I know you have unlimited potential as it relates to a job or as church pastor. I just wanted to make you aware. Even though it would require far less than your capabilities, this church could sure use someone like you. If you will, think about it and let me know if you have any interest in my presenting that option to our board. I plan to tell them about my call next week."

They both turned to the TV. "Looks like Davis is going to tie it up with a birdie," said Lewis. "He has certainly surprised everybody. This will be his first win." Davis birdied the hole, and, in the end, he won the tournament. It was fun to watch a young rookie win his first tournament. Lewis thanked the minister and his wife for the afternoon and took the short walk back to Aggie's.

Lewis shared the conversation with Aggie and was not surprised when she said that it was up to him. He questioned her further and finally did get her to agree she would like nothing better than to stay near home. That worked for him, as he had no family or place that he preferred more than this one. "I'm going to sleep on it and will talk with him again tomorrow. Also, I may ask the general what he thinks. He is a pretty smart guy. Besides, he will see it from my perspective, both of us having a military background. It is not much of a salary, but I have my retirement."

Aggie then responded, "Lewis, you have never questioned me about my finances. I think this presents the best opportunity for us to talk about them. My first husband, Gus…let me start again. Gus's family was quite well off. When his parents died, they left an estate that was worth over $7 million. That amount has grown significantly. Since Gus 3 died, all of that passed to me. Between the income those investments produce and the farms and some other rental properties, I have a very significant income. With all of that, I also own a nice house and one day that will be two. The bottom line is, that money is not mine. It is ours. Do not let money be a factor in any decision you make. We are fine." Lewis also had some other funds available so he knew money should play no part in their plans for the future.

Later that evening Lewis called General Hrabal and told him he would like to talk with him the next morning. The general suggested they meet at Nick's Diner. "How about 7:00?" the General followed. Lewis agreed that would work fine. Lewis could not help but chuckle as he thought about the 7:00 a.m. meeting time. That was typical for the military. *Guess I will carry those things now for the rest of my life too,* he thought to himself. *General Hrabal certainly does.*

He and the general got to the diner at about the same time. The general had just taken a seat at the table near the back. His regular spot. As he passed the waitress, Lewis told her, "Just coffee, black, please." They sat there a few minutes with no particular emphasis on any specific subject. Lewis then brought up the issue of the church possibility and explained the details. General Hrabal's association with G Johnson made him very aware of Aggie's financials. He knew enough to know that the salary he would make as a pastor should not be his decision-maker about whether or not he would like to take that job. He supported the concept. He was convinced that to become pastor of this church would be the most beneficial thing he could do for his future wife and for his new home. That is what made Lewis's decision.

Lewis stopped back by the church office on his walk home from the diner. The preacher was in and seemed quite excited that Lewis was stopping by. He already assumed that this quick response would indicate a positive one. He was right. The preacher breathed a sigh of relief as he was given the positive response. This made his having to tell his deacons that he was moving back to his home church much easier. He knew already that based on the acceptance of Captain Morgan in this community, he would be a welcome candidate to take his place. It all fit perfectly, the board agreed, and all that was left was a trial sermon for Captain Morgan.

A SERMON

Lewis had not been tasked with doing sermons for some time. In fact, hardly ever. The sermons he had done were onboard a ship in a hostile zone or in the worst of conditions in a faraway place. From his position, being the chaplain for the Joint Chiefs of Staff, he had done many opening prayers for events both large and small. He had loads of funeral experience. He had even done a few weddings. However, this type of sermon was not in his comfort zone. With that thought, he worked on it long and hard. The day came for his trial. Even though everyone knew who Captain Morgan was, the preacher gave an extensive review of Lewis's career to the congregation. General Hrabal sat on the front pew. The sermon would not be new to him. From his front porch, the general had heard it a number of times as Captain Morgan rehearsed it from his guest house quarters. Aggie had not heard it.

He rose and walked up to the pulpit. He did not wear his dress uniform but instead a blue suit. Just as he would have in his uniform, he stood tall and straight, his bright blue eyes enhanced by the blue suit. Aggie wondered if any of the other ladies there noticed those eyes. He preached about a life's path that had brought him to this point. He blended it into the path that each of them would travel. It was directed very much so at the younger members of this group. That was perfect, as the single thing that church needed was young people. Families with kids. The older group knew their congregation must be reinforced with a young and vibrant one so the church would not fade away. A group that would carry them into the future of the spiritual segment of the world that those same young people would soon inherit. Those listening that day saw and recognized that attribute he brought. All, with not a single exception, were sure he was the man for the job. He was accepted by a unanimous vote of the congregation.

After the service, a group from Aggie's Sunday School class approached her. It was both boys and girls and was, in fact, just about her whole group. One of the young girls spoke first. "Mrs. Aggie, we sure do think you are lucky. He is a nice man, and I can tell you, and all of us girls agree, that this is the first time we have really listened to a preacher and what he had to say. With those eyes, none of us could look away." Then one of the young men spoke up and said, "I don't get it about the eyes, but it is easy to listen to a guy who has been in a war." She smiled, because her question about who may be looking at those eyes was answered.

SPECIFICS

The good thing about all of this for Aggie and Lewis is that they seemed to be able to work together on almost everything that came up about their potential marriage. The wedding would take place in Aggie's church and would be on July 17. It would be a very small and private ceremony. Marylin would be matron of honor, and General Hrabal would be best man. Without question, she would like to make it possible for Marsha to be a part. The one extravagant thing they did agree on was that they wanted to take an extended honeymoon. General Hrabal had told Lewis that if they preferred not to travel, he could get the plantation home of Benard Leonard's located at the new USO site to serve as a honeymoon retreat for them. He was good friends with the owner. When Lewis mentioned that to Aggie, she was absolutely against it. She wanted to travel. That was okay with him. He had a number of places that he wanted to see, and now wanted her to see. Also, she wanted nothing more than to visit that statue located in a little village six clicks south and west of Nha Trang. He was fine with that as he felt no competition from those memories. Her love for him, as he knew, was unbounded. That would be their cornerstone.

HONEYMOON PLANS AND A WEDDING

It was just over two months before the wedding. First thing they did was to plan an itinerary for the honeymoon. Tickets were bought, and reservations were made for some of the nights. Part of the plan was to have a free and easy trip. No schedules to bind them. This would be a trip of a lifetime. It would be her first experience out of the country other than four days in the Bahamas. He had traveled extensively, and his experience made the plans work out just like what they both wanted. A chance to see some of the world and to enjoy each other without restrictions.

Marylin thought this was one of the most romantic things she ever heard of. She would certainly look forward to a play-by-play of everything they got to see and details about all they did. Aggie was a little more familiar with what Marylin wanted to know than was Lewis. Aggie shared none of that with Lewis. She wasn't hiding anything; some things are just best left unsaid.

Her current pastor would do the honors. She had known him for close to twenty years and felt very close to him. Mama and Da would sit on the front pew. A couple of Lewis's closest military buddies would serve as ushers and then stand with Lewis and General Hrabal. Marylin and Marsha would stand beside Aggie. A list began to grow about who should be invited. A small wedding was about to be big. It was all either one of them could do to hold it down. Each day, either Aggie or Lewis thought of someone who should be included. Finally, they agreed. There would be no invitations. The announcement would be made in the church, and put in the local paper and in the *Military Times*. That way, her friends nor his could say they had been overlooked.

It was made very clear that there were to be no gifts and that a reception would be no more than an afternoon gathering on the church grounds. It was the day of the wedding and no one expected such a crowd. His military associates, her friends, local and national USO committee members, and even those couples whose wives she had sunned with all came. The church was full, as were the church grounds. Somewhat unplanned, but carried out perfectly. A beautiful day, a beautiful bride, and a great crowd. By way of overdoing the refreshments for the afternoon on the grounds, Marylin had saved the day. She had enough for the large crowd and even some more. Marylin spotlighted her abilities as a planner.

CHAPTER 20

WORD GETS AROUND

A couple of the international papers that King Adjah read on a regular basis had picked up a picture of the event along with a short story. A wedding is something they would normally not have covered. However, when a member of the staff of the Joint Chiefs of the United States marries the widow of a decorated military hero, it becomes newsworthy. That accumulation of facts gave it international significance.

King Adjah knew the wedding was to take place. Nothing made him prouder than to see his beautiful mom with her new husband. On his mom's side were Marsha and Marylin. Beside her new husband was General Hrabal and two other soldiers Gus 3 did not know. He also did not know who in the world all those attendees were. He ached to see her. His heart was broken by the decision he had made to let her think he was no longer alive. He guessed she would be very angry when she found out. He knew he must do what was right for his country and others around the world. His father had done so and never had he heard a single person say a negative thing about his dad. If only he could have been in this picture. At that same moment, as Aggie looked at the photos, she thought to herself, *If only Gus 3 could have been in this picture.* At the same moment, all those miles apart, tears filled both their eyes and fell to the earth. It was on that earth that they were joined. Neither aware of that reunion.

SUNBURNED AGAIN

Captain Morgan and his new bride would be spending about a month in his apartment in Washington before the honeymoon. He would do all those things involved with "mustering out" and then could leave for what would be a number of months of travel. He would take over at the church the first of the year. Soon after that was about the same time that "Reach" would open. Robert was fine with Aggie's being gone for a few months. Marylin would take her place in the office for those months. That is, if he could stand it. Turned out she was pretty damn good at it. He was amazed at her abilities. He knew how smart she was but had no idea of her professionalism. She was really good at a lot of different stuff!

All the folks at the apartment, many of whom were at the wedding, could not have been more gracious to Aggie. Aggie developed what would be long-lasting friendships. Every Saturday that month she enjoyed the August sun from that rooftop deck. In fact, she turned it into a ritual. Her first words to Lewis as she would come in on Saturday after laying out with friends would be, "I think I am going to take a shower. I have a sunburn." He would always smile and respond, "Let me know when you are ready and I'll put some lotion on you." Neither thought that would ever get old. Hard to know which one enjoyed it the most.

His retirement was a big deal. There were receptions at the Pentagon and several at the homes of different members of the Joint Chiefs. His friends at the apartment building seemed to want to get together almost every night. The time was filled with parties, lots of food and drink, and three bottles of sunburn lotion. He signed out of his unit for his last time, and the trip of a lifetime was about to begin.

BON VOYAGE

They drove back to Aggie's mom and dad's house and left most of their stuff there. They were going to travel as lightly as possible. If they needed anything that they had not carried, they would just buy it. So far as a home to come back to or place to live, they would worry about that when they got back. Robert and Marylin would drive them to the airport the next morning. That night Mama and Da seemed to want to tell them something. At dinner, it was Mama who spoke first.

"We have something we would like for you to consider. This house holds wonderful memories. It has been in our family since Da and I built it in the late '40s, just after the war. It is our wish that it stays in the family. We are both at the age that makes it hard for us to keep it up. We need a little different lifestyle now. We have found a small cottage in the senior living center between here and Wilmington. We can move in there, and if either of us ever needs more care, they will provide it. It is a perfect place for folks our age. Some of our friends live there and love it. When you get back from your trip, we will have moved." Da made it known that he was in full agreement.

Mama continued, "It is our hope that you and Lewis will accept and use this house as our gift to you. Whatever you choose to do with it, it is yours. It has made a wonderful home for us and we know it could for you as well." Lewis and Aggie were both shocked. Where they were going to live had not been on their radar. This made things easy, and would provide a quick solution to that issue. Moving in the future would always be an option, but right now this was a wonderful gesture. Lewis could tell that Aggie was moved.

In a few minutes, he missed her but had an idea where she might be. He walked onto the front porch and stepped down the steps. He sat beside her on that bottom step. Her eyes were filled with tears. These were not tears about the house. These were the tears that flowed as she now understood that her family had reached this point. Soon it would be just she and Lewis. Thank God that she had him now.

Early the next morning, after tender goodbyes with her family, Aggie and Lewis joined Robert and Marylin in the Mercedes. Both had backpacks. That was their luggage for a two-month trip. Almost like teenagers off on an excellent adventure. Marylin pointed out that they were just not responsible to be going on a trip like this with so little luggage. Robert pulled in front of the airport and shook hands with Lewis as Marylin and Aggie embraced on the other side of the car. Marylin spoke into Aggie's ear and told her that her friendship was one of her life's greatest blessings and that she would miss her. "Please call as often as possible." She then handed Aggie a small book. Looking Aggie straight in the eye, she said, "This is a diary. I want to know everything, and I do mean everything."

Robert walked around and gave Aggie a great big old hug. "The best thing I ever did was hiring you. You must go and have fun. This will be your finest hour." He stepped back and looked at her with his usual "I got you" smirk, and he followed with, "Keep Marylin posted. I so enjoy reliving those adventures of yours." Aggie blushed and they parted.

NOTHING BUT A BACKPACK

The trip was going to be simple. Just two things mattered. First and foremost, it was a honeymoon. This was a time to be shared, a time to explore, and a time to learn all of the things that this new sanction could hold. Second, it was a time to share, a time to explore, and a time to learn all about places they had never been. Two things, totally different, but from an adventure point of view, just as glamorous and just as informative. Very much the same. They planned to do their very best to ensure both things were maximized.

The first leg would put them in London late that day. They had a room in centrally located Piccadilly. From there, all the places they wanted to see were close. They would take a train north to Scotland for a couple of days. He wanted to see the links at St. Andrews, and she wanted to see the gravesite that Greyfriars Bobby visited daily. They would then go south and west to Devon. There the two of them could sit in a thatched-roof pub and drink cider.

Then across the Channel into France. He must see Flanders Fields and the beaches at Normandy, and she had always wanted to visit the Eiffel Tower and the Musée Marmottan Monet to gaze at the Water Lilies.

Then it would be through the south of France to Spain. By boat to Palermo and then a ferry to the Amalfi coast of Italy, on to Rome and the ruins, then to Venice for a gondola ride, at night, on the canals. She wanted to do it at night so they could make out. Through the Alps into Switzerland where they would snow ski. That would be new for her, but Lewis knew she could do it and she was certainly willing to try. They would then travel into Germany. They would enjoy some of the famous German beer. It would be a sad sight, but both wanted to visit Auschwitz. Norway and Denmark maybe, but a train ride across several of the other countries in Europe for sure. They would end up in St. Petersburg, Russia, to enjoy the art and the vodka before boarding another plane to Manila.

From Manila it would be a quick flight to Vietnam to that small town near the coast. That would be the highlight of the trip. The monument erected to her Gus in that town would be the crown of her tour.

When they landed on the airstrip in Nha Trang, they got a room on the beach. The location was quiet and beautiful. The sand was white and clean, and the palm trees swayed ever so slightly overhead. It was as if they were nature's umbrellas keeping those beaches shaded and cool. It was much like a picture of a tropical paradise on a postcard. Using the hotel concierge, they made contact with a cab driver who could speak English and seemed to know exactly where they wanted to go. He would act as a guide and an interpreter. They chatted with him and from that conversation trusted him. He told them to just call him "Tobby."

He, just like Lewis, had blue eyes. Tobby told Lewis and Aggie that he was the son of some American soldier who had served here during the war. Many of those his age had that same appearance. When Lewis and Aggie asked Tobby about his experiences growing up, he admitted that the offspring of foreign soldiers were never really accepted by their own people. They were living reminders of the war and Southeast Asia's many casualties. Later, Aggie and Lewis discussed what Tobby had said. Aggie commented to Lewis that although the war had been over for many years, its tragedy was still being felt by people around the world: family members like her who had lost a loved one, the children of soldiers like Tobby, and so many others.

The next morning Tobby was waiting outside their hotel just as he said he would be. The trip down was to take only about an hour. "It only about five or six miles in U.S. measure," he said in broken English. It was a pretty ride down the coast and then a very short distance inland. They were soon at the entrance of the small village, which was easily identifiable to them as there was a monument as they entered through a wooden gate.

The structure was no more than a portion of the burned helicopter that had been embedded into a concrete base. The concrete statue of a man reaching out of the wrecked chopper stood intact. Tobby parked the car close by and they walked over. Lewis had to take Aggie's arm as they took those steps. For the first time in many years, she was about to sob and was having a hard time maintaining her composure. She had not felt this much pain since she had lost her son. Now standing within inches of where her Gus had actually died, she could almost see and touch him. Lewis was also emotional. Anything that caused his Aggie pain hurt him as well.

THE PAST, FOR BETTER OR WORSE, IS STILL THE PAST

They stood there a long time. After a while, Tobby walked up to them and told them that he had a found a lady who remembered the crash. "She say she will talk about with you. I go and tell you what she say." The lady was sitting on a chair outside a small block house. The house had no windows, only a door. An old man sat beside her. He looked directly at them as they walked up. His small dark eyes were haunting.

When they stepped in front of the couple, Lewis stuck out his hand to the lady and smiled as he said, "Chuc ngay tot lanh."

She looked wide eyed at him and responded, "Hello, soldier."

They had both used the total of their vocabulary of each other's language.

Aggie spoke and did so while looking straight at her. "I was the wife of the sailor on the helicopter." She pointed at the monument.

Tobby told her what Aggie had said and she responded, "So sorry."

Tobby continued to translate. "Can you tell me what happened?"

"He reach for her to help. Helicopter go boom."

"Do you know why it went boom?"

"Was be girl."

"What do you mean girl?"

The old lady then spilled off a long answer. Tobby looked at Aggie and said, "No tell."

"What do you mean no tell? I want to know what she said."

Tobby looked at Lewis as if to find relief. Lewis responded. "We have traveled many miles and this lady would like to know the truth about how her husband died."

Tobby seemed to shrink as he began repeating the story he had just heard. "Soldiers have girl's mama in hut. She and girl been used bad many times by soldiers. Girl and mama free if she throw heavy ball in chopper. She and mama want go home. She not know it would boom. Boom kill her then soldiers kill her mama too. It was no good day."

Aggie looked a few moments at this woman. She had probably seen so much horror during that war. She undoubtedly experienced it as well. Now all she had left was this block hut and memories. This woman could well have been one of the last people to see her Gus alive. With all the strength Aggie could muster, she bent over and kissed the lady on the forehead. She placed an envelope with twenty $100 bills in her hand as she reached and touched the old man sitting next to her. As she touched him, he looked up and without a spoken word, his eyes told her he also knew the pain of that horror.

Not another word was spoken as she turned and walked back to Tobby's car. Lewis found no words. He just joined her as they rode silently back to the motel. She looked over her shoulder as they drove away for one last glance at that spot. Finally, she looked at Lewis and said, "Thank God you were never in that war. I cannot stand the thought of what my life would be without at least one of you."

They lay on the beach in front of the hotel the rest of that day and said little. The next morning, Tobby carried them to their early flight. Through the reliving of a horror, he had become their friend. They paid him well. Lewis gave him his card and told him that if he ever came to America, he should contact him.

They boarded a flight back to Manila and would then fly on to Australia where Lewis was going to fish on the Great Barrier Reef. While he fished, Aggie would sun on the shores of Cairns. If they were lucky, she may need to have some sunburn lotion applied after that. Trout fishing in New Zealand and then back to Hawaii for a few days prior to returning to the mainland. They would stop in San Francisco and then on to Lake Tahoe where they would ski again.

The Glacier National Park was a must-see. It was in Glacier National Park that they confirmed there was no more beautiful place in the world than that spot. One of their must-do adventures included traveling by car north to a place near the Canadian border called Polebridge. It was not really a town, but a collection of about ten buildings. One of them was the restaurant. It was in that small community that they enjoyed one of their best meals. That meal and that place registered high on their "must-do-again" list. From there they traveled by rental car diagonally across the United States, stopping often. The last of the planned destinations was New Orleans. From there they would drive home. Aggie and Lewis had traveled around the world and brought home with them the dream of doing it again.

Marylin had followed them closely. Postcards told her where Aggie and Lewis were and where they were going next. Infrequent phone calls kept her abreast as well. Marylin still could not understand how anyone would even attempt to make a trip like this with just a backpack. She did understand the hint when, during a phone call, Aggie described lying on the beach at Cairns. Then she whispered, "I got a sunburn today." Marylin quickly responded with, "Careful not to fall in a creek." Lewis was nearby and overheard Marylin's response. When Aggie's conversation was over, he told his wife that he did not understand what Marylin had meant.

Aggie quickly responded, "Me neither."

CHAPTER 21

BACK

The next few weeks were full of getting their feet back on the ground. It was a little hard to get landed back in real life. The trip had been everything they had hoped. Already, they were planning to do it again. Mama and Da had moved into their new cottage and were doing wonderfully. Friends had already established them as part of their new community. Seemed that group was nothing less than a bunch of social butterflies, constantly moving and busy. They were happy, and that made Aggie happy. When Aggie was happy, Lewis was happy. It all flowed.

They were moving furniture around and setting up the house in a way that suited their younger lifestyle. Plenty of room in this house. Da had kept it up in a way that would meet any standard. He was an excellent carpenter and loved doing that kind of work. He had made sure the house was very livable and very secure. They were soon settled in. Aggie visited Mama and Da almost every day. Lewis had already started giving a helping hand with everything going on with the church. Every time he would become involved with an activity, he seemed to beam. He loved doing those church duties, and each one he did further confirmed that his decision to lead this congregation was the right one. Aggie was wide open catching up at Robert's office.

6,000 MILES EAST

A special group of United States leaders would be arriving in Nagorno-Karabakh in a couple of days for a meeting with the king. It was to discuss some possibilities that could really help King Adjah's country. He had assembled a group of his fellow countrymen and women whom he felt could have major positive input into such a discussion. All of his people were aware of this meeting as it was in keeping with his promise of absolute transparency. Local reporters would be allowed to observe and report on those meetings.

The group from the U.S. had landed at the airport in Antalya, Turkey. They would then board smaller aircraft for a short jaunt to the king's country. Only small dirt strips were available for air travel in his country. That was the heart of this trip.

Many of the formalities of handshaking and backpatting were photographed before the meeting could begin. Everyone was smiling and seemed very happy to be part of such an undertaking. The king started the meeting with a welcome to his American guests. Introductions were then made of those in attendance, and each would stand for all to see. All had name tags, and name plates marked each spot. There was an electronic interpreting device so that everyone could understand those words spoken from either side of the table. The king wore one just in case he had lost any of his English language abilities. It was all presented as 100 percent proper.

After some haggling over a few major issues, an agreement in principle was made. All on both sides seemed to agree. The United States would put up the dollars required to build an airport of international standards. In exchange they would get an adjacent area for the purposes of maintaining a small air force base and communications center. For the U.S., the location was perfect. For King Adjah's country it was a good move. All loans for the previous upgrades to his land from the U.S. were forgiven. This new adventure would provide many jobs both in the building and in the maintaining and running of this new airport. It was a win for both countries.

The details would be worked out by a panel representing both countries and then presented for signing the next month. It was during this month that some other plans must also be made. Just as in the case of inserting Cadet Johnson as King Renede's heir, he must now be removed. His mission was done.

SIGN AND GO

Just over a month later, a ceremony for a document signing was put into the planning stages. It would be formal, and it would be a significant event. The signing would take place in King Adjah Renede's palace. He had an area designed for such an event. A group of U.S. leaders including the secretary of state attended the ceremony. It was he who signed the document on behalf of the United States. King Adjah kept his assistant in the middle of all things having to do with this ceremony. On the day of the signing, the king praised the young man. He stated, "Jubada Hermana has been an important part of these negotiations. Without him, we would not have been able to proceed as we have to achieve this end." The U.S. delegation also praised Jubada as an outstanding diplomat with unmeasurable potential. At King Adjah's selection, Jubada was the king's primary assistant. He was intelligent and loved his country. It was all things that were in his country's best interest that motivated him.

The signing was done. News went out all over the world as to this new alliance. A number of countries raised concerns over the new agreement, and a couple even strongly opposed it. Too late. It was done and would now proceed. Many of those who would oppose had been taken by surprise.

A few weeks after signing, King Adjah made a decision that he would like to get away for a few days. He needed a break and would enjoy going to one of his favorite spots in Switzerland for a short ski trip. His adventure was planned. He would leave on Tuesday and travel on his country's only plane to Ankara, Turkey, and then by Swissair to Zurich. From there it would be a car ride to a favorite resort. It was one with few people and long and uncrowded ski trails. He and one of his staff members who was also a skiing buddy were the only two going on the trip. It was all kept very low-key and private.

They arrived late in the afternoon on a Tuesday. They skied a little that night but saved the long slopes for the following days. The next day, which was day two, they both skied most of the day. The weather and the snow were perfect. A new layer had recently fallen, and the trails were covered with a fresh powder that made skiing a pleasure. More snow was forecast for that night as well. Conditions would be just as good the next day. On the third day, the king arose early and hit the slopes alone. He left a note for his skiing partner that he was going to ski slope three early before anyone else had a chance to do so. The time alone would give him a good opportunity to begin plans for the future.

It was a perfect morning as the sun rose between the mountains behind him. The trail was over six miles long. After he traveled about a mile, he came upon an area of trees he must ski through. He was following a plan that he had received through a coded message in his country's only newspaper. He saw two men standing on the edge of the slope in those trees. One of them wore a red toboggan. That made him easy to spot. The king stopped as he came alongside where they were. He spoke. One of the two then posed a question: "How is the snow?"

The king responded, "Near perfect on the part I have skied. How is it where you have skied?"

One of those two responded, "Near perfect; you can fly on it." The code had been submitted and responses were correct.

He just nodded that he was their man, and they instructed him to follow them. He did so and they skied down a side trail to an opening about a quarter of a mile away. There they were met by another young man on a snowmobile. He had a second of the machines with him. The king was instructed to put on a set of coveralls and a helmet. He did so and then followed the first machine for about two miles. They went around the edge of a mountain to a small valley between two mountains that was not part of the ski area. A helicopter was waiting. He got aboard. The pilot said little but did instruct him to hook up his seatbelt and to put on his headset. The pilot then asked him if he had ever been on a chopper before. He indicated that he had not. The pilot told him the flight would be short. It would be only about 45 minutes. The pilot maneuvered between the mountain tops as they traveled. He did so to avoid any populated areas or possible sightings.

In a small building in the Midwest of the United States, a young female air force officer saw a message appear on her computer screen. Neither she nor her associate would ever have any knowledge of what they were doing or why. They just followed instructions and looked at their monitors. The screen flickered as the following words appeared, "Lift off confirmed." She then forwarded that message to another address who then responded with "Mission confirm." She reached over and tapped the airman next to her and gave a simple one-word order, "Execute." The airman pushed a button on his keyboard. Within a second, a missile no larger than a child's toy was released and pierced deeply into a snowbank before exploding. An avalanche was triggered and swooped down slope three. No one on that slope could have survived and it was probable that no bodies would ever be found. It was a six-mile-long drift and more than thirty feet deep. That morning, the beloved young king of Nagorno-Karabakh had been killed in a horrific ski accident.

The tragedy was soon discussed at the palace in Nagorno-Karabakh. King Adjah was mourned and would be missed. Many tears fell as the country learned of that loss. Jubada Hermana was to take the place as temporary ruler and would surely have no opposition in becoming King Adjah's replacement. The plan had come full circle.

HOME AGAIN

The helicopter ride finished at a small airstrip somewhere. Trip assumed he was still in Switzerland but was not sure. Wherever he was, he could see snow-covered mountains, and it was cold. A military cargo plane was waiting within a few feet of where the helicopter landed. The engines were running and the back ramp folded down so his entry could be quick. He was out of the chopper and into the plane in a hurry. Once inside, it was only he and the two pilots on board. One of them led him to the small passenger area of the plane, stuck out his hand, and stated, "Welcome aboard, sir." Trip acknowledged his welcome and then asked, "What now?" The pilot indicated that in the box on one of the four seats was a suit of clothes for him to change into. The flight would take about ten hours and for him just to relax and enjoy. There was a copy of the *Washington Post* and *USA Today* and some magazines for him to read. He showed Trip a fold-down cot that would serve for sleep. A blanket and pillow were overhead. The pilot ended with, "Again, welcome aboard, and I will see you when we land. If you need anything, just walk through this door to the cockpit."

He ate a few of the onboard snacks, drank a soft drink, and read part of the *USA Today*. Soon he was about to doze, so he pulled down the bed and pillow, covered with the blanket, and was then asleep.

Next thing he knew he was being awakened by that same pilot who had instructed him earlier. Now he was telling him that they would be landing in about ten minutes. Trip asked where they were, and the pilot simply replied, "Sir, all I can tell you is that you are safe and you are home." When they landed, it was dark. The plane taxied into an open hanger. The door shut behind them. There was a sedan with a driver waiting inside. When he got off the plane, the driver of that sedan led him to it and opened the back door for him. The driver went around and got into the car and told Trip that they would now have about a one-hour drive. Trip had no idea where he was.

They pulled out of the hangar and left the airport. It was not a large airport, and he still had no idea where he might be. He questioned the driver, who informed him that they were headed to a small farmhouse a few miles south of Silver Spring, Maryland. It was a safe house, and he would be there for no more than a couple of days. He could tell from the clock on the car dash that it was just after midnight. A lot had happened on this day.

CHAPTER 22

OPENING REACH

Over two years of hard work and planning was about to become a finished product. It was all that could have been hoped for. The interest in the facility had been unprecedented. The only thing the committee may have done wrong was to underestimate just how popular it would be. Based on advance reservations, there were already discussions about making the parking lot larger. So far, the buses could handle most of the crowd. The various motels and hotels in the area would provide shuttles from their facilities. The parking would be to accommodate day visitors. Mostly those with small children being brought to enjoy the water parks and the other amenities provided for the younger attendees. Like the advertisements indicated, "This place has something for everyone!"

The new general manager of the facility had been on-site for a couple of months. He had a great deal of expertise in these matters. He had been involved in the opening of the Disneyland Park in Paris. He was there when it opened in '92. His experience made him a perfect candidate for the job. The opening had been designed to bring in as many families of deceased military members and as many disabled vets and their families as could be. It was for everyone, but this time, those who had paid such a sacrifice would get first dibs. There was not one single activity in the entire facility that did not have disabled usage capabilities.

The date of the opening came and passed just as all hoped it would. The committee had decided that keeping this opening low-key would allow the best accommodation for those guests. They were right. You could tell by the smiles and laughter at the park that all were having fun. The most important of all measures for this place was the reactions of those guests as they were leaving. Watching their faces provided assurance that they had enjoyed a wonderful experience, one that they appreciated. It was a very small payment for the sacrifice they had made for this country.

A Vietnam vet had walked with his twelve- and thirteen-year-old sons and fifteen-year-old daughter to the area of the main gate. He knew that the bus would pick them up there so the walk would only have to be one way. He and his children had all had a wonderful day. It had been spent in the pool and recreation area, and then on the fishing dock. They were able to catch a number of fish and then enjoy the adventure of having to take them off the hook and put them back in the water. It was fun to watch as the daughter had no problem baiting the hooks with worms or crickets, but the younger sons did not want to touch them. By the end of the fishing adventure, they had learned from their sister that worms would not hurt them. It was a lesson that they could pass on to their sons and daughters. Reach was just that kind of place; they would want to come back and enjoy it again. When they got to the front gate, the veteran walked right up to the statue of the petty officer reaching down to help someone in distress. For a couple of minutes, he did not say a word. He just looked at it. Then he talked to his three children about how he had done that same thing. He had been a medic on a helicopter during the Vietnam War and had done many such evacuations. He explained to them that he had been lucky. It could just as easily have been him that this had happened to. He told them about how they were also lucky. If it had been him, they would not be here.

In an obviously broken voice, he spoke directly to them and said, "Promise to bring my grandchildren to this place and show them this statue. Tell them this is what their grandfather did. Tell them that your dad did not know why he was chosen to live while Gus Johnson died. Tell them that the greatest honor of my life was to serve my country. No matter what the history books may report, the men and women who fought alongside me were all American heroes. That is what I want them to know about me and my many friends who died or suffered in that war."

The younger son spoke up and said, "I promise I will tell them, Dad. I am glad it was not you." One of the shuttle busses stopped, the side door opened, and that group ended a special day.

Life had changed in the small town just fifteen minutes down the road from Reach. Those people who had been the vital link in making it all possible were doing everything they could to keep their hometown much as it had always been. No doubt that the jobs and dollars provided by this undertaking were welcome. So were those efforts made to keep their hometown's personality. The bridge clubs, churches, golf outings, and back-table meetings at the diner were still very much a part of this good town year-round.

Mrs. Osgood still kept a keen eye open for any activities she felt may need to be addressed. Her reports would make their way around town just as quickly as had the one about Aggie and the soldier in the Jeep.

Chuck Greely had been in several times over the last year as he was continuously looking for sites for new business facilities. He always made it a point to drop by Robert's office to speak. He would also sit and chat with Aggie. The conversations were always about current goings-on and the like. Neither he nor Aggie ever made any comment about that night at the playhouse. Aggie wondered if he even thought about it when they talked. She sure did. She had an idea that he probably did too. That encounter had been a special one in her life and she had no regrets about it, and she hoped that he didn't either. It happened at the right time and in the right place. It had turned out to be as good a night as she had ever spent. Just as good was the absence of any conversation or mention of it having taken place. That was a memory that would forever remain a memory.

Marylin and Robert had taken a long vacation and left his practice for Aggie to run, and she had no problem doing so. His clients trusted her as much as they did Robert. He and Marylin traveled to the many places around this country that they had always wanted to see. Marylin had done most of the planning. There was no surprise that spots like Niagara Falls, the Poconos, Key West, Martha's Vineyard, Las Vegas, and others were her go-to favorites. Her mind was forever on romantic and exciting adventures. Robert loved each of them and was eager to take part in all her various plans. They would be coming home in a couple of weeks.

Aggie and Lewis could not have been better. They were both enjoying every minute they shared. He had undertaken the task of visiting every member of their church during the last few months. The members loved him, and he was always welcome in their homes. He would always ask those older members if he could do something for them that they may not be able to do for themselves. Most often they would need a lightbulb changed or a leaky faucet fixed. He did it all and loved every minute of it. A younger group had begun to attend church as well. It seemed that Lewis appealed to them. He and his wife were the perfect pair to anchor this congregation in their path toward redemption.

Most of all, he cherished every moment he got to spend with his new bride. He and Aggie were still enjoying the honeymoon portion of their new life together. One thing he was excited about was that spring was just around the corner. That meant sunburn would soon be a matter that needed attention. Aggie felt the same way. Sometimes, though, she embarrassed herself. She felt a little guilty about the excitement she felt each time Lewis would take her into his arms. She enjoyed the wonder of what this time may provide. The things she was still learning and the experiences she was enjoying about her own sexuality were many. She had missed over twenty years of those encounters, but was making every effort to catch up. So far so good. It did not seem to hold either of them back that he was a preacher and she was a Sunday School teacher.

There was one thing in her life that seemed to always give her heart a tug. It was that bottom step, the one just outside the bright light on the porch. It was that step that provided the very best of all she could remember, but at the same time reminded her of those two loves she lost. She could still see Gus as he looked into her eyes and asked if he could call. She remembered about her mom telling the story of how Gus 3 wanted to be a hero. How she had cried on that step when she realized her mom and dad were now in their last years. How she had watched in absolute glee as Gus 3 had taken his first steps and they had been toward her. The talks she and Lewis had shared sitting there, and how he had looked into her eyes and then kissed her on the cheek that first date they had. It was on that step that she had asked her son to accompany her to the Christmas dance at the club. That last dance was one of her life's fondest memories. It was a wondrous place, and it was hers. The only thing she could wish to be different would be the ability to hold Gus 3 in her arms and tell him how much she missed him. Maybe he knew.

CHAPTER 23

THE FUTURE

Just over 350 miles due north Trip sat in a safe house in Silver Spring, Maryland. He had caught up on his sleep, been given an entire wardrobe of new clothes, and had indulged in his favorite meals. He wasn't sure how his host knew so much about what clothes he would like or what food he preferred. Seemed they knew him better than he knew himself. The couple he was staying with were just good people. They did not seem to know anything other than what it took to make him happy. He had heard of these safe houses before, but this was his first time in one. He could get accustomed to it. He thought about that restaurant in Wilmington where he and Marsha had enjoyed that high-dollar meal. How he had thought he could get used to eating that kind of food every day. It was a lifetime ago. He wondered about her and how she was. He did not even know where she lived or what she did. He also had a lot of questions he needed to ask about his mom and Mama and Da. He knew that generally they were okay, but he needed details. He also had questions about his mom's new husband. Most of all, he thought about how he would love to give his mom a big hug and tell her how much he missed her. Maybe she knew.

The next morning would be Friday, and he was told he should pack his bag and be ready for a car to pick him up about 8:00. When 8:00 came, he was ready to go. He had no idea who had been his host, but he gave the lady a hug and then shook the man's hand as he told them thank-you and what a great place they had provided for him. They both seemed to appreciate the gratitude. They did not usually get that much from their "guests." There was a knock at the door, and his car was there. Once out the door, he realized it was not a car at all; it was a pickup. That really did make him feel at home.

It was only about fifteen miles to the CIA headquarters at Langley. Just as at Fort Belvoir, they had little trouble getting into the area of the building. Getting into the building proved more of a task. Trip was made to take off his belt, his shoes, and empty his pockets. He had not realized it until that minute as he looked at it, but there was a wallet in his pocket with an ID and driver's license and a gold American Express. It also held an amount of cash; he could tell it was a good amount. He put it into the little tray and ran it through the machine along with his shoes and belt. He then walked into the arch where he was told to stand with his arms above his head. He could hear the whir of an X-ray machine as he was scanned for the presence of anything other than his own body. Once inside, another young man met him and escorted him down the hall and into an elevator.

When the elevator began moving, Trip could feel that he was descending. Soon he was in a conference room with about twelve others. When he came in, all of them clapped and got up and shook his hand. They were congratulating him on a job well done. He got pats on the back and what seemed to be some very sincere thanks. He recognized only two of them. It was the same two who had done the talking at his last meeting. That meeting where he had agreed to the mission that had consumed him for these three-plus years.

REVIEW TIME

The conversation with that group was very general. It was obvious that they all knew various details about those previous plans but there was little to no discussion about its total purpose. After about thirty minutes of an exchange of them asking him and then each other general questions about the mission, the meeting broke up. Trip was left with the same two men he had negotiated with those years ago. They chatted for just a minute and then told him that they knew he would have some questions for them. They indicated that they had a video prepared that would answer many of his inquiries and thought it would be best to look at it first. He did not disagree so the video began.

It began with his funeral. He was able to see who was present and the service. One of the two guys had a remote he could use to stop the video. During the funeral, he did stop it and said in an almost laughing way, "I bet you didn't know just how many people would be affected by your death." It was a compliment, but still a little crass in the way it was stated. The video moved on. It was stopped again, and Captain Morgan in his civilian clothes was pointed out. Trip was told that by the time of the funeral, Captain Morgan had been selected to be the one who was assigned to assure the well-being of his mom. It was for a reason.

After that he saw a short clip of when his Da had fallen in the backyard and the surveillance system was explained to him. He was assured that no person's eye had ever seen anything that would be embarrassing to anyone. He saw scenes of the building of Reach, saw how a statue of his dad was at the entrance, and how the president of the U.S. had read his dad's story at the ribbon cutting of that event. It was the first time he had ever heard that story. He saw videos of his Mama and Da at their new cottage home. He watched his mom's wedding and snaps of the honeymoon. He saw from a distant vantage point his mom talking with the old Vietnamese lady in the village where his dad had been killed. The video was informative, but he still had many questions. The most important thing he learned from the video was an assurance that his mom was being looked after.

The same man with the video remote then said, "Now, we will get more personal. I am Charles Hersey, and this gentleman is Victor Hawburg. We have been the primary handlers of your mission. We are stationed here at Langley. We are what is referred to as your 'inside contact associates.' We are more commonly referred to as 'ICAs.' For the last four years, we have been the ICAs assigned to M302. That identifies you. Our time is your time, and we imagine that you have a number of questions for us; you can start whenever you are ready. If you think of something later that you may have missed, feel free to ask anything you would like to know. Before you start, it is important for me to tell you that you are referred to here as 'Gus.' Just plain 'Gus.' That is the name we feel keeps your identity most undercover. We encourage that so long as you are part of this company you stay with that name. Most of the agents here do not use their correct last name. A check of the ID in your billfold will indicate that in the eye of this organization you are Gus Felding."

Trip had lots of questions. He would start asking now, but knew more things would come to mind later. He began, "Tell me about my mom…Is she happy? Who is this guy she has married? If he is your agent, then is he taking advantage of her by marrying her? Is her health good?"

Agent Hawburg responded, "Yes, she is very happy. The only real negative in her life now is having lost you. Captain Lewis Morgan was the chaplain on the Joint Chiefs staff. He was picked because he had knowledge of your mom. He was the chaplain who had been assigned to her case when your dad was killed. She was his first case. All indications from those interviewed were that he had very sincere feelings for her and had kept them through the years. We felt that he was the obvious selection for the purposes of keeping a close watch on her. He was told that his assignment in watching her was based on a secret mission your father was involved with. And the company was watching to ensure she had no knowledge of that mission. That was for her own protection. We knew there was a possibility that he may in fact attempt to begin a relationship with her. We also knew that she had no other men in her life and was probably ready to develop a lasting relationship as well. We put them into this box, and it worked out for the very best. Their love is sincere and mutual. A happy couple indeed. We got that one right.

"So far as her health, she receives regular physicals and is in excellent health. All in all, your mom is running at 100 percent. Minus only you.

"As to how her new husband goes, he is an outstanding man. You could not have picked a better companion for her. He does not know that you are alive. Also, we feel that since he and she have developed this relationship, he will never risk telling her she was an assignment. That would probably cause a rift in their relationship. He does not want that. Nor does she.

"Your mom continues to work for Robert Neece and has become extremely close with his wife, Marylin. Both your mom and Captain Morgan have many friends. He is now the pastor of your church. It has come to a point in their relationship and your knowledge of that relationship that we feel it may be okay to release him from his duties as a 'caretaker.' He is now her keeper based on love. The company no longer needs to be involved. It is up to you to make that call. We advise you to make that choice because the longer he remains assigned to your mom by the company the greater the possibility of her finding out about his association with us. That would not serve him or their relationship well.

"Your grandparents are doing well and living in a senior living center near Wilmington. Both of them are enjoying good health for their ages and enjoy their life in that center. They are, in fact, quite the social trendsetters among their group of friends."

Trip then asked about Marsha and General Hrabal, two of his closest friends. Agent Hersey spoke up and stated, "I am the guy to go there. General Hrabal is doing well and living in his same home. He and his wife are older, but still very active. He still plays golf on Saturdays, and, in fact, Captain Morgan plays with that group.

"So far as Marsha, and we knew this would be an important topic for you, she is also doing well. In fact, it goes beyond that. When you were investigated to determine if you would be a suitable subject to work as an agent, she was vetted pretty well. From what we could learn about her, it was determined that she also had many of the qualities we looked for as attributes in that agent role. She passed the muster and was seduced into applying for work with the CIA after her schooling. She is now an operative just like you. She has no idea that you are an agent or that you are alive, but you could be allowed to meet with her at some future date if you so desire and if it provides any potential for the company. In other words, there is a possibility that the two of you could work together."

Trip really could not think of any questions right that minute, but figured he would have plenty more later. He did!

WHAT NOW

After all of that discussion, some other general and incidental factual issues were discussed. It was decided to begin again the next day. Trip was told he would be staying in the agents' suite there at Langley. No need to get out in public and risk being seen. There were a couple of other agents staying in the same area whom he would probably get to meet. It was best to stay on a first-name-only basis. The other agents may have the same anonymity concerns as he. They would share a common dining room and dinner would be at 7:00 p.m.

His bags had been carried to his room, and he was not sure whether he should unpack them or not. So far, he had no idea what was next other than his ability to make a decision about where his life would go from here. It would be the processing of the details that made his decision a reality that would be complicated. It was that process that would take time. He decided that for the next few nights, he would just live out of his suitcase. As he emptied his pockets, he checked his wallet and did find that his new identity was in fact Gus Felding. His cards and his passport also confirmed that new identity. He wondered, *Just where do they come up with this stuff?*

Just before 7:00, he found his way into the dining area. He was the last of four to come in and introduced himself to the others as Gus. There was one older gentleman who gave his name as Wayne. Another was a woman of about forty. She had a British accent and was very attractive. She was to be called Georgie. The third was a guy just a little older than Trip. His name was James. The first thing Trip did was smile when he heard the name James. James could see it in his eyes and knew exactly what he was thinking. He got this all the time. He quickly said, "No, it is not 'James Bond.'"

After an excellent meal, they were all in agreement they would like to watch a movie. They told the attendant to just pick out something new. The area for the movie was much like a luxury movie room in some high-end home. It had leather recliners and a large screen. There was a bar with everything from popcorn to Bemka beluga caviar. Every sort of soft drink, wine, or alcohol was there.

"This whole thing is pretty damn first class," James stated. Both Wayne and Georgie chimed in that they had stayed here a number of times before and it was indeed very first class.

"After the movie, if you want a massage, you can just buzz from your room. Same is true if you want something to eat or drink. Better than any hotel around here," followed Wayne.

The movie began and the attendant had picked one that was a brand-new 1996 release. It may have been a joke by him, but the movie was good. A bit like a busman's holiday. It was *Mission Impossible*. They watched, exchanged ideas as to how it could have been better, and generally enjoyed their time together. None of them had any idea if they would ever see each other again. That was the nature of this life that they had chosen. Trip was the only one of them who had not yet made that choice.

As he waited for sleep, his thoughts were that it had been a good night. He had enjoyed his new friends, if he could call them that. He guessed he could; it was easy to see how the group of them could become the very closest of friends in another place. Or, he wondered, if it was only this time and place, this circumstance, that led them to this friendship.

In the morning there was a knock on the door and he was instructed that breakfast would be on the table in about twenty minutes. He enjoyed chatting with the three of them again. Soon, four young attendants came into the room and indicated that each of them would all be going in a different direction. Wayne spoke up and said, "Guys, don't say goodbye. That's bad luck. We will meet again." They all seemed to understand, and with little more than a nod of the head, went their separate ways.

Trip was taken to the same meeting room as the day before, but with more people. Four other agents were present. Agent Hersey spoke and said, "Gus, time to make some choices. Depending on what we decide here this morning, we will introduce you to two of these individuals. Please understand that we are not trying to hide anything from you. It is just best that any information any of us carry from here is held to the absolute minimum. Same is true with names. Now, before you are given the floor, you will need some additional information. I will give you some details that should help you in your choice. At the time you began your training, a piece of land was purchased in your name in an area in south France near the city of Marseille. A few weeks ago, it was sold, and you made quite a profit. In fact, over some $3 million profit. The monies have been placed in a numbered account that only you can access. The access information for that account is in the envelope laying in front of you. The taxes have been paid, and those funds are yours, free and clear. We also know that you have a significant inheritance from your grandfather. Your mom has done well with it, and you will suffer no loss with that if it is left in a way that does not flow directly to you. Regardless of your choice today, that money is yours. It serves to repay you for the sacrifice you have made. Now, you must decide."

"All of my options are good ones. I can be very happy within the confines of whatever I may choose," Trip stated aloud and then his mind weighed what would be his future. Trip continued speaking, "My greatest wish was to be with my mom. I do feel, though, that it could cause some issues with anger and trust. The only good thing about that specific issue is that the only person she could be mad with would be me." He knew she would get over that. "Also, she would want to know that I am alive, but that single fact would change her entire life. Her happy life.

"Second, I would love to rejoin the corps of cadets at the Point and complete my education. But with that, I would have to overcome being 'out of place.' The fact that I would be with an entirely different group of cadets would make it easier as none of them would have any knowledge of my death.

"I also like the idea of becoming a captain in the regular army, but wonder how I would be accepted among my peers. My rank would seem to them to be basically unearned. With that option, it would be easy for you to create a history that showed an ascension to that rank.

"The option of becoming an agent also has appeal, but I was bothered when I learned that the young man I had replaced as a future king had been terminated. I wondered how I would handle such an issue in the future, especially if it was me who had to be the terminator. Still, I really feel good about serving my country. All of my choices put me in a place that would still allow me to provide that service. Even if I went back into civilian life, I could choose a career like medicine or teaching. Those would require more school, and I have been away from that for nearly four years now."

Trip's mind raced through the different scenarios that lay before him. He knew it was a decision that had to be made. He also knew that at his young age, none of the decisions would have to be permanent. It occurred to him that instead of being in a dilemma, he was in a pretty good place. Money was not an issue, and he loved the idea of taking any of these options. None of the choices offered anything less than great opportunities, and each of them had more perks than negatives. It would be tough for him to pick a wrong path forward. But, pick he must!

ABOUT THE AUTHOR

I am a 77-year-old who has been blessed and lucky his entire life with good friends, good health, and good memories. I grew up in a small town in southeastern North Carolina called Burgaw. I still live there. I spent three years in the U.S. Army and was then gone for a number of years while trying to earn a living for my wife and three sons. As soon as I was able, I came home.

I have been blessed far beyond what I deserve. I am basically uneducated with the exception of the USMA Prep School while serving in the Army and a few courses I have taken over the years. I am very fortunate that I found a job that I love and am fairly decent at doing. I am a salesman.

My family is grown and have taken over the business that we started some 25 years ago. We are a brokerage company and sell just about anything you may find in a grocery store to a number of those stores up and down the East Coast of the U.S.

I have been very lucky in my travels. My business has allowed that. I have also been very lucky in having fished in many different locations and countries. Fishing is my favorite pastime. From a cane pole with a cricket in the black rivers near home, a fly rod in Alaska, a week on the Amazon, billfish in the Pacific, and even on the Great Barrier Reef, I have loved every adventure.

I have six grandchildren and one great-grandchild who are great. I had two grandchildren who lived for very short periods of time. They were born to a son I lost a number of years ago. He would be 56 now. His loss changed the life of our family. We have overcome that loss, but still feel the pain of losing him and his two children on a daily basis.

Made in the USA
Middletown, DE
13 February 2023

24568799R00146